MIDNIGHT WORLD

VOLUME ONE

MIDNIGHT WORLD VOLUME ONE

CUT FROM DARKNESS

DALIVIA PLAUT

DARK PLOT
PUBLISHING

● ● ●

First Edition, December 2018
Story by Dalivia Plaut
Written by Dalivia Plaut
Edited by Ireland Lelisio

ISBN: 978-0-9976453-7-8
Plaut, Dalivia, 1983—
Cut From Darkness
I. Title. Fiction. Dark Fantasy/Horror

ISBN: 978-0-9976453-7-8 pbk.

Cover Design by Low Key
Book Design by Dalivia Plaut
Cover Photograph by TheLux (istockphoto.com)

● ● ●

Author's Note

The world presented beyond this page is a fictitious one, as are its characters. Any resemblance to actual persons, living or dead, is entirely coincidental.

MIDNIGHT WORLD VOLUME ONE:
CUT FROM DARKNESS

ARE *we so different from them?*

The thought consumed Kid as he stared at the two black widow spiders tangled up in a messy web inside a dark crevice behind the anchored shutter next to the windowsill.

Intrigued by the violent nature of their species, Kid leaned closer to the shutter for a better look. The larger spider—or what Kid discovered, after an extensive research on his tablet device, was a highly venomous female spider that had recently mated with a smaller male spider—started to overpower and dominate the smaller one, forcing it into submission.

For days the larger black widow had been hanging outside his window, spinning its thick durable web that could withstand the brutal autumn winds that slipped past the corners of the shutter.

Every night Kid would poke his head from the window and shine a flashlight on the elusive spider, making sure it was still there. It was. At times he'd tap on the shutter and talk to the spider whenever Runt was too exhausted to play. Of course, the black widow never responded. But the spider did something that nobody on the farm would ever do with Kid—at least no human—it listened.

The other spider's legs twitched before it finally stopped moving.

Kid wasn't sure whether or not the spider was dead when the other larger one started to consume it. He knew that for any spider—either male or female—to hang around in one spot all the time probably had more disadvantages than it did advantages. But then again, he retraced his thoughts back to the female spider and the information he read on his tablet device.

What if she spun her web in order to lure in the other spider?

Kid's attention was drawn to both Unk and The Irishman, who were escorting one of the pigs, a butcher hog, a two hundred pounder, from the barn to the shed. He spotted what looked like a pistol dangling in Unk's left hand.

Dread came over Kid.

He leaned back inside his bedroom and turned toward the closet behind him.

He knew exactly what day it was.

ON these days, The Day of The Slaughter, Kid never left the house.

Kid cracked the window and carefully listened. He didn't hear a sound, not a single squeal from Alberto. They'd normally let out a grating squeal, which was much higher in pitch than any normal one, a last-second utterance of both fear and imminent death. All Kid heard was the sound of a soft *tha-thump* from the safety of his bedroom. Then, moments later, he watched the two lanky shadows of men pacing back and forth inside the grayness of the shed, diligently working with glistening objects gripped in their hands. He never saw Alberto get the bolt to the brain. All he saw of Alberto was a trail of blood slithering from the doorway of the shed. Kid watched the blood run like a red teardrop from a small ramp and drip onto the dirt pathway.

The most he observed was the aftermath of a kill, The Irishman hosing away puddles of blood, as well as random red streaks from the floor inside the shed. Then, he'd see whatever was left of the recent kill hoisted upside down, its entire body precisely split in two halves, the hair of its skin scolded away, giving off a slick and remarkably glowing appearance. Unless it was disease-ridden, every part of it never went to waste—even the ears; they, too, were used for consummation. By that final stage of the whole process, it was, as Unk stated to Miranda, "a means of income."

Kid didn't know why—maybe it was a culmination of things or maybe it was the curiosity of a young mind—but Kid wanted a better look.

As Kid stepped outside the house, it was deathly quiet on the farm. Normally he could hear the herd from the inside of the barn or one of the several sties outside, talking among themselves in their own peculiar way, farting or snorting or even squealing, nonetheless, communicating. Kid compared the pigs to dogs, and how they, too, were incredibly sociable animals.

After Alberto's death, they were silent, almost reverent.

Kid made his way to the red shed.

Each step felt long and slow.

Somehow, time slowed.

As he made it to the shed, Unk stepped outside with a red-stained towel in his hand.

The expression on Unk's face was one of great surprise.

"Kid?" said Unk, as he wiped the blood from his hands. "What you doin' out here? You know what day it is."

Quietly, Kid shrugged.

"I know," he mumbled. Then, he said more clearly, "I just was tired of being inside, that's all."

"You okay?"

"Yeah," Kid said and nodded at the barn. "What's wrong with the herd?"

"What you mean?"

"They're quiet."

"Yeah, well," Unk sighed, "they usually is on days like today."

"They're sad," Kid said over the strange silence.

"They don't have feelings, Kid."

"But they do."

Unk turned toward the shed and yelled out at The Irishman who was holding a bloody hacksaw in his hand, "Hey, Paddy, give me a minute, will you?"

The Irishman, who was a short fellow who made Unk look like a mythological giant, didn't respond as quickly as Unk wanted.

Unk once more: "McKellar?"

Finally, The Irishman responded with a wave of his hand.

Unk pointed at the barn and told Kid to follow.

Kid followed.

The tension between the two was awkward; Kid remained, like the pigs, reverent in the recent passing of Alberto while Unk fished around inside his head for something to say to Kid.

"So," Unk started, "where's your little iThingy," Unk said, referring to Kid's tablet device. "I don't see you on it that much anymore."

Kid followed with a shrug, as if it was starting to become an involuntary gesture on the farm.

"I dunno," he said shortly. "I guess I'm not interested in it anymore."

"Well, good," Unk snapped, "those damn things will rot your brain."

"It's not like that," Kid said defensively. "I just, I dunno. I miss home that's all."

Unk stopped walking.

Then, Kid stopped.

"Don't be talking like that, Kid," he said. "You just miss your mamma, don't you?"

"Yeah."

"Your momma's a strong woman, probably the strongest woman I've had the privilege of knowing, but you know she can't raise you on her own, at least not in her current condition. And don't be thinking it has anything to do with you 'cuz it don't. What your momma is going through is her own doing, you hear? She has her demons, Kid, and right now, she's at war with them."

"But demons don't exist."

"Well sure they do, Kid," Unk chirped. "They exist like you and me. You may not be able to see 'em just yet, but they're there, Kid."

"When will I be able to see them?" asked Kid.

"Well," Unk said, "hopefully, you won't."

They approached the barn.

Unk held the door open for Kid. They stepped inside where all the pigs were waiting.

"How about the pigs?" asked Kid. "Do they have demons?"

"No, Kid," he said. "They don't have anything—"

"—But they have each other."

Unk laughed.

"I swear, Kid, you something else."

They walked through the barn, occasionally stopping next to the rails which surrounding the pigs.

Kid posed an unusual question, which caught Unk by surprise: "If we didn't kill the pigs, do you think they'd evolve too?"

"Evolve?"

"Yeah, like us," said Kid. "Humans evolved."

"You talking about evolution?"

"Yeah, you know, like us and the monkeys."

"Kid, you know I won't tolerate that blaspheme in my household," Unk said, his voice louder. "We're here 'cuz the God Almighty put us here—

"—But according to science, *all* humans evolved from monkeys."

A grin broke free, stretching across Unk's glistening face.

"So, is that what these fools teaching you in school these days?"

"The scientists people even have one of them skeletons from way back when it began to walk upright. Actual physical evidence, Unk—"

"—How you know?"

All seriousness washed over Unk. He glared at Kid.

"I've seen one."

"Where? On that iThingy?"

"Yeah."

Unk leaned in close to Kid.

"If you can't touch it with your own two hands, then it ain't real, you hear?" He stood up and pointed at the herd before him. "You see that, Kid. That's real."

The words suddenly came to Kid, even came so close to reaching his lips, yet they dangled on the tip of his tongue.

What about God?

He thought about those words. He thought about this god-figure whom Unk always talked about whenever he felt His presence. Most importantly, he thought about the backlash in speaking those words, let alone even thinking them.

Unk towered over Kid and pointed his sharp, twisted finger at one of the pigs standing against the railing. "Go on," he urged Kid. "Touch it."

Kid was hesitant, but eventually he touched the backside of the pig.

"You feel that? That's real. Somebody put them here for us. And you know who did?" Unk didn't give Kid a chance to answer. "It was God. He's the One and the Only who put these creatures here on earth for us to survive."

"But, Unk, all I'm saying is *what if* it's true—"

"—Kid, don't you dare start with me."

"But I'm being for real, Unk," said Kid. "Think about it: pigs walking upright. That'd be so cool! What if they learned to talk? That'd be even cooler!"

"Kid, I tell you what," Unk said, shaking his head in amusement, "you're just like your momma, always thinking about wild stuff. But don't look at it as a bad thing; in fact, Kid, don't you ever lose that imagination of yours. You hold onto it as long as you can 'cuz one day it might vanish just like that and you might never get it back. Who knows? That imagination of yours might make you famous one day."

"Famous?" Kid puckered his face. "I don't wanna be famous."

"You don't want to live in a big house with lots of money one day?"

"Not really."

"You could have a house all to yourself. That doesn't sound interesting?"

Once more, Kid shrugged.

"Lemme ask you something, Kid. You like it here?"

"It's a'ight, I guess."

"You know when I was your age, my old man and I didn't get along too well. I admit there were times when I hated him. *But*, Kid, I respected him and what he did for a living. When he died, he handed this place down to me. I didn't own a iWhatever—"

"—My tablet," Kid said.

"I didn't have the opportunity to lose myself in technology. For me, Kid, this is all I really know. It's all I have, you hear?"

"I know."

"No," he said, his tone sharper. "I don't think you do, Kid."

Kid kneeled down and started petting one of the piglets.

Unk grabbed Kid's wrist and removed his hand from the pig.

Kid stood.

The abrupt movement frightened the piglet, causing a strange domino effect among the other pigs.

He said over him, "Miranda's been telling me she thinks you've been wetting the bed."

"What?" Kid blurted out over the squeals. "No!"

Unk backed Kid away from the pen.

"There's no shame in admitting it, Kid."

"But I didn't wet my bed," whined Kid. "I'm too old for that."

"Then, who did?"

"I mean," Kid backtracked, "I might've spelt milk or something."

"I'm not buying it."

"But it's the truth."

"The truth?"

9

"Yeah."

Kid struggled to look Unk in the eyes.

Unk sighed.

"So who's your Boogeyman?"

"Boogeyman? I don't have no Boogeyman."

"Don't lie, Kid," Unk said.

"I'm not."

"Every kid your age has one, Kid," he said. "I did."

"You did?"

"Sure did," Unk said. "I reckon, for me, it was clowns. My daddy once took me to the circus when I was around your age, maybe a bit younger. I remember being scared half to death by them clowns jumping all around, doing tricks, with their smiling faces and painted white faces. Ain't nobody normal be smiling that big. I remember I couldn't stop thinking about those faces, like they was etched into my brain. For weeks, I dreamt about them ghostly white faces with dark sinister eyes. I imagined them creepy clowns lurking in my closet, sneaking into my bed-room, stalking the dark hallways at night. Then, one night, you know what I did?"

"What?" asked Kid.

"I killed them."

"You killed them?"

"In my dreams, I did," Unk clarified. "They ain't haunt me since."

"I ain't afraid of clowns."

"Then, tell me, Kid, what you afraid of?" asked Unk.

Kid paused and thought about the question. He didn't think about clowns or giant arachnids lurking through the darkest corners of night. All he could think about was Miranda and how she, like them clowns Unk spoke of, had been sneaking into his bedroom to strip the sheets bare from his bed and washing them without his permission.

Would she ever find Runt?

What if, Kid thought, *she looked in my closet?*

As before, Kid shrugged his shoulders and did what he usually did whenever Unk had him under interrogation. He deflected. "I dunno," mumbled Kid. "I ain't afraid of any-thing."

"Is that so?" Unk asked.

Kid turned his shoulder and looked Unk in his murky eyes.

"Yeah," he said. "I guess so."

"I tell you what, Kid," Unk said as he picked up a candy wrapper sticking out of the hay, "I given you your space. I've respected your space, hadn't I?"

Kid bobbed his head.

"Guess so."

"Well, I think you're getting old enough to start helping out around the farm. You think you're up to it?"

Kid faced Unk.

"Help out like what?"

"Like cleaning the barn, maintaining the barn, feeding the herd," Unk listed.

"I can do that," Kid said cheerfully.

Unk stepped closer and kneeled down until he was face-to-face with Kid.

"If you're gonna help out," Unk said, "there's one rule and one rule only and every person who works here at the farm must abide by it."

Kid asked, "What's that?"

"Don't get close to 'em," said Unk as he nodded at the herd.

"Well, I can do that," Kid said, as he took another step back.

"No, Kid," Unk corrected. "Don't get close to them—emotionally. You best keep your feelings at the same door you come in. And don't you look at them as pets 'cuz they ain't."

Kid didn't respond to Unk's grim remark.

"André, am I making myself clear?" asked Unk.

He waited for Kid to make any type of response.

Eventually, Kid sold Unk a nod.

But Unk wasn't buying it.

"Kid," Unk said and grabbed Kid's chin, "we gonna have a problem?"

"No, sir," Kid said, clearing his throat. "I—I understand."

Unk stood up.

"Good," he said, still not entirely convinced with Kid's response. "I'm glad we have an understanding, Kid." He turned to a massive door at the far end of the barn. "There's somebody I'd like you to meet."

Unk walked Kid over to a dimly lit area. He opened a wide sliding door, revealing yet another pen separate from the other one.

"I thought I wasn't allowed to go in here?"

"You ain't," Unk said. "But if you're going to be working around here you need to know about Boris."

"Boris?"

"That's right," Unk said as he guided Kid into the dark, dusty room. "I don't have any names for the others. You can think of them as Boris's minions. Boris is the leader. And whatever Boris does, they usually follow."

Kid waved his hand in front of his nose.

"He don't smell like the others," said Kid.

"That's 'cuz Boris ain't like the others."

"What is he?" asked Kid.

"He's a monster," said Unk.

Unk walked Kid to a more secure pen where a shadowy figure awaited. Kid saw a pair of eyes glowing in the darkness. Then heard a low guttural noise, like a cross between a wet fart and a belch coming from the smelly darkness. The rickety boards surrounding the pen trembled as Kid stared at the two glossy eyes lift through the dark haze. Other pairs of eyes manifested inside the darkness, smaller in size but equally as terrifying.

Boris finally stepped forward into the dim light, revealing his scarred face. He had tusks nearly the size of Kid's arms. One of the tusks had been chipped during a recent skirmish, part of the tooth broken off, leaving one side of it serrated like a saw blade, making it twice as easy to slice through the toughest hide. Ropes of drool dangled from his fleshy swollen lips and as the monster took another step forward into the light, the drool swayed from side to side like viscous pendulums.

"Meet Boris and The Minions," Unk said, pointing at the boars.

"Sounds like the name of a rock band."

Unk laughed.

"Boris here is a reminder of what we're dealing with."

"Why you keep them separated from the others?" asked Kid.

"If I set Boris loose with the other hogs, there'd be absolutely nothing left of the other hogs."

Curious, Kid asked, "Why would he kill others like him?"

"Why does a man decide to become a politician?" Unk asked Kid.

Kid didn't answer.

"Power," Unk snapped. "Control. Eventually, it all leads to corruption, Kid. And Boris here, he's a master of corruption. A true artist, Boris is." Unk waved Kid in closer. "They ain't our friends, Kid. These here animals were put on this very earth for one reason, Kid, and one reason only. For us," Unk said. "Without them, there'd be no us. They're what keep us alive, you hear?" Kid didn't move his attention away from Boris, even though the sight of Boris sent chills through his body. "As for us, the workers on this farm, the town relies on us to make sure they're fed properly. That's our obligation. That's 'us' doing our part in sustaining human life."

"If animals were put on earth just for their meat, then why don't we eat dogs or cats? I mean, is their meat different from a pig's?"

"I'm sure it is, Kid," Unk said. "They eat dogs or cats in other countries."

"How you know?"

"I just do."

"Then, why don't people eat dogs or cats in this country?"

"People, especially groups of people, have a way of choosing what's wrong and what's right. When it comes down to it and there was no more pigs or cows or chickens or even fish left on this earth, who do you think people would turn to next?"

Again, Kid didn't answer. In a way, he didn't want to know the answer.

"My point exactly." Unk tilted his head as if he was tilting the very thought in his mind. "Then you got another group of people, people like that uppity white bitch we ran into the other day—"

"—Ms. Meghan?"

"Think about Kid," Unk said. "You think someone like that, someone who's living high off the hog, is going to strut her honky ass down here, roll around in the mud with us, and get those silky smooth hands of hers dirty?"

Kid stepped closer to the pen.

In return, Boris let out a sudden snort, the burst of air hitting the ground below and sending a cloud of dust through a ray of sunlight beaming from above.

"You understand the point I'm trying to make, Kid?"

Kid turned to Unk.

"Yes, sir," he said. "I think so."

As Kid turned back around, Boris was standing even closer to Kid. A sudden fear gripped Kid, draining the dark color from his face. His eyes, like his already gaping mouth, widened. Face went long, expression slack.

Kid found himself gradually taking a step away from the pen.

The other boars stepped forward into the light and stood behind Boris. Boris lowered his head, his sharp eyes focusing on Kid.

Unk placed his hand on Kid's shoulder, startling Kid.

"Don't you dare underestimate them," said Unk. "They'll tear you to shreds the second you drop your guard. To them, Kid, you look like food."

The sight of Boris standing so close to Kid spread fear throughout his entire body. Kid imagined if this was what it felt like when Runt first laid eyes on him. Yet, as Kid stood face-to-face with the boar that Unk called the monster, Kid couldn't take his eyes off Boris. The two locked eyes. In a way, he felt hypnotized by the large boar.

WITH Boris still on his mind, Kid went back to his bedroom. He walked straight to his closet and opened the door. To the right of the closet was a litter box with a couple of turds, which were coated with kitty litter.

"Runt," Kid said, "you in here?"

Kid heard a *rustling* of clothes.

On the other side of the closet, a pile of old clothes moved.

The head of a piglet "Runt" suddenly emerged from the clothes. It was much smaller than the other piglets in the herd, hence why Kid decided to brand it with the name, Runt. It was a white pig, its hair white as well, with black spots scattered over its body. It had a particular black spot around its left eye, which made it stand out among the herd.

Kid pulled Runt from the clothes and held the piglet in his arms.

He couldn't stop thinking about Boris, what Unk said about treating pigs as if they were pets, but mainly, he couldn't stop thinking about how wrong Unk was.

Kid petted the top of Runt's head.

Runt gazed up at Kid, its soft eyes attached to Kid's. It let out a sound close to a purr.

"I'm not going to let anything happen to you, Runt," Kid said. "I promise."

FOR the rest of the day, Kid holed up in his room and hung out with Runt.

They played all kinds of games together, apps, first-person shooters, even chess; and by the time they moved onto something else, the screen's surface on his tablet device was covered with white imprints of Runt's snout from where Runt had used its moist snout to tap on the touch screen. Together, they'd binge-watch a TV series. Whenever the piglet got hungry, he'd feed Runt milk through a baby bottle.

After supper, Kid sneaked Runt into his bookbag and carried the piglet to an open field on the other side of the woods where, together, they played catch; however, Runt never caught the ball. But he was a good kicker. Kid and Runt practically did everything together, and all of it was done in secrecy.

KID couldn't sleep.

He never did on the Day of the Slaughter.

Wrestling through the bed sheets, the images of gore plagued Kid's mind. In the red haze, he witnessed Unk hang a lifeless Alberto upside down on a rail, then he inserted a knife into Alberto's jugular vein. The blood poured from the pig and dripped into a bucket resting below. Once the pig was exsanguinated, it was then placed inside a pig scolder; the scolding hot water removed the hair from its body.

Then, from there, the gore came in hot flashes: the pig was first eviscerated, its bowels stripped from its body, then placed inside trays. Next to go was the pig's head. It was chopped off. Then, its body was cut in half.

Sweating profusely, Kid bolted upright from bed.

He rolled out of bed, walked to the window, and stared at the barn outside.

ONCE Runt was secured in the closet, Kid grabbed a coat and walked to the barn. He ignored the other pigs, as well as the piglets, and checked on Boris. He only made it a couple of steps into the dusty room before he heard Unk call out from behind, "What you think you're doing in here, Kid?"

Startled, Kid turned around.

At the entrance of the barn stood Unk with his arms folded across his chest.

"I—I was just—I wanted to see Boris."

"You have no business in there." Unk waved Kid close. "Come on. Back to bed."

With his head hung downward, Kid walked to Unk.

"You know you ain't supposed to be in here at night," Unk said. "What's a matter with you?"

"I couldn't sleep."

"Again?"

Kid quietly walked with Unk back to the house. Unk walked Kid to the table in the kitchen. He grabbed a pill from a bottle in the top cabinet, then poured Kid a glass of water from the sink's faucet. He held out both the pill and water in his hands and waited for Kid to grab them.

"What is it?" Kid asked hesitantly.

"It'll help you sleep," Unk said, holding out the glass of water as well as the blue mysterious pill. "There's absolutely no reason why a boy your age shouldn't be getting his rest. Now go on. Take it."

He grabbed the glass of water as well as the pill from Unk's hands. He didn't think twice about it. He popped the pill into his mouth and washed it down with a sip of water.

"That'll help you sleep," Unk said as he escorted Kid to the staircase. As Kid walked upstairs, Unk stopped him and said, "Sleep tight."

KID slept heavy.

By the time Kid surged from the blackness of his dreams, the sun was already high in the sky.

Feeling more energetic, Kid bounced from the bed and stretched his arms to the ceiling.

First, he checked on the black widow next to the windowsill.

The sturdy catacomb-like web with dozens of carcasses of dried flies and curled-up bugs was still tucked away in the cozy nook of the shutter, but the spider was gone.

Kid's attention was drawn to a commotion outside the house.

Below, Unk was marching toward the shed as if he was on a mission. In his hand he was holding a piglet—perhaps a suckling pig—by the legs. He didn't see any dark spots on the piglet; however, it was seldom for Unk to slaughter suckling pigs for their tender meat.

The piglet was squirming all around, kicking its front legs.

Kid should've been relieved, knowing the piglet wasn't Runt.

But he wasn't.

Glum shrouded Kid.

All of a sudden, Kid thought about last night. A distant image surfaced in his mind, one of Unk studying Kid trudge back to his bedroom as he stood in the dark shadows at the base of the staircase. For a moment, Kid wondered whether or not it was a dream. He recalled rolling out of bed in the dead of night to check on Boris. He never made it to Boris nor did he see Boris, only the thought of the boar which he held inside his mind ever since he saw Boris. Then, in the blackness of night, he saw the shifting eyes of the great monster.

Enraged, Kid rushed to the closet and swung open the doors but found Runt nowhere around. He grabbed clothes and newspapers and started throwing them back into the room. He checked underneath his bed but Runt wasn't there either.

AFTER combing his entire bedroom for Runt but coming up empty, Kid ran past Miranda, who appeared concerned by Kid's frantic state. She asked if everything was all right, but Kid ignored her and ran outside where Unk was carrying yet another piglet to the red shed.

"There he is," Unk said, as he spotted Kid in the corner of his eye, "you sleep well—"

"—What you doing?" asked Kid.

Unk furrowed his brow in confusion.

"My job, Kid," he said. "What does it look like I'm doing?"

"They're just piglets," said Kid.

"What's your point, Kid?" Unk said shortly.

"Can't you just kill Boris?"

Unk laughed as he handed off the piglet to the smiling Irishman whose apron was covered in random smears of blood. Kid peeked inside and spotted a mound of piglets, dead, at least thirty of them, all stacked in a dark corner of the shed as if they were about to be bulldozed into a massive grave.

Kid frantically scanned the pile for black spots but didn't see any among the other dead piglets. Unk nodded toward the barn. "I'm actually glad you're up. There's something I need to show you."

Unk walked Kid over to the barn.

Kid heard a thumping sound followed by a squeal behind him. He turned his shoulder and saw The Irishman whacking the piglet's head against the side of the cutting table. He flung the piglet on the ground where the piglet started convulsing, all four of its legs kicking as if it was trying to flee from the inevitable death that awaited it. The images of The Irishman slowly killing the piglet without displaying an iota of remorse enraged Kid to the point where he was tempted to snap at Unk and his willingness to stand by and let a massacre happen. For some reason, he thought about the spider consuming the other spider outside his window.

The walk wasn't that far, only a good fifty yards or so, but to Kid, it felt as if he was walking to the ultimate doom.

Time slowed.

His legs started to buckle. He could feel each step getting harder and harder. Muscles tightened.

"Where you taking me?" Kid asked, his voice, like his body, trembling.

"Did you not listen to a word I told you yesterday?" asked Unk. "I gave you a chance, Kid. Didn't I?"

They arrived at the barn. Kid could hear all of the *squealing* inside with that one particular squeal being the most prominent among the other squeals, the death squeal. Unk walked Kid into the barn. Kid frantically searched for Runt. He saw Runt inside a pen all by himself. There were many other piglets in a pen next to Runt and they, too, appeared mortified by the sudden commotion.

Kid ran to Runt.

Unk grabbed Kid by the arm and yanked him close.

"Not so fast, Kid," he said as he grabbed a knife from the table. "This is for your own good, André." Unk dragged Kid toward the pen. "If there is one thing you never—I mean, *never*—do, Kid, you never mess with another man's livelihood, you got that?"

"Don't hurt him," Kid whined. "Please. . . "

"What did I tell you, Kid?" Unk said, jerking Kid around. "These ain't pets! These things ain't to be played with, you hear! They're what puts food on the table! Do you understand me, Kid?"

Unk opened the pen and held the knife with an open palm in front of Kid.

"Go on," Unk urged, "kill it or I will. . . "

"I ain't gonna kill it," Kid cried. "Runt's the only thing I got here."

"I don't care," Unk said. "You went behind my back and you disobeyed me. Did you think there wouldn't be consequences for you actions? If I let you off, then how do I know you ain't gonna go behind my back and do it again?"

"I won't! Trust me!"

"No, Kid," said Unk. "That trust was broken the second you defied me."

"But it's just one pig, Unk," Kid begged. "I'll pay you for it!"

"This ain't about money, Kid. Don't you get it? You need to learn a lesson."

"It'll never happen again," Kid begged. He made his body go limp and fell to the ground. "Please, Unk! Don't make me do it. Please. . . "

"You ain't gonna do it?" Unk asked, as he waved the knife in front of Kid.

Kid shook his head.

"Fine," Unk said and walked into the pen.

Runt tried to flee, but Unk cornered Runt and snatched the piglet by the legs.

Kid yelled, "Don't!"

As Unk raised Runt in the air, Kid dropped his head and cried.

"I want you watch, boy!"

Kid didn't, wouldn't. He'd never watch. Kid knew that, if he did, then he'd never forget. He'd carry the image to his grave.

Unk screamed, "I said 'WATCH!'"

As soon as Kid barely raised his head upward, Unk suddenly drove the knife into Runt's chest.

Kid turned away, crying.

"No," he bawled into his hands.

All of a sudden, the rage was back. Kid balled his hands into fists; his body started to shake. With his teeth bared, Kid charged at Unk. But Unk was a rather sturdy man who stood over six feet tall. He was slender but he had what the folks around town called the "country-strength" of a black man.

Unk threw Runt's body to the ground and grabbed Kid by the collar. He was punching at Unk's legs. Unk tossed the knife aside and put Kid into submission with a headlock.

"You gonna stop!" shouted Unk.

"I hate you!" Kid shouted back. "I hope you die!"

"Oh yeah?"

Angered, Unk dragged Kid to Boris's pen.

"Lemme go!"

"You hate me? I'm gonna show you what hate looks like, boy!"

Unk held Kid close to Boris's pen and started banging on the side of the pen.

"Wake up!" he shouted out.

All of a sudden, Kid heard a low grunt.

Out of the darkness Boris charged directly at Kid and rammed his tusks into the side of the fence.

Kid screamed with terror as he tried to duck for cover but Unk grabbed Kid by his wrists and forced Kid to watch the rage that drove Boris.

"You hate me?" said Unk. "Well, too bad 'cuz they hate you!" Boris continued to ram the fence. Kid tried to jerk his hands away to shield not only his body, but also his mind from the primordial hunger before him. He thought about God, Unk's god, and asked himself what kind of God would bring such a beast into this world. Somehow, Kid managed to slip one of his wrists free from Unk's slippery grip. "Look at them eyes of his! Look at 'em! He's ready to eat you up!" Unk reinforced his grip around Kid. "You think he cares about your black ass?"

Trembling, Kid covered his eyes with his hand as he pleaded for the comfort of his momma.

Unk jerked Kid's hand away from his face and forced Kid to watch Boris.

"Boy," Unk seethed, "I said 'Look!'"

He pinned Kid's arms behind his back and with his free hand, steadied Kid's head upright and told him once more to look.

Kid couldn't—wouldn't—as he tightly shut his eyes.

In the red darkness behind his eyelids, he heard the sounds of rage, savagery, and hunger. Kid couldn't understand why Boris was so desperate to rip his body to shreds. A part of Kid didn't want to understand. A part of Kid didn't care.

Unk squeezed his hand tighter around the top of Kid's throat, his fingers curling around Kid's jaw like a vise.

Kid resisted, squirmed, tried to break through the chapped, calloused flesh that smothered him, but Unk overpowered him. Kid fought through his restraints, but Unk fought too and he was ten times stronger. Kid suddenly hurled his body into the air and attempted to kick Unk with the backside of his heels but Unk drove his boots into Kid's feet like coffin nails. Eventually, Kid tired himself out as Unk curled both his arms as well as his legs around Kid's body.

Weakened, Kid cracked open his eyes.

"You gonna stop? Huh?" asked Unk.

Kid didn't respond, too weak.

"I don't want to do this to you, Kid," said Unk. "I don't. But you must realize that these things ain't our friends." Boris ran back to the shadows, kicked the dirt below him with its hooves, and once more, charged at Kid. He battered the fence, loosening several boards. "When we're at our most vulnerable, Kid," Kid turned his head away but Unk straightened it for him, "Don't just look at it, Kid! Look through it! Do you see it? The evil inside it! *This* here is what your precious animals really look like." Boris backed off for a moment and as it paced around the halo of light inside the pen, he stared down Kid from the center of the pen while the other boars waited in the shadows outside the light. "They're animals, Kid, and the laws of nature forbid us to coexist with them."

"But Runt's different," Kid cried. "He's not like the others."

"He may be, for now, but sooner or later, this is what they turn into."

"No."

"Yes."

"I don't believe you," cried Kid, his body going limp. "You're wrong. . ."

Unk loosened his grip around Kid.

"If they're so evil, then why do you keep them separated? Why do you keep Boris back here, away from the others?"

"You can't be that naive, Kid," said Unk. "I thought your momma raise you better, but I was wrong."

Unk removed his grip from Kid, who, in return, fell to the ground. The very moment he found himself free from Unk, he stumbled to his feet in a blast of reserved energy and darted from the barn.

"Go on!" yelled Unk. "Run off to your video games! Reality can be a hard thing to deal with, Kid. The sooner you understand it, the better off you'll be!"

Kid ran and didn't look back.

Unk kept yelling at him from behind.

But all Kid heard was the beat of a pulse throbbing in his ears.

Miranda stepped in front of Kid as soon as he scurried from the barn.

She called out to him, but like before, all Kid could hear was his pulse.

His song.

The drumbeat of war.

EVENTUALLY, the beat could only carry Kid so far.

He was out of breath and struggling to stand once he reached the edge of the woods. He rested for a moment behind an oak tree while he caught his breath.

From a distance, Miranda was calling out to Kid.

The closer her voice grew, the more he thought about Runt.

The thought alone gave Kid the drive he so desperately needed to survive.

He gathered himself and told himself to stand.

He stood.

Then, when the moment came, he told himself to run.

He did exactly that.

He ran.

KID spent the rest of the day hanging out by a creek in the woods. He shed all the tears he had for Runt and when he thought he had no more tears left to cry, he reached deep down inside, throughout the gore and violence, and out came more. He thought about what he could've done differently—*if I hadn't been so scared*, Kid murmured to himself as he slammed the ball of his fist against the top of his thigh. *It's all my fault.* His thoughts were mostly consumed with his uncle, what he had done to Runt, how he drove a knife into Runt as if Runt was nothing more than a stuffed animal filled with wads of crumbled up dollar bills; and when his blade pierced Runt's carotid artery, the only blood that Unk saw pouring from the piglet's body wasn't blood at all but a glimmering flow of quarters, dimes, nickels, and pennies.

IT was getting dark outside when Kid returned to the farm.

From beside the porch, Kid watched Unk devouring a piece of meat over the kitchen sink as Miranda scraped away the leftover food on her plate into a trashcan, which would probably be used to help feed the herd. Kid thought it was ham maybe, but whatever it was, like most of the meat served around here, it came from a pig. Normally, Kid would just dismiss it and wouldn't think too much about it, as he pushed food around his plate as if playing hockey with his peas. The sight alone of Unk chewing through succulent meat sickened Kid to the point where he felt nauseous. Each bite his uncle took reminded him of a great white shark chomping through a hunk of rare chuck roast attached to a fisherman's hook.

In the cool darkness, Kid waited for Unk to leave the kitchen before he made his run to the front door. He crept inside, carefully shut the door behind him, and tiptoed his way upstairs. The hardwood floors creaked below him, forcing him to slow down his creep to a near cat's prowl.

As Kid finally reached the top of the landing, Miranda appeared at the bottom of the staircase.

Moments later, Kid heard the sound of footsteps thumping against the stairs. He could tell from the quickness of each step that it was Miranda. She had a distinct walk, opposed to his uncle, who was a man who moved slowly and often had others move for him. Miranda appeared at Kid's doorway with a plate of food in her hand. She tapped on the door, which was cracked open but not entirely shut, and glided into the bedroom.

"Leave me alone," Kid said, his face pressed against a pillow.

"I brought you some food, André."

"I ain't hungry," said Kid.

"You have to eat, André."

"I'm done eating."

"So, what? You going to starve to death? Is that it?"

"Yeah."

Miranda placed the plate of food on the nightstand. She couldn't help but notice the mud on Kid's feet and how he was getting mud all over the bed sheets that she recently washed. She turned to the plush toys on the ground, some of which were slick with slobber while others appeared as if they had been chewed through. She turned her attention back to Kid, his fragile state. Miranda leaned over the edge of the bed and touched the backside of Kid's shoulder. With his face buried in the pillow, Kid shrugged away her hand.

"Tomorrow is a new day, André," Miranda said, leaning away.

"I don't care."

"I'll talk to Cordell," she said. "Maybe we can work something out and find a new one for you."

"Runt can't be replaced," said Kid.

"Sure he can, André—"

"—Just leave me alone already."

"Okay," Miranda said and eased from the bedroom.

Once Miranda had gone back downstairs, he rolled over and found a plate of food, as well as a glass of milk, on the nightstand. On the plate were two slices of ham, a scoop of mashed potatoes and green beans, a corncob with a square of butter, and a wedge of homemade cornbread, which, un-like everything else, was still fairly warm. He could hear his empty stomach rumbling. His mouth even moistened from the sight of Miranda's homemade cornbread.

Kid reached over and grabbed the plate.

After taking two bites of cornbread, his eyes trailed downward onto a couple of strange-looking crumbs next to the green beans.

As he held a ball of cornbread in the side of his mouth like a mouthful of Big League Chew, he pressed the greasy tip of his index finger against the crumbs and held them up to his face for further inspection. The crumbs were the color blue. Kid thought about that particular color and only one thing came to his mind.

All of a sudden, Kid spat out the cornbread from his mouth!

He dashed into the bathroom where he thoroughly rinsed out his mouth with water. He noticed a couple of blue dots, no larger than the size of a speck of dirt, in his spit as well. He hadn't swallowed any of the cornbread. But he didn't take any chances.

IN the middle of night, Kid snuck out of the window.

Carefully, he tiptoed over the roof above the porch and used one of the pillars to climb down. He didn't know exactly how he was going to sneak back into the house. The climb was much tougher up than it was down. He told himself he'd cross that bridge when the time came.

Once Kid reached the ground, he pulled around his bookbag and checked the plate of food, which was sealed in clear clingwrap. The food on one side of the plate had shifted to the other side a bit but was still encased inside the clingwrap.

With his bookbag worn over his shoulder, Kid entered the barn. First, he decided to visit the herd. He placed the bookbag against a post and closed the door behind him. The herd woke from their sleep and they all circled around Kid. Kid dropped to his knees and strangely enough, the pigs dropped as well. He spoke to them and strangely enough, they all listened to him. Kid told them how sorry he was for Runt and how he felt responsible for Runt's death.

"I came here to make a deal," Kid said to the herd. "I have a plan, but in order to make it work, I need your help." Kid looked at each one of the pigs. "Will you help me?" asked Kid.

All of a sudden, Kid saw something moving underneath the pigs' legs. One of the piglets emerged from the herd, walked up to Kid, and rubbed the side of its head against Kid's leg.

In a way, they knew exactly what Kid wanted from them.

Kid turned to his right, to the dark room at the other side of the barn. There, he witnessed Boris, as well as the other boars, standing at the front of the pen.

They, too, knew why Kid came to visit them.

KID carried the bookbag to Boris's pen.

Boris's snort was much more phlegmy and deeper than the other boars; and to Kid, it sounded as if Boris was warning him to keep his distance or else. Kid had no interest in knowing what the "or else" part involved. He hoped not to put himself in a dangerous position where he teetered along a tightrope of life and death. But, Kid thought, *what other choice do I have?* Good thing for Kid, Boris was a predictable monster.

Using the same slow, almost sneaky movements Kid practiced with the other pigs, he pulled out the plate of cold food from the bookbag and inched closer to the pen. Kid was well aware that Boris's kind didn't like quick or sudden movements. So, he was slow in everything he did. Slow and strategic. With the tips of his fingers, he removed the clingwrap from the plate. Boris salivated. He looked up at Kid with dog-like mannerisms. His snout twitched as he sniffed the aromas of Miranda's home cooked meal. Kid brought the plate to the pen and found himself a couple of feet away from Boris.

Once Kid found himself face-to-face with Boris, he set the plate underneath the door and used the handle end of a shovel to slide it into the pen.

Kid backed away while Boris pounced on the plate and fiendishly swallowed the food quicker than he could chew.

"There's more where that came from big boy," said Kid, as he watched Boris eat in queer fascination.

Boris licked the plate clean and once more, looked up at Kid. For a moment, Kid actually witnessed Boris's tiny stub of a tail wiggle.

"You like that, don't you?"

Boris replied with a snort.

Kid inched closer to the pen.

"So," he said to Boris, "let's talk."

THE next morning, Kid beat Unk to the cereal. By the time Unk was awake, Kid had already finished his breakfast and he was ready to help out on the farm. Half asleep, Unk was surprised by Kid's complete one-eighty. He didn't put too much stock into his nephew's abrupt change in attitude. Kid was still too old to be considered a boy, even though he'd often be addressed as "Boy," whenever he goofed up, spoke out of turn, or made a mess; yet, at the same time, he was too young to be a man who carried the weight of responsibility on his shoulders. Decades ago, Unk was young, too, and every now and then, when he sat alone on the porch and relished the dying lights of twilight, he'd reminisce on his days as a young man, the warmness in his blood, the inexhaustible appetite to emerge unscathed from a word, like *boy*, a word that held so little influence yet the power of its unseen bite stung twice as hard and lasted equally as long as the many years it was thrown at him. He witnessed that same look he once had in his eye in Kid's eye. They both sat at the table in silence, Unk sipping on coffee Miranda had made while Kid gulping down a glass of orange juice. For the first time ever since Kid arrived at the farm,

Unk felt a warm sense of optimism. . . and fear of the un-known.

WORK began after breakfast.

Kid was tasked with a new role on the farm, which was to feed the herd. The task was normally designated to The Irishman. Instead, The Irishman trained Kid and showed him Pig Feeding 101. Kid caught on fast. The Irishman ghosted Kid for the majority of the morning. Then, once he felt comfortable enough to leave Kid alone to his task, he left the barn and tended to the shed.

Everything was running smoothly until Unk and The Irishman heard a shriek coming from the inside of the barn.

Both Unk and The Irishman rushed into the barn where they found Kid lying on the ground next to Boris's pen. Kid's arm was drenched in blood. He had two deep lacera-tions from where he said Boris bit him. Kid could hardly control himself for the pain was too great. Unk attempted to pick up Kid but Kid hollered out in great agony.

Unk specifically told The Irishman to watch over Kid while he grabbed the first aid kit from inside the house.

"No!" Kid cried out in desperation as he grabbed a hold of Unk with his good hand. "Don't leave me, Unk!"

Unk paused. He stood over Kid and they made eye con-tact. Unk witnessed a pain in Kid's eyes, a deep pain, not topical or one that belonged to the flesh, but a pain that ran much deeper than blood. Unk let out a noisy sigh. He turned to The Irishman. "Go grab Miranda," he said. "Tell her what happened—"

"—But Cordell," The Irishman started.

"Just do it," said Unk.

As The Irishman ran from the barn, Unk kneeled down and tended to Kid's injuries.

"I need to stop the bleeding," he said, as he pressed his hand against the lacerations.

Unk furrowed his brow from the shape of the cuts.

While Unk was inspecting the cuts, Kid's free hand slipped behind his back.

"These ain't bite marks," Unk said, a sudden coldness washing over his face.

Unk's eyes were drawn to a trail of blood. He left Kid and followed the trail of blood to the knife that rested in the hay.

"What's going on?" asked Unk, as he reached for the knife.

All of a sudden, Kid yanked on the end of a piece of string that was attached to the door of Boris's pen.

The door violently swung open, knocking Unk on his side.

Kid bounced to his feet, shoved Unk into the pen, and closed the door behind him.

Before Unk could open the door, Kid locked it shut and banged on the side of the pen. Boris, as well as the other boars, exited from the shadows. Unk rotated around and saw Boris closing in. He turned back around to Kid.

"Kid," he said, "André, open the door, you hear?"

Kid didn't budge. He stared Unk in the eyes. He watched the fear creep into them. Then, that old rage.

Unk bared his teeth. He suddenly reached his arm out between the openings of the fence and tried to grab hold of Kid.

Somehow, Kid must've known exactly how long Unk's reach was. Like before, Kid didn't budge, didn't even flinch.

As Unk hollered for help, the herd drowned out his voice, making it unrecognizable, a soft murmur among a symphony of harsh squeals.

Unk turned around once more and Boris was on top of him. As he grabbed Unk by the ankle and dragged his body deeper into the pen, Unk tried to fight off Boris and the other boars. But they had numbers. Kid grabbed the piece of string from the fence, as well as the knife from the ground and snuck them both in his pocket as The Irishman and Miranda rushed into the barn. Unk's screams turned wet. In a streak of sunlight beaming down from a hole in the roof,

Kid witnessed Boris sink his tusk into Unk's side while another boar grabbed him by the jaw and tore it completely from his face.

The Irishman pushed Kid aside, Miranda not too far behind.

Once The Irishman saw the horror inside the pen, he quickly grabbed a pitchfork from the wall and climbed into the pen. He shooed away the other boars. He ended up stabbing one of them. The other boars backpedaled into the shadows. Boris, on the other hand, stood his ground. He even placed one of his hooves on Unk's chest as if he was claiming Unk as his prize.

The Irishman displayed dominance by screaming and banging the pitchfork against the ground.

Boris backed off but now had The Irishman in his crosshairs.

He was ready to claim yet another prize.

The Irishman managed to grab hold of Unk's foot while Boris paced around, kicking his hooves into the dirt as if he was about to make a deadly charge. The Irishman pulled Unk's lifeless body close enough to the fence for Miranda to get a hand around Unk. Kid stepped in to help as well.

As they pulled Unk from the pen, Boris stomped his hooves into the ground.

Considering the weapon in The Irishman's hand, he'd more than likely win in a fight with Boris.

But Boris had his minions and each one of them was creeping closer to The Irishman.

As Boris charged at The Irishman, The Irishman darted toward the fence and leaped over in the nick of time. Except for a couple of scraps and bruises, he was unharmed. Unk was a different story.

MIRANDA rode inside the back of the ambulance as Unk was being transported to the nearest hospital, Saving Grace, which was located roughly thirty minutes from the farm, but with the siren blaring, they made it in twenty-five. Kid rode inside The Irishman's truck with his head pressed against the window and his body hugging the side of the passenger door as if The Irishman was infected with a contagious disease. Kid asked The Irishman what he was going to do with Boris, if he was going to put him down. The Irishman said he was going to do what was necessary. From that point forward, neither one of them uttered a single word to each other.

IT was late in the night. Doctors spent hours working on Unk, stitching up his open wounds, realigning and setting bones.

The doctors wanted to know exactly what happened to Unk, what kind of animal attacked him, what triggered the attack.

Kid, being the only one who was at the scene when Unk was attacked, had told Miranda, who then relayed to the doctor, that Boris, the boar, kicked open the door and dragged Unk inside the pen where he was ganged up on by the other boars. And the reason why the door was shut when she arrived in the barn was that Kid feared for his own safety.

Once Unk was stable, the nurse allowed those who were closest to him to pay a visit, Miranda being Unk's first visitor, then, Kid, second.

After spending a few minutes inside the hospital room, Miranda stepped into the hallway and told Kid that Unk wanted to see him.

Kid clung to his fidgety momma, Shakira, who had driven three hours from the city to visit her brother. He didn't want to see his uncle, nor did he have anything to say to him. He had a general idea of the extent of Unk's injuries based on all the questions the doctor was asking Miranda. Kid remained close to his momma's hip. She held Kid by the shoulders, nearly made a scene in front of everybody, and urged him to grow up and visit his uncle out of respect.

So, he did.

When he entered the hospital room, an overwhelming sense of dread washed over him. He was tempted to turn around several times. He wanted to run out of the room, ride home with his momma, and never *ever* think about what happened in that barn. In a way, he wanted Unk to be dead.

But he wasn't.

Unk was alive.

Miranda told Kid that he was able to communicate to her through hand gestures as well as blinking, one blink being *yes*, two blinks being *no*.

But he couldn't speak. His jaw was no longer there.

Kid walked to the edge of the hospital bed. He couldn't recognize Unk, but he could recognize the severe pain he was in. Miranda stepped outside while Kid walked closer to Unk.

He sat by his bedside and looked over his injuries. His left hand had been bitten off. His stub was dressed in white bandages. He had various cuts all over his face, neck, chest, as well as his legs.

Kid showed no emotion as he stared at the torn flesh, the broken bones, the cuts. He didn't feel anything, didn't shed a tear, didn't want to make a scene for that matter. He just wanted to go home. Kid moved his attention away from the injuries. He struggled to look Unk in the eyes. A part of him was just too ashamed.

He finally gathered enough courage to look Unk in his soft brown eyes.

In return, Unk opened his right hand, his eyes flicked downward. Unk's hand opened wider, revealing his palm to Kid.

Kid thought about a lot of things, sleeping in his own bed again, playing basketball and video games with his neighborhood friends. Mostly, Kid thought about the offer before him, his uncle's offer.

Eventually, Kid reached down below and sat his open hand inside Unk's hand. Kid didn't lift his hand away. A part of him just didn't want to.

So, he squeezed, not too hard but not too soft, but strong enough for his uncle to feel his presence pressed up against his.

Unk squeezed back, and Kid felt the subtle beat of life inside Unk.

A gesture, like the squeeze of a hand, was an action he never understood for he only saw the adults do it from time to time whenever they shook hands.

To Kid, the idea of one person grabbing hold of the hand of another person seemed so insignificant and, at times, so silly.

Yet, at that moment in time, Kid realized for the first time what it truly meant.

JANE often thought about what it'd be like to be hunted.
Stalked.

Then, *finally*, killed.

Or, as Chandler coined, the "Big Sleep."

Jane carried around these macabre thoughts ever since she became a collector of all things creepy. Her fascination began with the more vulnerable bugs. Black ants. Carpenter ants. Sugar ants. Caterpillars. Earthworms. Silverfish. Various types of beetles, including the ladybird beetle—the "ladybug"—longhorn beetles, the American carrion beetle, oil beetles, acorn weevils, fireflies, click beetles, tiger beetles, rhinoceros beetles, stag beetles. Earwigs. Phasmids. Then, various types of crickets—Jane was dumbfounded by the many different types of crickets. She kept all of these tiny beautiful critters in a Mason jar that once belonged to her grandma before it was handed down to her mother. Eventually, as Jane's diverse collection grew, so too did her "bug hotel." Jane replaced that old Mason jar with a shoebox and as with the Mason jar, poked holes through the top of the lid. Parts of the shoebox eventually became heavily saturated from the dampness of soil and other loose vegetation inside and started to break down and eventually, collapse. Jane upgraded to an aquarium that she bought with a brick-sized Ziploc bag of change she earned by secretly pawning away clothes that she outgrew on eBay.

As Jane's hotel grew, so did her fascination with bugs. Jane sought out those that didn't want to be sought out. The creepiest of crawlers. Spiders. Centipedes. Even reptiles like baby garden snakes and lizards.

She was a collector of God's banished children.

After awhile, the grasshoppers, the ants, and the worms—the smaller, more vulnerable ones—were looked at as more of a food supply rather than a friend or fancy she'd say, a "guest" at Bug Inn. Jane thought it was an incredibly bizarre idea for a living thing to consume another living thing in order to survive.

What savagery, she thought.

One girl's bug collection was another one's dinner.

On the contrary, the savagery of survival made Jane even more curious to seek out more bugs, as if the savagery in itself was her own little gateway drug.

Either way, she collected these creatures as if they were a part of one big dysfunctional family inside a fish tank which was layered with sand, rocks, and grass, as well as spruced up shrubbery and tree branches that she gathered from the woods behind her cozy yet, often times, obscurely deceiving peach colored Victorian-style house. She resided in a predominantly white neighborhood where the only crimes committed were soft dialogue, subtle prodding, invasive moments, and occasionally, a late night egging and rolling by the royally privileged high schoolers or a sexually frustrated spouse privately scratching an seven year itch.

Jane was an only child. Both her parents had decent jobs, content, itch-free. Both had comfortable six-figure salaries with 401ks, health insurance, including dental, and a weird and wonderful daughter who found companionship with those who dwelled in the most unlikely, yet dirtiest of places.

Jane didn't have many human friends whom she could call her besties. But she had her bugs.

Eventually, Jane looked upon her vast collection of insects and reptiles on a much grander scale and changed the name of her hotel from Bug Inn to Jane Cutter's "Brave New World" because she didn't want to offend the reptile or arachnid community. She even handcrafted a marquee-style sign speckled with glitter and plastic emeralds. Hung it up above the fish tank for all her imaginary friends to see.

But nature started to run its wicked course.

Through Jane's rougher side of adolescence—or what she branded her "mutant years"—she graduated to the ever so elusive praying mantis, which she kept in a special jar and would only let it play with the others during dinnertime. That was when those dark thoughts took shape, the stalking, the killings. The praying mantis was, in a way, the "King" of all stalkers, a natural born hunter who put any cockroach to shame. Even though the mantis was related to the cockroach, it was anything but. Jane knew it as the bug's predator. Graceful yet deadly, unlike its ugly cousin. Blended into its surroundings as it stalked its prey. Most of the time its prey would ease right next to the praying mantis and not even realize it was about to become dinner until the predator was right on top of it.

Then, as Jane started to develop into a woman, her bugs got bigger and more deadly. Tarantulas. Scorpions. She'd go well out of her way to locate these tiny monsters.

By the time her junior year rolled around, Jane was spending most afternoons combing the deserts with a backpack full of jars, rather than studying. Jane wasn't the type of student who excelled in one particular subject. She was your average student who put in an average effort. Precalculus, world history, English literature: none of these subjects appealed to Jane.

Every now and then, she'd even skip second period to search for tarantulas at an old desolate quarry, which, over time, had eventually turned into a lake known as Quarry's Lake. But the kids called it "Devil's Throat." Over the years, Devil's Throat had become a go-to spot for kids to cool off the hot boredom of summer. However, after one of the kids from Jane's class died from hitting his head on a rock in the shallow end, Devil's Throat had become more of a safety hazard than a fun hangout spot, which meant the quarry attracted fewer humans and more animals.

Even the highly evolved kind. . .

Throughout most of Jane's senior year, Devil's Throat was Jane's own personal paradise. She had a world of creatures at her disposal.

The tarantula was one of her greatest discoveries. During the day, she'd keep it famished. Same with the scorpion. She'd place it a separated jar and have it facing the tarantula. Only at night would Jane put them in the same arena and let them spar in a battle royal to a bitter death.

Night was a cruel child which brought out its most strange mysteries.

On some mornings when the air in her bedroom felt slightly dense, her collection would be disturbed. Several bugs—sometimes, a lot of bugs—would be missing from the fish tank. Later, she'd find them throughout the house: cowering under the fridge, chilling on the kitchen countertop, or making a desperate flee to an open window. Other times, she'd listen for an inevitable scream from her mother.

"Spider!" she'd shriek from the downstairs.

Then, Jane would sweep in before her mother would splatter the spider's guts all over the floor with a broom.

Jane was left baffled as to how—and why—her bugs were escaping from her "Brave New World."

Determined to catch the miscreant red-handed, Jane decided to hide a camcorder in front of the fish tank before she went to bed.

When Jane woke the next morning, the fish tank had been tampered with, as predicted. She noticed some of them were dead. She rewound the footage on the camcorder. That was when she soon realized the bugs weren't escaping.

She was setting them free.

Back to the very world that she scorned.

Or, as the film showed, smashed with a rock.

Jane's mother took her daughter to the doctor where they ran extensive tests on her. But the doctors couldn't find anything wrong with Jane. After bouncing around from one specialist to another, Jane was diagnosed with a sleeping disorder. They gave it a name for it: *somnambulism*. But she knew it best as "sleepwalking."

A once diplomat of the insect world who waged wars or brought adversaries together in unity by constantly welcoming new members to her secret society of creepiness, Jane was no longer allowed to collect any insects or reptiles—parents' orders. Her "Brave New World" was no more. All of the insects that Jane kept inside the fish tank were liberated back to the woods—or as she hopelessly put it, exiled. The fish tank was left on the side of the road for the local garbage man to collect. One girl's world had become another man's trash.

By the time Jane reached her roaring twenties, she finally got a handle on her sleepwalking. The insect world started to fade like a fad. During her first couple of years at Western University, she'd often go on bug hunts between classes. But it wasn't the same. Jane met another friend, a human one, whom she could genuinely call a friend: Ruby, a brazen tattooed chain smoker from Wensburg, Virginia. She, too, could relate to Jane, not because they both had more love for the animal kingdom than the human race, but because she, too, was a victim of the harshness of scrutiny. The boys hated Jane because she was too much like *them* in certain aspects. The girls hated Jane because she was nothing like *them*.

"Them."

Two different sexes used in the same naming: them, *they*, you people.

But Jane wasn't the only person who called her relentless oppressors, as well as her abusers, by the same pronoun.

Ruby had an eating problem. Like all doctors, they gave it a name just like they had given Jane's sleeping disorder. Bulimia nervosa. Which kids often mistook for anorexia.

When Ruby was sixteen, the "popular years," as she called her peak of fame, she started to shed weight so fast that those who often ignored her in class started to pay attention. "Popular years," as in the worst years ever. But at that age, what was the difference?

By the end of the year, Ruby was a stick figure. She'd binge-eat in private, in the bathroom, in her car, at the park; then, she'd find a bathroom and purge it all away. She always kept a bag handy wherever she went out in public just in case there wasn't a bathroom in the vicinity. Ruby pulled this shady act for the entire year. She'd binge and purge. Purge and binge. The vicious cycle had drawn the kind of eyes that Ruby had feared. At the rate she was going, she was going to be dead by the age of twenty-five. Finally, Ruby got the help she so desperately needed and gradually put the weight back on.

By the age of seventeen, she was a brand new person. Ruby no longer cared about "them"; in fact, she wanted absolutely nothing to do with them—and whenever the topic of "them" came up, she'd often speak of *them* as if she was speaking of something less than human, less than a bug. Like something as primordial as evil itself. Like something that couldn't be seen with a trained eye, only sensed through human intuition.

Before Ruby enrolled at Western, she got herself a dog.

Jane wasn't into dogs, at least not enough to look at their kind as a friend because she always carried around this image of dogs being ushered down sidewalks by humans, but she fell in love with Gorgomite. He was a wild dog, free spirited, unleashable. Gorgomite was a Great Dane named after a ballsy sorcerer from one of Ruby's underground fantasy books and he was about the size of a small horse.

Gorgomite—or "Gorgo," for short—had unequivocally erased the image Jane once had of dogs: these small yappy battery operated things wearing cute tailored sweaters and colorful hair ribbons and scuttling around on leashes while scouting out a good piece of Bermuda or a lovely flowerbed to squat over to do their business and then afterwards, their owners picking up their smelly prize with one of those black poop bags and disposing it in the proper doggie waste bin as if ironically the roles had been somehow reversed and it was the humans who were loyal servants and the dogs were their pampered masters. That, of course, and sniffing or humping assholes *was all dogs were good for,* Jane once thought. However, Gorgo was neither small—obviously—or yappy or a nuisance; in fact, he was Ruby's most loyal companion. He was the love of her life.

Jane had her bugs.

Ruby had Gorgo.

Eventually, Jane stopped collecting bugs altogether, stopped looking for them throughout the slower parts of her day, stopped tending to them, stopped talking to them. She found a bond with a beast of a dog named after a fictitious character and developed an appreciation for its fellow canine pals.

After Jane graduated from Western, she spent the following year hopscotching from one shithole job to another. A part-time bartending job where the drinks were dirty and the men whom she served were even dirtier. A job as a waitress at a trendy restaurant in a newly gentrified area where ninety-nine percent of the clientele were either pretentious Silicon Valley wannabes, overeducated and underpaid hipsters, or shaggy-haired freeloaders; then the other one percent were manboys who still held a grudge against George Lucas.

If there was one thing Jane learned during her brief stint in the food industry, most of the guests were no different than the bugs she used to keep imprisoned in her jars, waiting to be feed.

All in all, the food industry wasn't for Jane.

She tried several other jobs. Retail jobs. Cashier. Sales associate. But they were no different than those food industry jobs. Catering to giant bugs.

Since Jane had a new appreciation for dogs, she started to walk dogs for other people. She'd take them to parks or open fields and let them frolic around as if they were in paradise.

Surprisingly, Jane earned enough cash from "walking dogs" to pay a month's rent, but it wasn't enough to pay the bills.

As the bills started to pile up, Jane stopped walking dogs. But she still loved them. And cats, too. She got into them after the whole Internet craze. Had two. Named them after the two characters in her favorite book, *Fight Club*. Tyler Durden was a Russian blue. Marla Singer, a sweet tortoiseshell. They, too, had fallen witness to Jane's mounting frustration with the workforce.

She had a major in political science, which was like accidentally dropping a hot french fry on her résumé and all that remained under college education was a smudge of grease forever stained into the paper. Since Jane's parents had paid for most of their daughter's college—Jane promising her parents to pay back her debt as soon as she found a decent job—Jane wasn't too concerned about the money. She was more concerned by all the time she had wasted. Time she could've spent finding a job. Time she could've spent finding her own unique voice without it being stifled by college mobs who chased after trends.

After weeks of searching for jobs related to her major, Jane simply gave up. She started to feel as if the last four years of her life was all for nothing, as if the four years weren't a part of a "growing up" phase. Instead, they were taken from her, stolen. All the money that her parents spent on her for college could've been loaned to her for an investment or a business venture or opportunity. Jane started to question whether the experience of something, like college, was worth the price.

Was it any different than trying to buy friends?

It wasn't until a couple of days after Jane returned home from visiting Ruby, who was visiting her parents for the weekend in Virginia before heading back to New York where she was doing a six-month long internship at a highly respected magazine, when she got the idea to work at an animal hospital. She was motivated by the horrid thought of moving back home with her parents. Jane could visualize herself sunken into the couch, hugged by it as if she only received hugs by her parent's criminally expensive furniture, then her body prematurely wilting like a recently bloomed flower after spring's last freeze, as she lost herself in reruns of *The Real Housewives of Atlanta* while her passive-aggressive parents, too timid to confront their own daughter whom they had spent their life's savings on for college, routinely shot her age-old glares from the other side of the living room; whereas on other days, which seemed longer and less bright, her mother would accompany her patent glare with stingy spoken criticism, yet not entirely directed, at her daughter. The remarks stayed with Jane well after they were spoken. Often times, she'd fall into a trapdoor of the worst scrutiny a young woman could ever endure whenever Jane didn't respond to her mother in a timely fashion, which, consequently, was met by disguised lingual assaults, such as "our daughter is so friendly, isn't she?" Jane's mother would sarcastically say these words to her husband as if their clueless yet fragile daughter was in another room pounding her head against the wall. Jane's mother would randomly spit out playful yet internally damaging lines such as, "you're never going to get married" or "it's no wonder you don't have a job," whenever the two had a trivial disagreement about a dinner arrangement or with very little disregard of her daughter's attempt at building confidence, speak for Jane whenever she was in the company of strangers or distant relatives, as if her daughter was a closemouthed mute who didn't possess what humans referred to as a tongue; these incredibly strategic yet manipulative remarks lived with Jane throughout the pauses of the day, constantly plaguing the rest of her day, ruining her day, destroying her day. Ever since Jane was a girl, she displayed, from the trials of ridicule, a natural, altruistic ability—one that Jane harvested at an early age from her grandma who had been shunned from the family as a Bohemian recluse who lived deep in the woods—to use whatever was spoken to her as a shield to protect her from the outside world. The last time Jane visited her parents, Jane was only half-there. Her body was present, but her mind was off somewhere else. For Jane, it was better this way. The sly remarks would only ricochet off her. In the past, though, it'd only take one *word*, one remark, to send Jane into an internal war of suffering, then the words taking shape into other mysterious forms, battering against the corners of her skull until she felt as if her mind had been reduced to atom particles. The words would *still* be there, though, even after her parents were gone. The words living inside her, lingering like a cool villain in the back of a dark, smoky lounge.

But her mother was running out of insults, and Jane knew every single one of them before they were flung her way.

The last thing Jane wanted to become was a cliché.

While Jane and Ruby were visiting Bush Gardens, Ruby was actually the one who made the suggestion of Jane working at an animal hospital. From there, the wheels started to turn. She found a vet not too far from her apartment. There was an opening for a veterinarian technician. Without even knowing what the job involved, Jane applied for the job. Easily got the job. Lived happily ever after.

End of story, right?

Wrong.

Jane spent just shy of a month as a veterinarian technician before the strange events started to happen. Jane didn't exactly know when it really began. But she knew things started to change for her after she heard the story about a Rottweiler not only killing a baby, but also attempting to eat a baby after the baby died from its injuries. Having spent time around dogs, Jane was well aware of the power of a canine, its bark often being louder than its bite but when provoked its bite could make its bark sound like a murmur underneath the average scream of any individual and would pale in comparison to a human's bite. That was the one thing Dog had over Man: its bite. Even the bugs Jane used to collect could pack a real punch. A tick spreading Lyme disease; a snake injecting lethal amounts of poison into a human body, making it extremely deadly if untreated; even mosquitoes carrying a range of diseases such as malaria or encephalitis. There had been cases of hairy scorpions killing humans. Jane read online about a baby boy dying from a hairy scorpion's poisonous sting in the middle of the night when he was sleeping. She also heard on the news about an elderly woman who got stung but didn't even know about until it was already too late. But a dog, a Rottweiler, not only killing a human being, but also eating one: for Jane, this was like uncovering another side of life. A darker side.

The macabre thoughts returned, slowly at first.

Scattered deeply in a lost dream.

Jane warded off these violent thoughts by experimenting with the one thing she had always wanted to do but never had the courage to do.

Dating.

Again, Ruby's idea.

"Start off small," she'd say. "Coffee. Drinks. Work your way up to 'Dinner and a Movie.' The ultimate test for a young bachelorette like Jane was the 'Day Date.' Go on dates that involve outdoor activities, like bike riding, hiking, even camping. Let him show you that he's a man who has blood pumping through his veins. If you can stand sharing each other's company when you're both as sober as monks, then you might just have a chance at being somebody's girlfriend."

Jane took Ruby's advice and played the field. She had never been on a date before. Never even had a drink with a person of the opposite sex. Growing up, Jane had never been comfortable around boys. Jane had never been comfortable around girls, either. Except for Ruby. Jane was "physically" attracted to Ruby. After Ruby's health crisis, she did a complete one-eighty and turned into what the boys called a "gym rat." Twice a year, she ran a 5K. She cut bread from her diet and only ate meat, veggies, and fruit. Never once indulged, not even a crumb of a cookie. She was a walking cliché of a full-time health nut. However, Ruby was clueless when it came to Jane's feelings toward her. Sometimes she'd often appear unclothed in Jane's mind. Jane and Ruby once shared an intimate kiss on the way home from a Pi Kappa Alpha party, which ended up getting busted by the campus security after one of the Pikes set a sacred tree on fire. That night, Jane and Ruby were both wasted from slurping body shots of bourbon and pounding down skunky keg beer. Ruby hardly remembered it the next morning—in fact, she spent the most active parts of the morning with her head buried in the toilet—while Jane, on the other hand, couldn't get it out of her head even if she tried. The kiss. *That kiss.* Their relationship was strictly platonic, no chaser, no regrets. That, they both understood, especially Ruby. After Western, Jane looked at their relationship, more or less, as a "fantasy friendship," as if there would soon come a day when all Jane had left of Ruby were fond yet distant memories, only touchable via mindscape. In a way, Jane always looked at what she and Ruby had as "too good to be true." Something only discovered in a timeless fairy tale patiently sitting on the back of a dusty shelf somewhere in some dusty library, waiting to be digested. Even when Jane was attending Western, she had a feeling in her gut that she and Ruby's relationship, like all beautiful things, wouldn't last. A part inside Jane—a darker part—wouldn't let it. The time being separated from Ruby eventually turned Ruby into a voice on the other end of her phone, nothing more than a voice to listen to whenever Jane was lonely or needed pointers. Jane wanted more from Ruby, more than her voice, but she knew the closest she'd ever have with Ruby was exactly that, just a sound.

The first date Jane went on was a disaster. Drinks with a guy named Jeffery Maiden—or "Just Jeff," as he introduced himself. She met him online through a dating app called MINGLE. The guy was a real jerk, Jane thought, had the wrong kind of arrogance that made his perfectly carved jaw and cheek structure look annoying, as if she was tempted to punch him in the face during his hour-long bragfest about his job in advertising. Throughout the entire night, he didn't ask Jane one question about herself; and whenever Jane did talk or strategically divert the conversation away from Just Jeff, he never followed up with interest. Instead, he went back to kneading his own ego with a cat-like satisfaction. He looked at her merely as an object with two holes for releasing himself—three, if Jane was into the kinkier recreations, but he'd never bring up the subject on a first date.

By the end of the night, he only got to first base with Jane after he "purposefully" fed her shots of Jägermeister.

His goal for the night was to round first base and do an in-side-the-park homerun, but Jane wasn't at all waving him to home plate. And that was all that remained of "Just Jeff," a self-absorbed man who hit a routine single up the middle but got way too cocky by squeezing that single into a double and getting thrown out at second base.

Jane's second date was equally as poor as the first; how-ever, she was starting to master her curveball. The guy made a half-ass attempt at bunting: a small peck of a kiss on her lips. Jane turned her head at the last second and re-ceived a dry, thorny kiss on her cheek instead. To Jane, a dog could kiss better.

Some of these guys—and girls—hung around for a couple of days, shooting her text messages laced with selfies, insin-cere compliments, and innuendos of sex or copulation. One woman she met on Mingle talked about how much she wanted to adopt a kid. Even said Jane make the ideal part-ner. Jane had only spent a couple of hours with her at a lo-cal coffee shop and by the time she was done with her caramel macchiato, the woman was already talking about touchy subjects normal couples didn't even bring up until they moved in together or mutually committed to raising an animal by rescuing an old Golden Retriever named Waggles from the pound before they decided to raise a human life. Even the good guys, preppy or non-preppy, who acted de-cent enough to keep their minds from the gutter folded after a week; however, they couldn't hit Jane's wicked curve, which usually came barreling by with first, a cordial hug then followed by a swift "good night' as soon as her date was about to lean in for a kiss. Most of the dates on Mingle, Jane realized, turned out to be disguised booty calls or fore-play into much carnal activities cloaked with a phony inter-est as to what Jane was getting herself into that day, as if it was reverse psychology 101. These deviants certainly weren't going to "get inside" Jane anytime soon. She made sure of it—or at least, tried to.

Despite dozens of dud-dates that turned out being a bust, Jane ended up getting lucky a handful of times. The relationship only lasted for two weeks until the fire was put out, but it was Jane who did most of the extinguishing. Again, it was that darker side of her, a vengeful, ruthless darkness that had been living with her ever since high school, her "mutant years." Two weeks of putting up with Jane's resilient optimism was all it could endure before it killed any desire she felt about sharing a life with another individual. Several guys—and girls—had come along and showed prospects of being that person her fantasy-friend, Ruby, could *not* be. After two weeks, the light changed. All of a sudden, Jane started to see her prospects in a much darker, less attractive light. Like the Darkness wanted Jane all to itself and it was deceiving her by showing her what "these people" appeared like underneath poor lighting. She'd pick out a flaw on their face or in their personality or whatever, highlight and then exaggerate it to the fullest, so much that, after those two weeks, it was all she saw. Eventually, she gave up on the dating scene, dropped the whole online dating thing, dropped "seeing" other people in general, and just "got around." *But* there was only so much of "sleeping with strangers" she could condone until she wanted something more.

Something real and right.

But her dreams started to turn on her.

The thoughts became more vivid.

Red and deadly.

This time around, those curious thoughts had become a reality.

Later, Jane would go on to call him by the name, Mr. Moonlight, because his eyes looked like tiny moons, at times full and bright while other times, keen and sickle-esque, like a waxing crescent. She had once heard the name on the night of a rare lunar eclipse when both her drunken parents were singing the hazy lyrics to The Beatles song, *Mr. Moonlight*, on their fuzzy-sounding antique vinyl record player. Jane remembered stretching her seven-year-old body over the banister along the staircase and gawking at the tall, wavy shadows of her parents swaying back and forth like buoys over the glossy hardwood floor in the kitchen as they repeatedly howled that one name, "Mr. Moonlight," in the candlelight, occasionally laughing while doing so, as if they were performing some kind of ritual downstairs—*a sacrifice*, Jane would later consider, maybe even satanic—as she was strangled by the sweaty teeth of night. Cowered between her covers, she visualized the shadow of a disproportionate arm of her father striking down with a strange, twisted blade of some kind on a much smaller shadow strapped to the kitchen table. Followed by the stabbing motion was the deafening yelp of an animal. Then the Shiraz that her mother had been supposedly drinking spilled over the hardwood floor. But was it red wine that had been spilt? Or, Jane thought, was it something else?

Maybe that was where the name came from, a young girl running away with an imagination so rich and wild that would make other girls her age jealous.

Maybe she just liked the name when it rolled off her tongue.

Mr. Moonlight.

Jane never actually saw him, Mr. Moonlight, well enough to identify him to a sketch artist. For one, Jane had seen him only at night; and two, Jane didn't even know what race he was because he looked no darker than a silhouette.

A dark, faceless figure.

Watching her.

After the second time Jane saw him outside her apartment window, she called Ruby long distance and told her about the stalker. Ruby told Jane to call the cops. But the guy had committed no crime.

Another month passed.

Jane was starting to hit her snooze button more often.

Each and every day, her passion for animals started to diminish, like the bugs she once collected. Going to work everyday seemed as if it was becoming an unwanted choir, something to be put off, inevitably neglected. She even started to change the way she felt about her cats, Tyler and Marla, once thought of as two lifelong pals; but after awhile, they became these burdens as if she was taking care of two upset babies that forever remained upset babies, never at all cute and cuddly, just ugly and upset. Even the sounds of their meows started to have a piercing wail of a baby.

The thought that kept nagging at Jane: When would her violent thoughts turn to action?

Then, one day before work, it happened.

Jane was scrambling around her apartment, racing from the dryer to fetch her clothes and then back into the kitchen to grab a breakfast snack to go, when all of a sudden Tyler snuck up behind her and gently pawed at her ankle.

Not thinking, Jane reacted.

To Jane, it felt more like a shove than a kick, a way to keep Tyler in check by showing him who was boss. Tyler didn't see it that way at all.

Tyler's eyes swelled with blackness. His pointy ears folded over the sides of his head. Everything about Tyler folded, his body and soul, as if he was winding himself up to spring himself into an attack. Jane saw these defensive gestures and yet, she did it anyway. She "shoved" Tyler once more. Tyler let out a high-pitch hiss and scratched Jane across the shin, drawing blood.

Jane snapped from her red haze and ran to the bathroom, crying.

Soon after, Tyler poked his head into the bathroom. Jane welcomed Tyler; in return, he rubbed on her leg in the most deliberate act of forgiveness.

Jane couldn't apologize enough to Tyler. She didn't know what happened or even *how* it happened. She was beginning to feel as if these behaviors alone had come straight from the deleted scenes cut from another movie where she, the star of the movie, was no longer a relatable character.

Later that night, when Jane was driving home from work, a deer suddenly ran out in front of her car.

With no time to react—no time to even blink—the deer struck the side of her car. The side airbags deployed, forcing Jane to swerve the car off the side of the road. She managed to slam on the brakes before driving into a ditch. It was dark out, late. The accident happened on an empty two-lane road in the middle of the woods where the only life forms came from Jane's imagination. She switched on the caution lights and pushed open the door, which had a massive dent. She saw the blood on the door, a chunk of hair wedged between the hinges. She found the deer sprawled out on the side of the road. But it wasn't dead. She, Jane realized, was still alive. But barely.

With no car in sight, Jane looked around and realized that she only had two options: *Let the deer suffer to death and eventually, die alone out here on the road and hope that possibly someone will come along to "finish" off the deer or do the one thing that she most feared, put the deer out of her misery?*

Jane didn't think twice.

She chose option number two.

However, it was the way she killed the deer that disturbed her the most.

This wasn't a deleted scene, Jane soon realized once she made it back home and tossed her bloody shoes into the trashcan.

This was the moment in *her story* where everything changed.

After Jane had confessed as to what she had done, Ruby made a suggestion that Jane join a club or even go out more during the day, do anything to keep her mind away from what took place that night.

Jane decided to give love a second chance.

"No more hooking up," Jane told herself in the mirror. "Find someone who sees you for who you are."

Jane tried one of the easiest places on earth for human interaction. The bar. Literally, the placed was named, "The Bar;" however, the word *the* was replaced with the slang word 'Da. The bar read: 'Da Bar. Kind of the stereotype of a Chicagoan saying 'Da Bears. So, 'Da Bar. A sketchy lit joint, which was located not too far from her apartment. Everyday, Jane passed by the place on her way home from work. Every Saturday night, a local band played at 'Da Bar. However, 'Da Bar received most of its business on Thirsty Thursday nights and Sunday Funday afternoons, Thursday nights typically drawing the rowdy football crowd and Sunday afternoons pretty much drawing the same crowd, only younger. Jane decided to rid any stereotypes that she had about 'Da Bar's regulars and try Thursday night.

For the first twenty minutes or so, Jane wasted away the time hidden at the end of the bar while randomly looking over parts of her body as if she was giving herself a self-examination or making minor clothing adjustments or primping herself. Jane did all these tiny movements as if it was a nervous tick. At times, she acted as if she wanted to leap out of her own skin, like some junkie falling into a wicked pattern of fidgety movements. She'd take a bird-like sip of her bitter gin and tonic; then she'd sweeten it up with a squeeze of lime; then she'd take another bird-like sip; then she'd watch a couple of minutes of some game that she wasn't the least interested in on the idiot box; then she'd check her wristwatch that she only wore on special occasions; then she'd check the time on her phone to make sure it matched the time on her watch; then she'd take another bird-like sip of her drink; then she'd dizzily swim back into her phone and act as if she was texting somebody, like her bestie or business associate, when she was only pretending to text another human being to make it look as if she was normal and that she wasn't alone but instead anxiously waiting on her bestie or business associate whom she was meeting up with for drinks (depending on the sex of the party involved, bestie if it was a man and business associate if it was a woman) when, in fact, she'd use the common excuse of being "stood up" if she was ever asked why she was drinking by herself.

By Jane's second drink, she finally mustered the nerve to talk to an older man who sat down next to her. The conversation started out like any other small talk. Weather analysis. Unseasonably cold conditions, cold fronts, and whatnot. Then, he acted like a broadcaster on TV and gave his own one-sided commentary on the overpaid football players on TV.

Then, after he plowed through his third drink—Jane still working on her second—he started to get political by bashing the specific players who kneeled during the National

Anthem, comparing the sport to a job, and how his ass would get fired in a heartbeat if he brought his politics to the job and started kneeling during the Monday morning staff meeting. The old man had what Jane thought was the attention span of a goldfish. He even forgot her name twice; and by the third time she told the old man her name, he misheard it—probably not—because he started calling Jane Lorraine.

Riding on her smooth buzz train, Jane wasn't the least interested in anything the drunken man had to say to her, but it felt good just to talk to somebody even if the old man was incredibly mouthy and full of shit and most of the conversation felt like Déjà vu.

It wasn't until a couple of minutes into his rant when Jane wished she hadn't opened her mouth to say hi in the first place.

Jane excused herself, shouldered her way to the bathroom, didn't relieve herself yet hung around in front of the mirror for a moment and gathered herself; then when she made her way back to the bar, she found another seat far away from the local drunk. The night barreled along like a hurricane along the Gulf Coast.

Waves of people flowed into 'Da Bar in intervals, at times, overflowing.

Jane ended up talking to several other people among the crowd, but they, too, had nothing interesting to say to her. Most of what they had to say was the same stuff the other guy was saying, as if their conversations were being controlled by what they heard on TV or read on social media and that they, too, all watched or read the same stuff. More stuff about stuff. Stuff on stuff. Weather stuff. Sports stuff. Hollywood stuff. Then, the stuff did a full circle and wound up back at political stuff like a vicious feedback loop. The night gained momentum, more stuff upon stuff, loops upon loops. For some reason, Jane thought more about goldfish, the internal design of a goldfish and that *old myth* about them being masterminds of their own brutal short-term memory and being able to forget just like that, for instance, like being trapped inside a glass fishbowl and tediously swimming circles into what Jane could imagine was an end-less ocean where the only predators came in the wicked shape of warped eyeballs and fingertips.

At one point in the night, Jane unfocused her eyes as if she was staring at one of those stereogram posters where, inside the image, there was a visual illusion of a three-dimensional picture. She'd blur out each pale face and in that white blur, she'd witness puckered lips forming into black dots.

They—the people—actually looked like goldfish.

The talk became looser, so did the crowd—or in Jane's eye, the school.

A couple of men complimented Jane on her ass and how nice it was. She was tempted to slap one man; but after Jane decided to cool off with a stiff drink, she rid any notion of doing so.

Another man smelled her hair and started talking about lions and how the male lion would smell the scent of a lion-ess right before he was about to mate with her. Jane laughed off the man. She needed another drink, a stiffer one.

Another man came along and bought Jane a whole bunch of shots. He acted as if it was his sole mission to make sure Jane wasn't taken advantage of by any of the other men. Yet, the man bought her shots without any re-gard for her personal safety, as if his whole angle of being the "only gentlemen" at the bar who made enough money at whatever make-believe job to afford expensive shots of extra rare Crown Royal—the top shelf stuff—was his stealthy scheme to convince Jane to come home with him before the last call. On several occasions, Jane attempted to brush off the guy like a pesky fruit fly. He kept lingering around her, either eye-flirting with her from across the bar or "mistak-enly" bumping into her as soon as she turned a corner. Jane wasn't at all interested in the guy getting in her pants by the end of the night nor was she remotely interested in his issues and his overly sentimental behavior towards her; in fact, Jane wished the man would disappear—or better yet, Jane thought, wished the man would shrink in size, like an action-figure. Then, she'd pick him up by the back of his collar, his tiny, stiff action-figure arms and legs aerobically winding all around, and then she'd flush him down the toilet and watch him go 'round and 'round.

Her eyes still remained unfocused.

Her body swayed.

At that point, Jane felt it was best to call it a night.

But when Jane left 'Da Bar, she wasn't alone.

As she stumbled to her car, she witnessed him, her avid follower, her stalker, "Mr. Moonlight." She didn't know if it was him or not for the lighting was poor outside 'Da Bar and the moon was nearly full, too, with its pale light casting over parked cars, causing certain metallic areas to faintly glint and deceive. Her head was also heavy from the house gin that she had consumed in short time. Her eyes red and burning. Her thoughts extra swampy.

She strangely extended her head forward and looked twice at the dark figure. Did the one eye trick and steadied her Cyclops-gaze.

It was him . . .

Mr. Moonlight.

It was on this particular night Jane had officially branded him with that name, *Mr. Moonlight.* Maybe it was the alcohol distorting her vision. Maybe it was all of the bar-folks who wore down her spirits into an old, cracked nub with all their crassness, rude ambiguity, and flaming contradictions. Maybe all of those nasty things they said to her directly and indirectly had come straight from alcohol, as if the alcohol itself had the power to make people extremely mouthy. Jane considered herself a social drinker, the ever-so elusive "When in Rome" type drinker, a featherweight who easily got knocked out when it came to throwing back shots of hard liquor. Besides attending a few parties in college, she hadn't been around enough drunk people to fully understand the power of influence that the bottle had on weaker saps who were bewitched by its liquid spell. Maybe Jane was only listening to things *they* had secretly kept locked away inside their skulls throughout the sober hours of the day; and alcohol—for some—was that key to unlocking that dark, foul chamber of demons.

Maybe it was just a whole bunch of things.

Maybe it was what went down on the road the night before.

The dead deer. The crushed skull. The eyeballs. The leaking brain matter.

Maybe it was nothing.

One thing was certain: Jane didn't see these people as people, but rather saw *them* as another "them."

Throughout college, she saw people, other walks of life, other figures open to the world, like Ruby, who shared a kinship with Jane, a person who lived in the moment. After they shared their first kiss, Jane questioned if she overstepped her bounds, if her being human was too much to ask from Ruby. She felt something for Ruby, that, she was certain of. Whether it was the flesh or not, Jane longed to feel what she had felt when she was with Ruby, to see life. She used to study the other students whenever she wasn't preoccupied with her tiny fellowship; and despite all of their differences, Jane saw these other walks of life for everything they were so ready to be and nothing they were trying to be in order to fit into the societal contract of normalcy. Throughout the day, she observed all of their unique quirks, mannerisms, and independence charging through as she overheard native tongues slip through group conversations. She observed clingy high school bullshit being removed from their shoulders like hooks; and at night, sitting alone in her dorm room, she heard sounds of life roaring in the night darkness. Her skin pulsed. Pulsed hard. In a way, Jane envied them, not as docked vessels eager to embark to a new world without rules, but rather ones charting a path feared by their ancestors.

Being back in her small town, she started to feel small again, irrelevant. She didn't see people anymore, only "them."

When Jane looked at herself in the mirror, she saw a young woman without any color. Her skin translucent like a jellyfish, revealing a complex nervous system, as well as a skeletal structure and the organs she kept inside. Everything was starting to blacken, shrivel, and warp. She was dying, but regardless of the factual evidence of her slow decay, she was still working overtime behind the scenes and doing everything solely in her power to escape death by reaching for something that seemed unreachable.

Mr. Moonlight was *that* something who saw Jane.

She saw him too.

In a perverse way, Jane longed for him and his tireless observations.

At first glance, her head lowered, shoulders hunched, eyes honed. Her upper body went hanging, like her left wrist whenever she buckled the strap of a watch. Jane's body, like her wrist in some way or another, was loose and limp, as if she was waiting to be secured by time.

Jane peered closer.

The sight of Mr. Moonlight made her skin pulse and throb, despite the inability to act upon its very urges.

She was the girl who used to stick her hand into a sketchy burrow in the desert and pull out whatever creatures resided inside it. At times, she was stung in the arm or hand, her body filled with poison. She'd ride out the rush of poison, at times sweating it out throughout the day like a cruel fever, while, other times, feeling great arousal from it. Over the years of collecting, Jane had become immune to the creature's poison, never at all frightened by its sting or bite.

But when it came to being in the presence of Mr. Moonlight, Jane's body was left in a state of paralysis. Not once did Jane ever approach him nor think about doing so. Even the liquid courage had no effect on her. She was too mortified by his ghostly aura.

As Jane fumbled for her car keys, Mr. Moonlight stood behind the bed of a truck parked at the other end of the gravel parking lot.

With her eyes never leaving his, she managed to get a grip on the keys while Mr. Moonlight remained in the shadows outside a flickering halo of an amber colored floodlight. Not doing much, just staring down Jane with those glossy moonlit eyes. Dressed in all black. Faceless. A rather lanky man with arms as knobby as tree branches. *Around six feet tall*, she guessed, maybe even a couple of inches taller.

Trying not to make a sound, she carefully opened the door and eased into the car as if she was stepping into a tub of ice-cold water. Jane inserted the key into the ignition the same way she opened the door.

Once she started the car, Mr. Moonlight was gone.

She checked all around her, checked her blind spots. Lastly, she checked the rear view mirror, thinking maybe he might've slipped into the backseat of the car without her knowing and she'd find him seated directly behind her, not saying a word, not doing much, just staring in the rear view mirror with those empty white eyes of his. She felt almost feverish by the thought.

This time, she turned fully around and checked the seat behind her.

Then, as Jane faced forward, the sudden thought of Mr. Moonlight standing directly in front of the grill of the car flashed through her mind.

But he was not there.

He was nowhere.

He was gone.

Mr. Moonlight didn't show up until a week later when Jane decided to join a tennis league. The morning after her run in with Mr. Moonlight, she determined that the bar life wasn't for her anymore not because of the cold dis or the political spats and camouflaged racist rhetoric or the lewd behavior or the other countless insults she received through-out the night, but because of the hangover she experienced the morning after. The worse part: there wasn't a magical pill to cure a bad hangover. A hangover was no different than a virus. It just had to run its course. Even worse: the hangover could've been avoided.

But if she hadn't gone to 'Da Bar that night, would she have seen him?

All Jane knew was that he wasn't a hallucination brought on by alcohol.

He was real.

Mr. Moonlight.

Doing that thing he does.

Just staring at Jane.

He was standing behind a picnic bench underneath a canopy not too far away from a playground.

His body was hard to make out for the night darkness.

But his eyes, though, were like distant headlights burning in the dark.

Several times Jane found herself distracted during the match. Every now and then, she'd take her eyes off the ball or remain in a trance-like stare during breaks or catch him in the corner of her eye while chasing down the ball. She was playing doubles and her teammate, a retired lady who spent her entire week preparing for these Thursday night gatherings, grew irritated by Jane's lack of interest.

Once, between games, she pulled Jane aside and asked her if everything was all right. Jane mentioned the strange man watching her. Even asked her teammate if she saw him standing underneath the canopy. Her teammate couldn't see him. But Jane figured the lady had glaucoma or something. That was her excuse.

The following week, Mr. Moonlight was back.

Jane made quite a scene. She spotted him during her serve. Distracted, Jane took her eyes off the ball as she was about to swing. The ball struck the corner of her racket, darted off to the right, and plunked her doubles-teammate in the back.

Her teammate went down hard, wincing and grabbing her back as if she had broken it.

Jane didn't care about her, about what she had done.

She had her eyes on Mr. Moonlight.

Without apologizing, Jane hurried off the court and did the one thing that she said she was going to do all week.

She approached Mr. Moonlight!

Her adrenaline had taken over and she was jacked up. A couple of the tennis players tended to Jane's teammate, Ms. Walsh, while the others stood in awe and watched Jane storm directly to the canopy.

Jane suddenly flung the tennis racket to the ground and curled her hands into fists. Both of her eyes were wide and mad. Her jaw clenched so tight she could crack a filling.

Jane yelled to the top of her voice: *"For crying out loud, what the hell do you want from me? Why are FOLLOWING me? Why can't you just leave me alone? WHAT DO YOU—"*

Once she reached the canopy, the fire she had burning brightly in her belly turned all to smoke. Everything about Jane had fizzled out, as if the sight alone of the dangling canned light fixture underneath the canopy had burst her balloon.

She pushed the fixture once, then it responded by swinging back at her. She stepped closer to the canned fixture and touched the light bulb inside. The bulb was as hot as fire. Yet, the bulb was dark and dead inside.

Jane quickly recoiled from the flash of pain.

Even when she tapped on the bulb, the spring inside rattled like a maraca.

More intrigued, she removed the scrunchie from her ponytail and used it as a glove to twist the loose bulb clockwise.

Surprisingly, the light bulb turned on!

She suddenly flinched.

The light nearly blinded Jane.

Once she knew it was safe, she leaned closer to the light and stood there more surprised not by the sight of the light but by the other players staring at her from the tennis courts.

Like the bars, Jane's tennis days were over. Even though she enjoyed playing tennis more so than drinking and at least trying to socialize at bars, Jane knew she couldn't go back to the tennis league. She was the one who hurt Ms. Walsh—or as Jane saw it, the Mother Theresa wannabe who bent over backwards to make sure everybody was hunky-dory by lending spare rackets to those who didn't have one or bringing extra Gatorade and granola bars for everybody. Jane was the one who went on a psychotic fit after "accidentally" hitting Ms. Walsh with a ball.

In Jane's mind, she was the one who just didn't belong. The elephant on the court. Jane did her research on the Internet and found another league that met on Tuesdays. But they played all the way in Bentwood, which was on the other side of town. Jane wasn't about to drive out of her way just to smack around a tennis ball for an hour or two.

She went back to her daily life, to movies, to her cats.

The one perk about tennis was that, like dating, it helped ward off the nightmares.

But now, with no tennis, no more dating, those nightmares were back with a vengeance.

The nightmares started to bleed into Jane's job. At times, she'd drift off into the reddest daydreams and fantasize about killing animals. Strangely, something darker had manifested itself inside her nightmares.

Somehow, Jane was no longer a prey, but rather the opposite.

The darkness spread into her day. Jane found herself in serious trouble while she was clipping the nails of Mrs. Keddlemen's boxer, Ali. All of a sudden, Jane fell into one of her violent daydreams—sunk, really. Her hand felt as if her hand no longer belonged to her body, not even loose or limp, but vanished; yet, she felt as if it was being controlled by something else, as if the nerves themselves were stuck on a GIF-loop. The violence swelled inside her and all of that red fury had somehow. . . moved. She tried to speak but all that came out were noises, barks? For a moment—and just a moment—it felt as if her soul had been cut, copied, and pasted into Ali. Jane wasn't aware of what she had done until she heard poor Ali howl out in great pain. A part of Jane had embraced that pain as it rippled across her body like a shockwave. Jane snapped from her red thoughts of chopping and looked down at Ali's paw and its fur drenched in blood. One of its toes was partially severed and hanging on like a baby tooth.

Baffled, Jane couldn't figure out whether or not it was an accident.

Ali, being a dog who was adored by the entire staff for his charming personality, ended up losing its toe.

Mrs. Keddlemen came from old money and white privilege. She was a sassy lady who'd make the most villains on soap operas look like kindergarten teachers. For Mrs. Keddlemen, her happy hour began at one o'clock with Pinto Grigio and smoked salmon and cream cheese on gluten-free crackers. She obsessively dolled herself up everywhere she paraded, including the animal hospital. As if a gust of wind followed her everywhere, the doors would swing open for her. She'd roll up in there as snobby as a horse with her pencil-point chin raised high in the air as one of her obedient assistants—usually a handsome boy toy who got paid in game tokens—carried a personally tailored Gucci bag. Ali's head would be poking out of the bag licking the pungent aroma her proud "master" Mrs. Keddlemen left behind. She was the type of benefactor who was not to be messed with, Jane knew. After the incident, Jane pleaded with Mrs. Keddlemen, couldn't say sorry enough. But on that day, Mrs. Keddlemen was in a rare mood.

Jane kept her job.

But after the whole incident, everybody at work was watching Jane.

It seemed like everywhere Jane went, everybody was watching her, studying her, waiting for her to snap or lose control.

Jane had to act fast; otherwise, she'd be out of a job. She started looking for nightly activities, something—anything—to keep her mind off violence. Jane hit the streets, scouted out flyers hanging on street posts, and then, when she didn't have much luck, she got lost in the good ole Internet. She went on Facebook and found a page for a cooking class. *Looked fun*, she thought. In the photos, the students were smiling from ear-to-ear while preparing gourmet food that you'd see on the cover of *Bon Appétit!* The students looked so carefree, as if through their warm hospitality, they were welcoming Jane to join them and show her what she had been missing. The class was called "Be a Chef."

Jane was in.

Be a Chef started at seven o 'clock, which gave many of the students time to get loosey-goosey. The class was located in the historic district, which, like most American towns, had been revitalized to appeal to a needy generation. The night started out optimistic. Jane was looking forward to cooking. However, when she arrived, her spirits were surprisingly dampened from the sight of the students in her class. Most of the people were either newly wed couples or retirees or cliquish Soccer moms trying to spice up their lives with fancy dishes that most of them could hardly even spell or even pronounce. In a way, Jane was desperate to find human connection with "them," but they ended up shunning Jane as if she was a damaged product. It was there, at Be a Chef, when Jane started to feel like one of those old, smelly dogs rescuers took in off the streets.

When she'd scrub away the street grime and pull off the dingle berries hanging from their rears, she couldn't help but think about the dogs' former owners. What kind of person would agree to take on the sole responsibility of caring for another life, then reject it or cast it aside as soon as it showed the first signs of trouble.

Through the mistreatment of these dogs and even cats and other animals, Jane saw firsthand the sheer laziness of society. Yet, she felt as if she was no different than these people whom she started to detest. Like with Mrs. Keddlemen's dog or even the neglect she had shown Tyler and Marla, Jane wondered if it was she who was behaving so out of character.

Was it I, *Jane*, who accidentally kicked Tyler after he scratched me? Was it I who accidentally cut off Ali's toe?

Or, she thought, was it someone else?

Someone—or something—*inside me?*

That was when Jane thought about him.

Sure enough, he showed up as if he was there all along.

Her own personal phantom.

Outside the window of the kitchen, he was standing behind a street post and watching Jane as she learned how to make the popular autumn dish, squash soup.

Jane went about her business, gutting the squash, going by whatever the instructor told her to do. Then, Jane switched stations. Her next task was "How to properly cut an onion," which didn't seem so difficult; however, there was an art involved in thinly slicing an onion, which would be used for the classical French-inspired side dish, potatoes au gratin.

As the instructor guided Jane to curl her knuckles into the center of her palm like a fist and press down on the onion using the same hand, she sliced the onion as thin as a sheet of copy paper. The whole goal was to prevent Jane from making an amateur move by chopping off her fingers—hence curling them into her palm and keeping them from exposure. She did the same for the potato, held the potato down with her hand shaped in a fist-like position, and sliced it as thin as a potato chip with her other hand. While she was working through yet another potato, she looked up and took a glance through the window. She'd make yet another slice, look up, and see him watching her. Jane didn't ignore him, though, Mr. Moonlight. She didn't let him entirely distract her, either.

She, more or less, accepted him for who he was.

Her stalker.

The very next morning, Jane woke up seconds before her alarm clock sounded off.

Energized, she struck the snooze button with authority and rolled out of bed.

The red light cast from a new dawn was burning bright through the windows, causing the blinds to glow. She felt drawn to that red light. She cracked open the blinds, peeked out her window, and fell witness to a red autumn sky. The clouds around the sun lit up with shades of reds and soft pinks and purples; the closer to the sun, the brighter the color red. She felt as if a small part of her was at peace with the world, as if the red light was telling her to be patient, that her *final* peace was ahead of her.

Riding the early morning high, Jane glided into the kitchen, no rush or panic. Most mornings usually consisted of Jane frantically scrambling around the apartment, making last minute wardrobe adjustments before grabbing a biscuit and coffee from one of those eat-at-your-risk fast food joints on the way to work because she didn't have time to prepare herself a decent breakfast. Unburdened, Jane decided to cook one of her most frustrating dishes: the omelet.

For eight years Jane had been a vegan and except for maybe being tempted to eat a slice of bacon that her mother deliberately cooked every Saturday morning as if it was a tradition, not once during those eight good years had Jane ever felt persuaded to hop back on the meat wagon. When she originally gave up on all things meat at the age of sixteen and converted to a life of veganhood, Jane told herself that she was in it all the way. Her parents went out of their way to cater to Jane's new lifestyle. She substituted the meat with protein shakes and supplements. She tweaked her diet accordingly, did it for the little ones, maybe to prove to them that not all humans were the cold-blooded killers like they played out to be. When she *finally* got a place of her own after she graduated from Western, she bought a carton of eggs every week. Every week, Jane kept her fridge stocked with eggs; and every week, she ended up throwing away the eggs. Her only explanation was that she bought the eggs "just in case" she went hungry, as if the eggs were some kind of life raft, an easy "go-to" meal when fruit, salad, tofu, or veggies weren't cutting it for her. Jane was ready to let those eight years slip away. In a way, she felt no different than a recovering alcoholic who feared, yet worshipped, the number zero.

"Just two eggs," she told herself.

After all, it was *only* two eggs.

Jane was no Julia Child when it came to cooking the perfect omelet; in fact, every time she tried to make one when she was younger, she'd end up overcooking the outside or undercooking the inside or, the most common mistake, ruining the physical structure of the omelet after the first flip and then, in most attempts, the final product turning out like roadkill. For as long as she could remember, she looked at the finished result of her infamous omelet like that half-eaten Big Mac, only it'd look twice as messy and falling apart before she'd even take a single bite of it. It would always break down midway through eating it, she recalled her days from her youth.

When cooking an omelet, the onions or bell peppers or mushrooms or spinach would somehow, like the middle bun, lettuce, pickles of a Big Mac with that special sauce acting like lube, wiggle its way out midway through cooking it.

After Be a Chef, Jane realized she was doing everything right, except for one minor yet crucial part. The temperature of the stovetop was too hot. The whole time, she realized, all I had to do was turn down the heat of the burner to its lowest setting. Just a slight twenty-degree turn of a knob separating a sloppy, uneatable omelet to something of great beauty.

While she was gliding around the kitchen and gathering last-second ingredients she needed to finish the perfectly cooked omelet—not too brown on the outside, not too yolky on the inside, but just right, Jane could hear the foodies say—Jane caught a familiar face in the corner of her eye.

She stopped dead in her tracks and turned toward the TV in the living room.

For some reason, she thought about *him*.

A sudden hopelessness washed over her.

On the TV, there was a news report about a man whose body was discovered last night in a car parked in the parking lot of an abandoned strip mall. His wife, Heidi, had reported her husband missing when he didn't come home from his recent book tour. His name was Mark Sakowski, a former executive director of the nonprofit, Green, which promoted sustainable farming, turned bestselling author and controversial filmmaker behind the book, *The Takeover*, which pulled back the curtain on an outdated conspiracy that the food agencies inside the federal government were carrying out covert operations known as "Population Control" linking cancer to many food additives, as well as certain preservatives used for processed foods and other food products. His earth-shocking documentary, *A Side of Arsenic*, focused on pesticides and the dangerous levels of arsenic and carcinogens and banned drugs, such antibiotics, antifungal medications, anti-inflammatory drugs, and even drugs, like the hallucinogenic party drug, ketamine, which were discovered in contaminated meat such as beef, poultry, and pork, and showed levels well beyond the cutoff of the Food Safety and Inspection Service (FSIS). Sakowski was widely known for calling out big corporations and how they were making the public sick in order to take advantage of them. "First, they poison us with their food," Sakowski wrote, referring to CEO, Luther Sims, of *Feature*, a well-known pharmaceutical company, as well as one of the largest beef producers in the world, "then, they heal us. It's a win-win for all parties." In *The Takeover*, Sakowski compared America's corporations as "chiefs who cook high-cholesterol foods for a living, then sale cholesterol drugs as their side hustle." Sakowski left behind a wife and two children. The police were notified after a street sweeper found the body slumped over the steering wheel of a luxury Mercedes Benz. Sakowski had been stabbed to death; in fact, the reporter said he was stabbed over sixty-four times. Police were officially calling it a crime of passion.

"Personal," one investigator stated in an interview.

Jane didn't exactly know where she had seen this man, Mark Sakowski, before, but she had *seen* him somewhere.

As Jane directed attention back to her omelet, the stovetop was smoking. She removed the scolding hot pan from the stovetop with an oven mitt, tossed the pan into the sink, and ran cold water over the pan. Steam rose from the sizzling pan. Jane picked at the omelet, trimmed over the dark spots, and tried her best to salvage what was left of it, but one side of it was black and inedible.

Throughout most of the workday, Mr. Sakowski's face was seared in Jane's mind, as if it was surrounded by so much darkness. It wasn't until a similarly profiled middle-aged man strolled into the animal hospital with his gray Scottish terrier that Jane remembered where she had seen Mr. Sakowski. She was immediately dumfounded when the notion struck her.

But *how?*

Jane had a stark image in her mind of a slender dark skinned man with blue eyes and shoulder-length purple hair pulled back tightly in a ponytail stabbing Mr. Sakowski in the chest with a pair of scissors. Even the windows sur-

rounding the two men were foggy from the hotness that ra-
diated from the killer's body.

A *crime of passion*: those were the words that came to
Jane.

Another detail that stood out inside the car: Mr.
Sakowski's pants, as well as his underwear, had been pulled
down to his ankles, exposing himself.

Rather trying to defend himself from the attack, Mr.
Sakowski was too occupied shielding his manhood. The
news report didn't mention anything about sex or any kind
of sexual transaction between both the victim or suspect,
only that it was "personal." They did say, however, that
most of the victim's wounds were located around the chest,
as well as the neck and shoulder region, not on his arms,
which, Jane assumed, would make sense if a man was leaning forward trying to pull up his pants instead of using his
arms to block the scissors from severing any major arteries or
striking any vital organs.

Jane had indeed seen these graphic images before.

But she was more intrigued by the notion of seeing these
images in a dream.

But how?

Throughout the remainder of the day, the thought alone
of Sakowski's final moments were followed by two words
that remained hovering in the dense air like a cloud of smog.

But how.

Later, the police would reveal to the media that a witness had come forward, a homeless man who saw a woman
in the vicinity of Sakowski's vehicle and possibly interrupted
the killer from disposing the body. He claimed she stepped
into his car and then exited with a knife. "Ran away once
she made eye contact" with the homeless man. These were
his words used to describe the situation. He also described
the young woman as short and sickly thin, had long hair
worn in a *ponytail*. Jane remembered the ponytail from her
dream. However, the witness said it was a she, *not* a he,
and her hair was blue, *not* purple.

Jane didn't know whom to believe: her dreams or the
witness.

An entire week passed with no leads into the death of Mark Sakowski. Each day of the week went by like the day before, with Jane spending most of the day trying to recall a dream from the night before. She'd occasionally drift off at work, as if, at times, she was trapped in the cell of her own mind.

Each night, Jane's dreams became redder, darker.

Each dream, she saw a new face.

Each face, she saw a new death.

Each one of the victims' faces from her dreams was filled with more detail, each feature attached to scrambled fantasies and haunted house-style flashes of horror.

The killer, however, remained as elusive as a leopard.

Throughout the latter part of the week, Jane found two of the same faces from her dream reported "MISSING" on TV by loved ones, both friends and family.

One of them being Jake Durbin, a police officer. Like Sakowski, he, too, had two children.

Then, the other one, Mary-Anne Simmons, married to Jonas Simmons, made her own jewelry at home, lived in a wealthy neighborhood.

Having grown up in a small town where everybody knew each other's business, Jane immediately recognized both their faces from high school. But she wasn't friends with either of them. The two were part of the whole "in-crowd." The sight of Jake and Mary-Anne's face on TV resurrected a lost memory. Mark Sakowski. Jane knew him, and not only from her dream. He was her eleventh grade horticulture teacher. He was creepy-quiet, Jane recalled, socially awkward. Every time she tried to dig deeper into the memory of Mark Sakowski, the darker the memory of him became. He was a man shrouded in darkness.

Which made her wonder if he had any connection to Mr. Moonlight.

Did they know each other?

The next time Jane saw Mr. Moonlight was at a family owned café called Hot Java. Like 'Da Bar, Hot Java was an older establishment that recently overhauled its interior decor, which used to be as bland as a doctor's office, as well as its entire brand in order to appease its more vocal fan base while, at the same time, trying to bring in the younger generation of coffee drinkers by sprucing up the café with the whole island theme inspired by Java, the island in Indonesia, in particularly the active volcano, Mount Bromo, and making it safer and more inviting and adding free wi-fi connection for its customers, which would come in handy whenever a customer ordered a cup of coffee through Hot Java's own personal app—this particular feature allowed its customers to place an order through their phone without having to go through the trouble or inconvenience of looking another person directly in the face. Hot Java was way more laidback than 'Da Bar, drew more of a diverse crowd, more PC but less cliquish, and moved more at Jane's pace.

After a long day of work and mind games, Jane wanted to treat herself. She arrived at Hot Java during a post-dinner rush and ordered a caramel macchiato the old fashion way by opening her mouth and speaking her order.

While Jane waited on the barista to concoct her drink, she grabbed a seat near a cozy fireplace and researched other activities to do on her laptop.

When she looked away from the laptop and rested her eyes for a moment, she smelled something burning in the kitchen.

Suddenly, she heard the sound of a cooking sheet crashing to the floor. The sheet danced around for a while until it finally came to rest like a spun coin.

A young baker darted out of the kitchen, a cloud of dense smoke trailing behind him like the one in a Wile E. Coyote cartoon. The baker was coughing and fanning away smoke.

Jane overheard the baker saying something about burning a batch of brownies. She couldn't quite make out the rest of what the baker was mumbling for she was paying more attention to the customers around her. Some of them were filming the baker with their phones and posting their recently shot videos online and then constantly wiping their thumbs down their screens of their phones, refreshing their pages for new LIKES or comments. Jane wondered if they were receiving gratification out of exposing another man's humiliation—*in this day in age,* the Age of Narcissism, *of course they did.* His cheeks were red and cloudy and he was hanging his head downward like one of those same dogs that had been brought in from the streets. Jane looked around in both amusement, yet confusion, and thought if these people's lives were so bankrupt that they went back home, sat in the comfort of their Lazy Boys, and watched these videos they recently recorded instead of capturing the moment with their own HD eyes. Jane knew that, unlike a video, a memory could *never* been deleted.

The more Jane wondered about these things, the deeper she started to delve into her laptop.

Before she lost herself in the Internet, the baker swung open the back door in order to air out the bitter smell.

Jane saw a tiny orange glow coming from the doorway and thought it was a floater in her eye, but it was only the glow of a cigarette the baker was smoking behind the café.

As the white cloud of cigarette smoke faded into the air, Mr. Moonlight revealed himself standing still in a dark alleyway outside Hot Java's.

Jane's head gradually rose from behind the laptop, her keen red eyes cutting through the pale blue haze of the screen.

She locked eyes with him.

Like before, he was watching Jane. And like before, his pale eyes never left Jane.

To Jane, the baker looked as if he wasn't aware of Mr. Moonlight's presence as he continued to puff away, probably replaying the recent goof in his head. Jane thought it was strange, though, how the baker didn't pay any attention to Mr. Moonlight. *Was it because he didn't see him?* He was only standing a couple of feet away from him. *Or was Mr. Moonlight that good at disguise?* Jane only caught a glimpse of his face, but in that brief glimpse, she saw more detail on her stalker's face.

Mr. Moonlight was, in fact, a man. She only had two choices to choose from; and all along, she had been leaning toward male. He was young too, but feminine in the way he posed for Jane. She thought that he could pass as one of those models on the front cover of a glossy magazine, stern and striking face, chiseled body. He was sneaky, thin, yet cut, his shoulders broad like a farmer; he appeared fragile, yet strong. He stood out, yet he blended into the night like a shadow.

He had the perfect color, Jane thought, *black.*

He had the perfect cover: night.

Jane guessed he was around twenty years old, but maybe younger than that, maybe even Jane's age or older. She couldn't put a number on his age because of the clear-rimmed glasses he was wearing. The man was dark skinned, as Sakowski's killer in her dreams, his hair was long, purple, and silky; and it hung over his shoulders like a horse's mane. He was also wearing a silver looped earring that glinted whenever it moved around the oversized collar of a sequined turtleneck he wore underneath a sleek-looking black duster.

Later that night when Jane fell into her dark slumber, she dreamt of death.

Murder.

A woman's murder.

She didn't know her name, yet, beyond the blackness of her thoughts, she felt as if she knew her from somewhere, maybe a run-in at a store or a place opened to the public, like a movie theatre or a park. Her face was so clear to Jane it seemed as if Jane was right there with the killer. She could even smell the faint aroma of shea butter under the killer's pungent funk. Jane picked up more detail than any other dream, especially the woman's face, as well as the horror etched on it. The face had been imprinted on her, as if she could easily point it out in a lineup. The woman was black-black. Everything about her was bold and voluptuous, even her personality; she also wore her hair was like one of those rockers from a hair metal band. Jane remembered seeing the hairdo in an old music video on *VH1*. She was also wearing a jeans jacket underneath a zebra-spotted shirt. Jane didn't know why these details had popped the most, but the clothing attire didn't reflect the fashion style of the current decade.

Both of the woman's shoulders were being pinned down by two pointy knees. The last detail was the pair of holey jeans that her killer was wearing. The kind of deliberate holes that were considered fashionable or dare Jane say, chic.

Then, the killer hushed the woman with a black-gloved hand while brandishing the pair of scissors with the other hand. Strangely, Jane could feel the grip of scissors in her own hands, *not* the killer's, as he playfully ran the tip of the blade down the sweaty woman's face.

Snip, snip!

Made the sound of the scissors as he opened, then closed the scissors in front of the woman's face.

Panicked, the woman's eyes swelled and stilled on the killer towering above her. The tears were like shrink-wrap covering her murky brown eyes.

As the killer struck, Jane's eyes snapped open! She never fully witnessed the violent parts, only the highlights of the moments leading up to the woman's death.

Jane gathered herself. She was sweating profusely, the bed sheets around her were as wet and wrinkled as an old dishrag.

Sitting against the headboard of her bed, she wondered where such violence had come from.

A couple of hours later, when the morning sun cut through Jane's windows and lit up the apartment in an eerie reddish haze, Jane finally rolled out of bed and grabbed the TV remote wedged between the cushions of the couch.

At first, Jane stared at the remote, tempted to put it away, even hide it.

After second thought, she turned on the TV.

She cycled through several news channels until she found one that caught her eye.

Her name was Shanique Willis, Jane had later learned.

Hours after Shanique's mother reported her missing, a pair of brown eyes was discovered at Hot Java.

One of the baristas was reaching for a blueberry scone when all of a sudden a customer screamed out, causing several other customers to dash in a frenzy to the door. Somehow, the word *gun* was shouted out and moments later, it was all pandemonium inside Hot Java. The word traveled from one customer to another and by the time the word reached the back of the line, the customers thought there was an "active shooter" inside Hot Java. More customers sprinted out of the café while others cowered under tables, earthquake drill-style, and started praying to the god of their choice. There wasn't an active shooter inside the café, people would soon realize after the barista called the cops and told them about the eyes sitting next to the cinnamon coffee cakes.

Once the excitement fizzled out, the brave barista picked up one of the eyes with his gloved hand, the eye as slick as the stone of an avocado. Still bloody. At first, the barista thought it was a gag or something, an immature employee pulling a gag or a disgruntled employee's prankish way of quitting the job, the big middle finger to the boss man.

Then, he held it underneath his nose and took a whiff of it.

He suddenly recoiled from the smell and dropped the eye to the floor.

The barista looked at the other customers standing around and they, too, were equally as repulsed.

Later that very same morning, a dumpster had been lit on fire directly behind a nail salon, which shared the same alleyway as Hot Java's. Before the firefighters arrived at the scene, workers from other nearby stores managed to put out the flames with buckets of water that had been circulated through a human chain.

Once the smoke *finally* cleared, the workers discovered a dead woman without eyes buried underneath piles of trash. The next of kin later identified the body as Shanique Willis, the same woman missing earlier that very same day. According to the autopsy report, Shanique's eyes had been cut out postmortem (meaning they were removed after she died).

Like the other victim, Mark Sakowski, Shanique was stabbed multiple times with a pair of scissors.

Based on the report, the coroner determined that Shanique died from a massive hemorrhage. She bled out.

Investigators interviewed those close to Shanique; and according to her closest friends, she was a regular who frequented the café.

The motive would be later speculated through the gossip queens and the true crime enthusiasts of social media that the serial killer—or "copycat," investigators weren't still convinced it was the same killer—was trying to make a bold statement for his or her audience. The exact position of the eyes was clue number one. The eyes were positioned at an angle inside the pastry case, pointed directly at the same seat Shanique always sat in, as if the seat itself had her name on the back of it. Shanique's murder was the first of many other murders to raise eyebrows. The criminal analysts on TV would say, "The killer is evolving."

The next victim resulted in the local newspaper, *The Messenger*, branding the killer with the name, "The Snipper," because of the killer's modus operandi—its method. Gary Worthington was discovered by an elderly woman who was out on one of her routine walks at the crack of dawn. Sugar, her cocker spaniel, was first to notice Gary, initially barking for the entire block to hear, then attempting to run over to Gary for a quick hump or lick. Sugar's owner stepped closer for a better look. Gary's injuries—or injury was brought out in vivid detail underneath the streetlight. Gary's ankle was shackled to the fire hydrant. The galvanized chain wrapped around his ankle had left it black and blue. He was exhausted, famished, his face as pallid as a ghost, his lips dry and crusty from extreme dehydration; and from all the head-bobbing he was doing, he appeared to be drugged.

(Later in the investigation, it would known that Gary Worthington had been, in fact, drugged; and after blood tests, it was revealed that Gary, as well as several other victims, had traces of a common animal tranquilizer in their systems, which made the investigators believe that the killer was drugging his victims before the final *snip, snip*)

Gary's other injury, the most noticeable one, came from his mouth. His chin was caked with blood as dark as tar from where the oxygen had hit it.

As soon as she realized he was still alive from his sloth-like movements, she tended to Gary. That was when he cracked open his mouth and revealed his injury to her.

A rope of blood gushed from the corner of his parched mouth and dribbled down the side of his chin.

Gary tried to speak but couldn't.

All Gary spoke were vowels for his tongue had been cut out—snipped away with scissors by a new threat on the block known as The Snipper. But Jane had a different name for him. Jane didn't exactly know why Mr. Moonlight had spared Gary Worthington's life. No words were exchanged in her dream; in fact, during each dream, Mr. Moonlight's voice, like his identity, remained a mystery. A part of her thought maybe he kept Gary alive to tell the world about his tormenter—or punisher; Jane was still on the fence about the killer's motives. But Gary couldn't speak; however, he could still paint. Gary was this famous artist from New York. Had a lifetime of success throughout the more productive side of his twenties but that premature fame dimmed significantly when Gary reached the wrong side of thirty.

Of all the victims, Gary had stayed with Jane the most. She couldn't help but wonder why Mr. Moonlight didn't cut off Gary's fingers or hands since he was an artist. If Mr. Moonlight was trying to punish Gary, then wouldn't the ultimate payback be to take away the very tools that he held most dearly. She wondered if he was shining the spotlight on Gary for all the wrong things, carry out Mr. Moonlight's bidding or legacy, provide Gary with his own inspiration to paint again, act solely as one, the great muse.

Then, perhaps later, a pivotal curator.

The next day after Gary was targeted—according to police, the word *targeted* was purposefully used during a press conference because Gary confirmed through a series of head nods and written statements that he had been followed prior to his abduction, which made investigators believe the killer knew Gary—Gary's partner received a blank package in the mail: Gary's tongue.

When Jane had dreamt about Gary the next night, she felt as if she knew him, like the killer, but only the façade the two hid behind. Oddly, Jane didn't feel the least amount of pain for Gary despite how the media had treated him as this kind of sympathetic figure. She didn't even know if it was her feelings that she was feeling or someone else's. Like Shanique's face, Gary's muffled voice was imprinted on her mind, as if Jane could access it at any time of the day; however, she could only hear the low end of his voice which sounded like the trailing resonance of a cave echo, like an overlapping mumble. She pinpointed certain *words* among the noise, heard nothing but bigotry and menace behind it. He sounded jealous of Jane or Mr. Moonlight. She couldn't quite tell if Gary was speaking to her or Mr. Moonlight.

But why, Jane wondered.

Gary was an artist struggling to rediscover stardom.

Was Gary jealous that Mr. Moonlight (?) was soaking up all the limelight?

Either way, Jane sort of liked the way it made her feel after she woke up from a dream. A feeling of power that she had only felt when she was a little girl carrying around a jar and collecting whatever creatures she could find in the desert. If Mr. Moonlight was punishing his victims, Jane thought that he could've been a vigilante. In her eyes, though, her Day-eyes, Mr. Moonlight was a monster. Like all monsters, they did their best work in the dark.

After Mr. Moonlight's next victim, Jane realized Mr. Moonlight was becoming even more complex.

Dylan Canto ran a podcast about true crime stories called *The 187*. Each episode involved old, unsolved murder cases, as well as kidnappings; and every now and then, Dylan would stray away from old cases and focus on new, more trendier ones, or as for "The Snipper," an ongoing case. Dylan didn't do much investigation per se, like the widely known stereotypes displayed in Hollywood movies as self-loathing men—or women but mostly men—adhered to the drink while obsessively tracking the movements of a killer at large. Dylan called up former detectives or journalists who once worked on old cases—solved or unsolved—over the phone and incorporated their conversations into a weekly podcast where he'd profit from it by spreading it all over the Internet for entitled, gullible kids to devour. He was, simply put, like many who thrived in the Internet world, an opportunist. And once Dylan heard about The Snipper, he couldn't help but jump all over the story.

When Dylan's sidekick, Gumshoe, found Dylan's body in a makeshift studio inside an older rented out building downtown, which used to be home for an insurance company before it went bankrupt, Gumshoe thought Dylan was pulling a twisted prank.

After all, Halloween was right around the corner and like they all say, everybody was entitled to at least one good scare.

Dylan wasn't moving, wasn't breathing.

By the time the paramedics arrived, Dylan was dead; in fact, Dylan had been dead for over twelve hours. The initial cause of death was mysterious; however, Dylan was missing a part of his body. The details of the autopsy report were left for the late night shows, past nine o'clock, when the children went to bed. Apparently, The Snipper had snipped off Dylan's genitals, the whole works. However, the genitals weren't mailed to anybody close to Dylan or lying around somewhere for some poor schmuck to find. After a surprising discovery while examining the contents inside Dylan Canto's stomach cavity, the coroner determined the victim had choked on them. The medical term was asphyxiation.

Through a rigorous investigation, investigators unearthed Dylan's latest podcast where he designated an entire episode to The Snipper and his recent killings or no-killings. On his podcast, Dylan blasted the killer with false information and bogus allegations. Ridiculed The Snipper. Even provoked The Snipper by filling in the gaping holes of The Snipper's background and suggested he was a toothless backwoods inbreed who burned too many ants with a magnifying glass as a child. The investigators determined that Dylan's podcast would come in handy and used it solely for their benefit. The Snipper had a glaring weak spot, so they thought, and maybe they could use what they learned from the podcast to their advantage. The investigators tried a couple of days later with Dylan's trusty sidekick, Gumshoe, not to draw any suspicion. Had Gumshoe record a new podcast to lure out Dylan's cold-blooded killer. Had Gumshoe rail against The Snipper. Had him read off from a shit blender of insults, as if he was hosting a roast and The Snipper was his roastee. He even went so far as to pull out a hefty supply of "Your momma so fat" jokes from his back pocket and slung them all over the stream-waves as if it was a national hashtag day. Gumshoe's tirade was so derogatory that it was even trending across every digital corner of the Internet.

For weeks, Gumshoe had a security detail covering his every move, a team of rough and tough bodyguards following him around everywhere he went. Watching him. Waiting for The Snipper to make a move.

For weeks, though, no sight of The Snipper.

The Snipper had moved onto other victims: a mother of two daughters named Camilla Hayes. Camilla's dead body was found underneath the blenchers behind Clover High. Her nose was missing.

Investigators believed The Snipper lured Camilla to the high school where he killed her.

Another clue: investigators found a half-pound of Oxycodone on her person.

After Camilla, it was Travis Pierre.

Then, Relene Applegate.

Sandra Cotes.

The list went on and on. Each one murdered by the same exact modus operandi: a body part removed before or after they were stabbed to death—or what the investigators refereed to as the most exaggerated yet vaguest statement that would literally and often times, metaphorically highlight a stigma of each victim.

For instance, a detective had a theory that Camilla's nose was cut off because she was prying into The Snipper's business—being "nosy." The only evidence he had to back up the wild theory was a ghostly photo posted on her Instagram page. In the shaky photo a dark blurry-faced man had one hand in front of his face while the other one was trying to shield the dotted lens on the top right-hand corner of Camilla's phone. The photo appeared to be taken at a nightclub due to the various colored lasers and mega-screen graphics slicing through the photo like distorted street glares and what appeared to be fog-like smoke hovering over a wavy crowd of intoxicated people standing shoulder-to-shoulder around the strange man.

Of all the victims, perhaps Camilla knew the identity of The Snipper.

Or, as the detective pointed out, was "onto" The Snipper.

Or, the man could've been a drunk who was giving Camilla a hard time at a nightclub—who knows?

For weeks, the nightmares had become exceptionally vivid for Jane.

In the darkness of her bedroom, she'd hear the distant sounds from her nightmares echoing through reality.

Snip, snip.

She'd hear those very sounds—*snip, snip, snip, snip*—from another room or, even at times, inches away from her ear at the most random times of the day; and every time, they'd cause the hair on her bumpy skin to rise.

She'd hear, as well as smell, such noises accompanied by the sudden squeals of a businessman sporting the smelly head of a dead pig. She could see and smell the man as if he was sitting directly in front of her. He wore a loose blue tie like a noose around his neck. Scratch that. The outfit changed. All of a sudden, he was wearing a cliché black hacker's hoody. With the fuzzy glow of the screen highlighting the shadows of his pig-face underneath the hood, he was hunkered behind a laptop, typing and squealing.

Whenever Jane closed her eyes to go sleep, she murdered inside the confines of a dream and yet, it felt as if she was the one being murdered in a way, as if she could feel each stab, hear each *snip*; then, the next morning, she was awakened to an unearthly creation, reborn for the masses. During each wake—each revival— Jane brought a piece of Mr. Moonlight with her, as if she had somehow stolen a memory from him.

At night, Mr. Moonlight would still visit Jane. During whatever activity, if it was grabbing a nightcap with a pity-friend from her work or catching a late night movie by herself, she'd find him standing at a distance, like always, staring at her, as if she possessed something that belonged to him; but he'd never ask for it. Either standing on a desolate street corner or sitting in an upper seat of a theater, Mr. Moonlight was the one constant in Jane's life.

Twenty-four days after The Snipper first struck, The Snipper made it to number one on the FBI's Most Wanted List.

But it didn't stop The Snipper from spreading terror all over the town.

The day after the lead investigator pulled Gumshoe's surveillance, The Snipper struck yet again.

The Snipper's next victim: Othello Brown, also known as "Gumshoe."

Gumshoe's severed head was found by a groundskeeper on the fifty-yard line Viper's logo in the center of Blight National's football field. The rest of his body was eventually found at a construction site, which led investigators to believe the body was meant to be found. What other reason would a serial killer dump one of his victims' bodies at a well-trafficked sight? Or, one investigator theorized, The Snipper was toying with them. Stretching the limits. Seeing how far he could go.

After extensive research into Gumshoe's social media pages, the investigators learned that Gumshoe was an avid Viper's fan. Went to games. Sported the Viper's logo, decals, and clothing. Trolled opposing teams and frequently started twitterwars with fans from rival teams.

The grisly details of both podcasters' murders were nearly too much for Jane to stomach.

"The final straw," she'd say.

The more Mr. Moonlight killed, the less she started to know him.

Which was strange, to say the least.

Jane became more paranoid and thought maybe she was The Snipper's next victim. Maybe the other victims had experienced Mr. Moonlight prior to the big *snip, snip*, but they didn't say a single word about it to friends or family members. Maybe Mr. Moonlight was the harbinger of death. There were a lot of maybes to throw around. One *maybe* Jane overheard while at work—another ridiculous theory—was that The Snipper was making his own personal Frankenstein's monster, constructing other body parts to form a singular body. Of course, the theory then evolved with more absurdity; and after Jimbo, one of the part-time techs, joined in the conversation and started brainstorming through that head of his, he proposed that The Snipper was making himself a skin suit, like Leatherface, only the whole body. As ridiculous as it sounded, it made perfect sense the more she had thought about it—the Frankenstein part. Jane wasn't certain if she had teamed up with the rest and bought herself a one-way ticket to crazy town. But Jane was certain that, if anything, something—maybe something positive—was going to come out of all of this. She didn't exactly know what, but she knew deep in her bones that somehow she was connected to Mr. Moonlight.

The morning Jane decided to drive to the police station to inform the detectives who were working The Snipper case about her "official" stalker, Mr. Moonlight and his possible connection to The Snipper, The Snipper struck yet again.

He was no longer killing his victims.

He was removing their eyes.

Each statement victims had given to the police was a near carbon copy of one another. At first, the investigators couldn't help but notice the oddity of it all. The Snipper was a killer who didn't show any mercy for his victims. At first, they thought it might've been a copycat—for real this time—who was inspired by what happened to Shanique

Willis. However, as with the case of Gary Worthington, The Snipper was known to make statements and what better way to make a bold statement than to have the victims live through probably one of the worst moments of their lives. As the victims retold each one of their stories, the details remained the same: The Snipper snuck up behind them whether it be leaving work or walking to a car or running errands; then, each one was blindsided by a sudden dizzy spell, and then blackness. Each one woke up in a strange and dark place.

The black world.

For weeks, The Snipper and FBI played this cat and mouse-type game. The closer they'd get to catching The Snipper, the more he'd evolve. He was one step ahead of them; and to the FBI, it was as if The Snipper was one of their own.

Soon, the FBI started looking inward, doing internal investigations, but all of the witch hunts led them nowhere, only back to square one.

Forty-nine victims later, the detectives received a break in the case.

Hykem Thistle.

"Internet Troll."

Thistle spent his entire day trying to make himself a name on the Internet by trolling users and making up lies to feed, as well as distort the public's perception. It wasn't just the name-calling that set him apart from other trolls. He'd post false accusations backed up by professionally photoshopped photographs. He had multiple accounts and usernames, created all kinds of memes that went viral in hours, reeked havoc across social media. Each victim shared the same pattern as Thistle. The ages of each one of the victims ranged from twenty-one and up. The Snipper wasn't gender bias, either. He targeted males, as well as females. Allen Starnes, who was a failed YouTuber turned so-called "journalist," reported bogus stories on celebrities, headliners, or whoever was currently (hashtag) trending in order to whet his own farfetched agenda of rallying up mobs to publicly shame those considered "hot" at the moment.

The news broke that The Snipper was targeting trolls on the Internet, specifically "bullies," those who were inclined to promote or push their agenda of toxic masculinity, low-lifes, even the office rats who exhausted every hour of their days as a Clark Kent-type figurine around the office, only to become Trollman behind the confines of their cubicles. One of The Snipper's latest victims, a woman, not a man, Kirsten Maiden, turned out not being a "victim" after all. She served eight years in jail after she was charged as an "accessory" to the death of her classmate who died after she was bullied into committing suicide. Three years after Maiden was released on good behavior, The Snipper paid her a visit. With Maiden's background at the forefront of the investigation, FBI combed all of her twisted social media pages and found suggestive language broadly used at other individuals and groups. FBI profilers concluded that The Snipper was removing the eyes of his victims as if it was his subtle way of branding them with his own "scarlet letter." These sudden revelations had made it easier for FBI to narrow down their search for the killer—or, as in The Snipper's eye, vigilante.

Eventually, the public created a persona behind The Snipper and he became a myth, this imaginary figure like the Tooth Fairy or Santa Claus, only he was very much real.

"If you wrote something bad about somebody or if you did everything in your power to make somebody feel awful or unworthy of life or hinder their pursuit of happiness, The Snipper was going to track you down and send you straight to the *black world*."

Whenever Jane grabbed a caramel macchiato from Hot Java or ran errands or picked up groceries, she couldn't help but notice the "change" in people's behaviors. People were way more observant of their surroundings. Instead of having their head buried in their phones while waiting in checkout or pumping gas at the gas station, people were looking over their shoulders. People were awake.

Jane thought about Lady Justice, the blindfold she wore over face.

The Snipper was preaching.

About what?

For Jane, the young introvert who, in her dreams, often found herself trapped inside the mind of a killer, the answer couldn't have been more obvious.

Jane *finally* decided enough was enough.

She had to track down and *finally* face the man from her murderous dreams.

Her stalker, Mr. Moonlight.

Jane thought the real reason as to why she couldn't confront Mr. Moonlight whenever she saw him stalking her in public was that he wouldn't let her confront him. There was an invisible line wedged between the two, separating them from two completely different realms or dimensions. Even when Jane first *tried* to confront Mr. Moonlight at the tennis courts, Mr. Moonlight was no longer standing there and it was as if he *never* was standing there. Somehow, Mr. Moonlight disappeared in the nick of time. However, to Jane, she sensed that he was *still* there even though she couldn't actually see him with her own eyes. Like a feeling deep inside—a gut feeling—she felt as if it was the *feel* of the air all around her, another world in that very air she breathed; even the way the cool air pressed against her body, it was as if she was wearing the air like a heavy fur coat. Jane was certain that she wasn't his next victim. Jane wasn't part of social media—at least not enough to draw attention—wasn't a member of Twitterverse, the Facebook scene, Snapchat, or any of the mind-manipulative outlets to alternate realties controlled by The Silicon Valley Overlords. She was hardly plugged in, except for the entire month of September when she quit her job at the animal hospital. She spent the late night hours researching past murders and violent crimes in and around, of all places, the West Virginia area. Jane scrolled through hundreds and thousands of mug shots available to the public, scouring the pits of the criminal database. The entire month of September was dedicated to research; however, Jane didn't know who she was looking for. She was just doing exactly that, *looking*. Maybe a part of her was consumed by the idea of wanting answers as to why she was so special. Jane certainly didn't fit the description of The Snipper's victims, didn't have a mean bone in her body—at least, not advertised. Yet, Mr. Moonlight habitually followed her around like clockwork.

Jane brainstormed an "old idea" the Feds tried with the late podcaster, Gumshoe. She had no other choice than to be a victim. She was going to be the bait.

Unlike Gumshoe's plan, which had backfired in his face, she wasn't going to lure out Mr. Moonlight by insulting him or trying to belittle him. Jane didn't have her own personal bag of insults lying around somewhere. No good punchlines or zingers or jabs or cheap shots to fling at the one whom she apprehensively called Mr. Moonlight. Wasn't her style. However, Jane was in a particular position that set her far apart from all the others. What made her so unique—and qualified—to carry out her mission successfully was that she had boatloads of material from her dreams. After all, she had been *inside* his head. She used it.

The day before her big plan, Jane went into the city and bought herself a gun. Something lightweight. Easy to carry. Only ten ounces. Like the ones the prostitute carries in his or her purse or the ones a well-endowed agent straps to his ankle. She liked the name of it too. Ruger. It sounded like a man's gun. Carried six rounds. Which meant, if he made a move on her, she had six attempts to put him down. But Jane was hoping for it *not* to go down like that. She took the Ruger for a spin the same day she purchased it with the money from her last paycheck. Used the shooting range below the ammunition shop to pop off round after round. During that time, an instructor shadowed Jane. Showed her the ropes. The do's and don'ts while handling a loaded gun. Jane caught on pretty quickly, though; in fact, she was a good shot.

"A real deadeye," the instructor told her.

The remark stayed with Jane for the rest of the day.

Deadeye.

Jane liked the name.

With her newly licensed weapon in possession, Jane spent her days glued to her laptop. She created a blog, which was sort of like her own journal, only every word was written for the entire world to read. She signed up and logged onto various social media pages in order to spread the word.

Mr. Moonlight was out there and it was only a matter of time before he found Jane.

On her blog, Jane recounted every little thing she knew about Mr. Moonlight, starting from the moment she first saw him hanging around outside her apartment to the time she encountered him at 'Da Bar. She was viciously candid in her blog. She wrote about how she could relate to him. The solitude she felt whenever she fell asleep and put herself into his mind. The loneliness. How awful it felt to live in such a ghastly place where its only inhabitants constantly went out of their way to stroke their own prerogative by picking apart, ridiculing, and trying to destroy anything that didn't belong to the starry-eyed world *they* observed behind their eyes. Jane didn't know whether or not the parts about loneliness or the feelings of being completely miserable in a world that she could no longer recognize anymore were totally true. In a way, the words came out like a hiccup. But she ran with them. She also wrote about the candid memories that had surfaced deep inside her dreams. Dreams within dreams. Deep slumbers, REM sleep. Sinking past the black place and experiencing the kinds of memories that made Jane question whether or not these memories were her own or somebody else's. She wrote in full detail about an "Uncle Cordell," or *Unk*, as she recalled. Certain traits and smells had come to Jane while she slept: the metallic smell of his ulcerous-laced breath, a tall and lanky man whose knobby fingers were always sticky with butterscotch, and the noises he'd make with his mouth as hard candy knocked against his teeth like a hockey puck. She carried all of these *little* things locked away inside her mind. However, Jane had never "physically" met Uncle Cordell before. But Jane *knew* him. *Knew* that he used to take her to the aquarium when she was a girl. Jane had these stark images inside her head and even though she wasn't a hundred percent sure if these images were hers or somebody else's, she knew they had come from a real place, not a black place. She also recalled the horror of the one-day she was bombarded by a horde of pigs. She remembered being smothered by them. She remembered hearing all those high-pitch squeals stinging her ears as they battered her body to the ground, their coarse hooves pushing her face into cold mud.

Jane hashtagged it—her memories or fantasies, whatever they were—for everybody to see.

After a full week of putting her thoughts out there, Mr. Moonlight started to take on a life of its own. Like The Snipper, Mr. Moonlight became a myth. Like all myths, they start out with a single buzz. Unlike The Snipper, Mr. Moonlight appealed to the underground scene, the cultists and theorists. He wasn't nearly as "mainstream" as The Snipper. But his name was out there. In a strange way, Mr. Moonlight's followers felt as if they could relate to Jane, her story. Some of the commenters mentioned that they, too, had encountered Mr. Moonlight at night.

The week after Mr. Moonlight became a new "thing" to talk about, Jane received a strange email in her inbox.

As soon as she read the email, she knew it was him, Mr. Moonlight.

First, the name of the email read:

POOCHYQUEEN@PAPURREMAIL.COM

Poochy, spelled with a *y*, not *ie*; however, she once saw it spelled *i* dot *e* dot.

She had also heard the name, *Poochy*, before, twice in her dreams, once when she had a dream about watching a YouTube video on "How to Make the *Purrfect* Cosplay Costume," and then, once again, when she dreamt of Camilla, one of Mr. Moonlight's victims, murmuring the name right before she received the *snip, snip*; then, another time, she overheard it being spoken when she was waiting on an airplane inside LAX. Once the plane touched down in Charleston, she was going to take another flight from Charleston to a smaller airport just outside Wensburg, Virginia, where Ruby would be waiting to pick her up. However, the airplane experienced engine failure, resulting in the plane having to make an emergency landing at the O'Hare airport in Chicago. Eventually, Jane made it to her destination, visited her friend for the weekend, and then flew back home. Jane suddenly realized that *he* was on that flight to Charleston. *He was!* She recalled this young yet extremely confident man, a similar profile as Mr. Moonlight, strutting down the center aisle of the airplane as if it was his own personal catwalk. Another passenger stood up from his seat two rows in front of Jane to stow a personal item into the overhead storage bin, the passenger not only temporarily blocking the aisle, but also blocking the young man's path. He had a silver Bluetooth in his ear and he was talking to somebody over the phone; but to Jane, it appeared as if he was talking to himself due the hands-free device. He was wearing lots of jewelry on his ears, hands, and all around his neck. What stood out the most was his pink hair which he wore in pigtails, as well as the light-colored cutoff jeans jacket worn underneath a holey top that matched his pink bubblegum-pop sunglasses.

The young man not only grabbed Jane's attention, but also other passengers' attention, not by the way he looked, but by the way he was acting.

Displaying an attitude for everyone to see, the young man stopped dead in his strut and deliberately shifted his weight to one side of his body as he waited in the most obvious exaggerated annoyance.

Once the passenger sat back down in his seat, he continued to strut toward his seat a few rows behind Jane. She couldn't forget the particular name that he said to himself— or at least, it had sounded that way.

Poochy.

Secondly, the email service.

Pa-per-email, the word per replaced with *purr*. Their logo was a cat dressed in a saddle with an emoji of an email riding on the back of the cat as it delivered an email. She reckoned the email service appealed to "cat lovers." She used to be a cat lover herself, back when she saw them as mutual friends instead of whining burdens. Mr. Moonlight had a thing for cats, she remembered. When Mr. Moonlight chained Gary's ankle to a fire hydrant and left him there to be found, he was rocking a lime green shirt with a flamboyant Siamese cat dressed in a sparkling gold dress and high heels. Above the Siamese was a cartoon bubble, the dialogue inside it reading something like "How you like *meow?*" She wasn't entirely sure, but she remembered the word *meow.* The image was distorted from the reflection of Mr. Moonlight in the tinted window of his car.

Thirdly, the contents of the email itself.

The email read:

I no wutt u doin. STOP it. Or elles.

Jane had only heard him speak several times in her dreams and she knew he wasn't the type of person who often used longhand or proper grammar. He was a visual monster who was *keen* on fashion.

For a moment, she pulled herself from the laptop and paced around the room.

Poochy.

Jane marched back to the laptop and googled the name, *Poochy.*

She came across the YouTube page of Drenelle St. Croix, the name *Drenelle* a combination of his birth name, André, and his "coming out" name, Shenelle; but most of his avid followers knew Drenelle as a famous Cosplayer who went by the persona, "Poochy Queen." Drenelle was a clothing designer who owned his own clothing line called, Cut and Paste. He was also known for designing his own extravagant costumes, which he showed off at Cosplay events. Drenelle was a celebrity among the tweens and teenyboppers, as well as the trans community, a role model who was an inspiration to our curious youth. But from recent comments Jane read in the comment board, Drenelle was also a subject of sharp criticism.

Once more, Jane pulled herself from the laptop and paused for a moment.

Was it really a dream?

Or, had Jane really been on Drenelle's page before?

Jane looked up Drenelle's profile, looked up his recent Cosplay events.

The last Cosplay event was at Hexacon in Huntington, West Virginia.

Drenelle went as Kilobit, a dark warlock/hacker from the *dΛ®κ Night* series.

Jane researched the date Hexacon was held.

The convention took place the same weekend she visited Ruby.

Without hesitation, Jane replied to the email.

Be at The Bullring tonight. Eleven o'clock sharp.

The Bullring was the nickname of Forsyth High School's football stadium. If "Poochy Queen" was the real Mr. Moonlight, then he'd know exactly what Jane was referring to when she used the word *bullring*.

Forsyth's mascot wasn't a bull, as most expected.

It was home of the Matadors.

The Forsyth Matadors.

WHEN Jane arrived at Forsyth High ten minutes earlier than the time she arranged in the email, Mr. Moonlight was already waiting for her. Jane couldn't see him, though, but she could definitely sense him.

She parked her car close by. Just in case something happened. Like her gun jamming or whatever. If so she'd beat Mr. Moonlight in a foot chase, although she hoped it didn't come down to that.

With her gun concealed behind her back, Jane stepped onto the football field. A distance floodlight shone its light on a dark lanky figure standing at the opposing team's end zone. Jane stopped in the end zone as well, her eyes slowly adjusting to the darkness. She spotted the eyes—or at least thought she did.

As she started to walk to the five-yard line, she noticed the dark figure getting closer to her.

Once she reached the twenty-yard line, she realized it was Mr. Moonlight and he, too, was walking forward. She made sure to keep her hands down by her side, inches away from her gun. Again, just in case the meeting turned hostile.

By the time Jane reached the forty-yard line, she didn't really know what she hoped to get out of the meeting.

Once, during her slow walk, she actually hesitated for a moment with a stutter-step and questioned her reason for being here.

She didn't have a reason—or did she?

In a way, she just wanted to talk to him.

Face-to-face.

Jane stopped in her tracks as she reached the fifty-yard line.

Mr. Moonlight stopped as well; in fact, to Jane, it looked as if he was mimicking her every move. His face was shielded by the night darkness. However, his profile remained the same from her dreams. He was wearing hippie-style sunglasses with small circular lens, which barely covered his pale eyes. The lenses made his eyes appear like lunar eclipses behind the wiry frame of his vintage sunglasses. Jane was also baffled as to why he was wearing sunglasses at night. She didn't bring up his taste in clothing attire or his need to accessorize. She started to focus on the *real* reason as to why she wanted to meet Mr. Moonlight.

Once she found herself in Mr. Moonlight's presence, the reason was simpler than she thought, as if the reason was there the whole time, dangling right underneath her nose.

The memory that she had been running from for so many years flooded over her thoughts. She turned her shoulder toward the field goal post in the end zone.

Jane nodded at the post and said, "That's where they tied me up. Right there. That's where they *killed* me."

She turned back around and faced Mr. Moonlight.

"The part that really counts, that is."

Strangely, Jane didn't expect him to answer her.

A part of her—a dark part—knew he wouldn't.

"I was only a sophomore in high school," she said as she started to tear up. All of a sudden, she found herself in deep thought. Reliving the moments from her teenage years, the mutant years, the awful years. "I had my entire life ahead of me," she said. "*They*, they took it all away from me." Jane paused for a moment to catch her breath. "When I saw that man's face on TV, I didn't recognize him at first. I suppose he put on all that 'daddy' fat. But his eyes, those reptilian eyes, those I recognized. The students used to call him Mr. Sakowski, aka Dr. Greenthumb. But I called him Mark. At the beginning, Mark was nice. *Socially awkward*. He once said that he was like me when he was my age. He didn't have many friends at school. Most of the students looked up at him. He was the 'cool teacher,' although misunderstood. Some of the students poked fun at him because of his nervous ticks and oddball analogies. He went out of his way, pulled strings to get me in his horticulture class with the juniors. There were like this 'exclusive group' untouchable by the rest of the school. I guess, at the time, I wanted to be a part of their group. To fit in, I guess. I used to hang out around the quarry not too far from school. At times, I'd skip school to hang out at the quarry. Once, I saw them there. They seemed so. . . alive, so untouchable. Mr. Sakowski brought me into his class, introduced me to them. And for a couple of weeks, they acted as if they truly cared about me. They all took me under their wing. We hung out at the quarry together, went swimming. Partied the nights away. Little did I know they were all using me, included *him*." Jane pulled herself away from the tragedy that consumed her for so many years and focused on the one good memory she shared with her horticulture teacher, the moment when Mr. Sakowski was no longer Mr. Sakowski, but Mark, the guy who talked a good game but was equally as cruel and wicked as the rest of them. There was only so much light and kindness in Jane's memory before it all turned to darkness.

Jane remembered staying after class to learn more about the plants inside the greenhouse. It started out as a harmless touch on Jane's shoulder. But to Jane, it was more than a touch. To Jane, Mark acted as if he was the only person on the planet who not only saw Jane, but also listened to Jane.

"On the night they brought me here to hang out or better yet, *lured* me here, I saw him standing across the field. I wasn't sure whether or not it was my mind playing tricks on me. But I saw those eyes of his in the dark," she pointed beyond the blenchers, "hiding in those shadows past the light, receiving some kind of sick pleasure from watching me in pain, not doing a goddamn thing to help me while they. . . *defiled* me. They knew about Mark and I—our relationship—and yet they acted as if they knew he wouldn't do anything about it. The next Monday, I saw him talking to them in the hallway, slapping hands with him, joking with him, acting like it was just another day, like what they did to me was okay, like it was a 'normal' thing to do to a girl. Even if Mark wasn't here that night, he knew what those people did to me. *He knew.*"

The tears streamed from Jane's eyes.

She never wiped them away.

"When it came down to having my back when I needed it the most, he chose to protect himself by denying any relationship we had rather than facing the consequences of what he had done to me. I was partly to blame, I know. But I was young, vulnerable. He was an adult. He had a choice to do the right thing. But he didn't. He chose to be *silent.*"

Jane sharpened her red-eyed gaze on Mr. Moonlight.

"All this time I was searching for the answers as to why I could never get a handle on my life, why every road I took— or every relationship I've ever had—ended up at a dead end. My road leads here and it'd always lead right back here if I didn't *finally* do something to stop it. It was 'them,' you see. *They* did this to me. *They* did this to *you*. *They* did this to *us*."

Mr. Moonlight started to tremble as if he was feverish.

"I know," Jane said sympathetically as she studied Mr. Moonlight's weakening condition.

She took a closer step toward Mr. Moonlight.

In return, he mimicked Jane and took a step forward as well, only this time he looked as if he was strutting through a gale of wind, his knees about to cave in.

"I know how it feels to have your voice stripped away from you—from your soul—only to be made into a mockery." Jane stepped closer. Mr. Moonlight attempted to step forward but couldn't, for he was too weak. "I know *exactly* how it feels to have ev-ery-thing that makes you who you are reduced to something not even worth being picked apart and it feels as if you're nothing, less than nothing—"

Mr. Moonlight tightened his jaw, the muscles along his face stretched into his neck, and he finally uttered the words *release me*.

"I'm sorry," Jane said flatly. "I can't. Not now. But soon, maybe."

She reached behind her back and pulled out the gun from behind her back.

Hesitant, she felt the weight of the gun in her hand and readjusted her grip.

She looked up at Mr. Moonlight and said to him, "Do you believe two people can share the same conscience?"

Mr. Moonlight didn't answer, couldn't. His jaw was starting to tremble as if he was standing half-frozen in a meat locker, and he was too feverish to speak.

"Right," Jane said with utter deflation and once more, looked down at the gun loosely gripped in her hand. "*Crazy world*, huh?" She took her eyes off the gun and looked at the empty stadium around her. "I remember when I was a little girl my father used to say this ridiculous expression all the time. 'Here goes nothing,' he'd use to say. He used to say it whenever he was about to do something that he knew would result in failure. Like the time the lawnmower broke down on him. He tried everything to fix the damn thing, checked every part. Finally, he thought it needed a new spark plug. So he drove to the hardware store and bought a brand new spark plug. Came back home. He changed out the spark plug. I remember I was like his little helper that day, doing everything he asked me to do. I watched the frustration slowly mount inside him, as if it was starting to take over his body. I watched him waste away an entire day toiling away at that piece of shit lawnmower when the easy fix would've been to buy a brand new lawnmower instead of a spark plug because the lawnmower he had was old and falling apart. Just as he pulled on the cord, he turned to me." Jane drifted in thought, her face slackened. "He had this light twinkling in his eyes—I'll never forget that look." Jane paused for a moment and readjusted the gun in her hand. "Then, he spoke those words to me, *'Here goes nothing,'*" she said to Mr. Moonlight. "I wondered why someone, like my father, a person I looked up to for so many years, would say or do something when he knew it would result in failure. He did it anyway. Why? I guess it's because he believed."

She suddenly pressed the barrel of the gun directly to the side of her temple.

With her eyes open, Jane said to Mr. Moonlight, "Here goes nothing—"

And then she squeezed the trigger. . .

As Jane fell to the ground, Mr. Moonlight gradually stopped trembling. His posture changed as well, going from weak and badly hunched to tall and straight. Everything about him had changed.

Cool and collected, Mr. Moonlight removed the sunglasses from his face and looked over his arms and hands and then checked the rest of his body in awe. He moved his eyes to the body lying before him. Jane's body.

Mr. Moonlight kneeled over her and studied the gunshot wound and what it had done to the side of her head.

Throughout the gore, Jane's left eye was still fully intact.

The eye was pinned open and staring directly up at him.

The pale light gradually went out in his eyes, softening like a dimmer.

He turned around and walked back to where he had come from, to a cool and dark place where he'd always be welcomed, never neglected.

⤕

IN the autopsy's report, which was conducted immediately after the body was discovered, Jane Cutter's death was ruled a suicide. The townspeople had their own little stories as to what really happened to Jane, why she killed herself. Most of them blamed her suicide solely on her type of character. "A troubled young girl who couldn't cope with reality," they said. "A loner. Didn't have many friends." These comments mostly came from those who didn't have the privilege to speak to Jane. Words like *quiet* or *nice* or *different* were thrown around a lot to describe Jane—the word *"different"* usually met with slight hesitation in respect to Jane's family. For the most part, Jane was a quiet character, strangely quiet, different as most had spoken; however, Jane was loud inside, bold, roaring.

Her parents tried to honor Jane's wishes the best they could. Jane once mentioned to her mother that, if she died before her parents, she wanted her body not to go wasted. Jane claimed it was her way of giving back to the land. After all, she said it was the earth that created her. It was the very least she could do. Jane didn't own a will or anything, never had any plans to instruct those who survived her on what to do with her remains or possessions. She had nothing written down in contract, only the sacred words she left behind to a mother whose memory and temperament was drastically failing her by the day. Jane's mother thought maybe her daughter was saying all of those absurd things about death because she played around in the dirt too much or hung around too many bugs as a child or wasn't as social with her own kind and maybe didn't understand that no human being wanted their body eaten by worms. Jane's parents decided to cremate Jane instead and have her ashes scattered over Mount Newman. They had a small but polite gathering at the house, nothing pretentious. Jane's mother, a devout Christian woman, corrected herself on several occasions that it wasn't exactly a wake, considering Jane's beliefs in religion or lack thereof, but it was exactly that, just a gathering of those who knew her daughter, Jane.

The turnout reflected the way Jane Cutter lived her life, surrounded by people—strangers, really—who, other than her name or a faint glimpse of what Jane looked like, hardly even knew anything about Jane. Most of the guests were distant relatives from Upstate, second cousins and whatnot, mostly her mother's bookclub buddies, basically "strangers" who had used the rare opportunity as an excuse to either get wasted off free booze and eat fancy hors d'oeuvres or try to buy a ticket into Heaven by using Jane's name to startup scholarships or charities.

Only a handful of people from Western showed up at the gathering. The only close friend was Ruby, who took the loss the worst. One person in particular caught the attention of Jane's mother. Not once had she ever seen the queer man before, but, in a strange way, she felt as if she had. He stood out among the crowd of guests with his bright red hair. Yet, he reminded her of Jane in the way that he, too, looked out of place.

✂

THREE days after Jane's ashes were scattered over Mount Newman, detectives, who were tirelessly working on the missing person's case involving Jane's former classmate Mary-Anne Simmons, received an anonymous tip about Mary-Anne or, someone who looked like Mary-Anne, being spotted at Devil's Throat.

When detectives arrived at Devil's Throat, they saw no sign of Mary-Anne. It wasn't until they got an overhead look of the quarry that they realized "something was in the water." *Something* not right. It was Detective Sharpe who found suspicious-looking tire tracks along the edge of a bluff. He put the two clues together, the tire tracks painting a stark image of a car driving off the ledge and then a murky shadow of a vehicle in the bottom of the lake.

Divers ended up finding not only Mary-Anne's car at the bottom of Devil's Throat, but also "other" cars. Six cars in total. Inside each car was a corpse. The marks on each one had varied. One victim, an attorney named Stephan Brodrickheimer, had been stabbed multiple times in the chest. All of the other bodies had less injuries. "There was a pattern," detectives learned from the condition of the bodies. Brodrickheimer's injuries had matched those of Sakowski's, most of the wounds being consistent around the upper torso region. However, some of the other victims' wrists had been zip tied to the steering wheel. One of the victims, Jay Carter, like the others, also Jane's former classmate, was strapped down to the driver's seat with a belt tied around his neck and secured around the headrest. The way they were murdered matched The Snipper's slow evolution. Detectives believed Sakowski and Brodrickheimer were The Snipper's first two victims; and then after that, it was Jake Durbin, Audrey Knox, Mary-Anne Simmons, Edward Lee, and, *finally*, Jay Carter. The victims' connection was obvious to the detectives. They all went to Forsythe High School. Four of the victims were on the high school football team, two were cheerleaders. They all knew each other. They were good friends. But it turns out the detectives were chasing a ghost. All fingers pointed to Jane Cutter, the recent suicide who shot herself in the head on the same football field where their recent victims played every Friday night.

However, there was one major **hole** in the story. . .

The Snipper was *still* out there.

Snipping away.

THE next morning the remainder of the missing persons' bodies were pulled from Devil's Throat. Drenelle, as he did most mornings, was doing his ritualistic pass through one news outlet to another. He reveled in the way each news outlet provided their own unique narrative to Jane's story when, in fact, there was only one story. There wasn't two, three, or four. There was one story. *His* story.

Drenelle left his studio, which was located in the basement below his auntie's townhouse, and met up with his friend, Latona.

"About time, Diva," she said, all sassy.

"That's 'supreme' diva to you—"

"Well, *Supreme Diva*, I've been waiting on you for a minute."

"You know me," Drenelle said, laidback.

"Yeah," said Latona. "I know you. Always taking your good easy time, like you always gotta look like you trying to impress everybody."

"So what you think, gurl?"

Drenelle opened the flaps of his bright orange blazer, did a twirl for Latona, and showed off the yellow meshed tank top, which matched his bleached blonde hair, as well as his green contact lenses.

Latona snapped her fingers.

"Flawless and fabulous, as always."

"Peaches and cream, baby gurl."

"Hey, ain't nothing wrong with dressing with the colors of the season."

Drenelle tapped Latona on the tip of her nose.

"Whoever said there *was* anything wrong?"

Latona shrugged her shoulders.

"I dunno."

"Hey, lemme ask you something."

"Yeah."

Drenelle and Latona started to walk toward the café.

"What you think of the name Mr. Moonlight?"

"Mr. What?"

"Moonlight?" Drenelle pointed to the sky. "You know, *moon*light."

"*Mister* Moonlight? You and I both know, Drenelle, you ain't no mister. Far from one. As a matter of fact, you said it yourself you against labels."

"I said that?"

Latona furrowed her brow until her forehead wrinkled and looked at Drenelle through the corner of her eye.

"You feeling a'ight—"

"—So, Mr. Moonlight. What you think?"

"You want to know what I think about Mr. Moonlight?"

"Yeah."

"Well, sounds like the name of an old Sinatra song."

"Sinatra?"

"Yeah," Latona drawled. "Frank Sinatra."

"How you know Frank Sinatra?"

"Drenelle, quit treating me like I'm dumb."

"I didn't say you was. You just did."

Latona smacked her gums.

"Anyway, you be thinkin' of that *Fly Me to the Moon* jam on TV."

"TV? Who 'da hell watches TV anymore? I get my shit from my phone."

"And where you think your phone gets its shit?"

"Whatever. It sounds 'old fashioned,' you think. Why you be askin'? You ain't thinkin' about retirin' Poochy Queen, is you?"

"Poochy Queen be *Poochy Queen*," Drenelle said, "and there will always be 'one' Poochy Queen. But I be thinkin' about another name, like something on the side, you feel me?"

"Nah," Latona said, shifting her weight to the side. "I don't really."

"All the great artists be changin' their names all the time. Look at Tupac. He did it. Prince did it—

"—Prince changed his name into a symbol."

"Yeah. So?"

"So, what 'da hell people gonna be callin' you if you change your name into a symbol?"

"Whoever said I was gonna change my name into a symbol?"

"You just did."

"No. I didn't," Drenelle said. "I'm just sayin'."

"What is you saying, Drenelle?"

"All I'm saying is I'm ready to—I dunno—expand."

"Expand? Like in doin' commercials and advertisements and goin' all mainstream like some sellout? Like that kind of 'expand?'"

"Not sellout," Drenelle said. "Just doin' something different."

"Drenelle, sweetie, you be makin' bank from all them subscriptions on your YouTube channel. You got the kind of fan base that most people your age would kill to have. They be showing up at all your shows. They be buying your clothes. You got it made, really. I'm jealous myself. Seriously."

Drenelle stopped underneath one of the many red maple trees along the sidewalk. Latona followed suit and stopped as well.

"You serious about this?"

Drenelle tilted his head in heavy thought.

"What about the name Moonbeam?"

Latona didn't respond as quickly as Drenelle liked.

"A'ight then," he said. "How about Moonstone."

"What's up with you and moons?"

"Moonbreaker."

Latona suddenly giggled at the name.

Once she realized the seriousness in Drenelle, she concealed her laugh.

"Moonbreaker? Seriously? Sounds like very *MCU*, don't you think?"

"Shear Solider."

"Shear—ah, no."

"Black Dragon."

"You ain't no dragon."

"Firechild."

"Child, please."

"Nightstar?"

"Drenelle—"

"—Black Night."

"Okay, Batman. We done here? Can we please grab something to eat already?"

"No," Drenelle said.

"No?" snapped Latona.

"That's Dark Knight. Knight spelled with a k. I'm talking about night as in the time of day."

Latona rolled her eyes.

"I get it."

"You ain't being helpful, you know?"

"Well, all of these names you keep spouting off sound like ridiculous superhero names, Drenelle, like. . . RE-DICK-U-LOUS," Latona emphasized for Drenelle. "You ain't no superhero, is you? Besides, what you planning on doing with this new side hustle?"

Drenelle noticed something hanging over Latona's shoulder.

"Don't move," he said abruptly.

"Don't move? Now, that's kind of catchy. 'Don't Move.' Like I'm 'Don't Move.' Which could act like some kind of reverse psychology shit. Your name's 'Don't Move' and all, yet the people who follow you would be the ones not moving 'cuz they too busy checking your fine-ass out. Sort of like the effect that lame band you be bumpin' to the other day. What'd you call them?" She paused for a moment and thought of the name of the 80's band Drenelle played for her yesterday while a spider started to crawl over her shoulder. "Oh yeah, *A-ha*! Like those fools who listen to them be like 'A-ha!' This is like some great music, dude!"

"Don't you dare talk about A-ha like that or else—"

"—Or else, what?"

The spider inched closer to Latona's neck.

"Don't move."

"You messin' with me, ain't you? What? You got you another one of them stalkers following you? I be tellin' you, Drenelle, you just you be paranoid from all that Internet fame. It's gonna straight to your head—"

"—No, Latona," Drenelle said clearly, his eyes attached to Latona's shoulder. "I mean, DON'T. . . MOVE. . . "

Without moving her head, Latona's eyes slowly moved to her left shoulder.

Next to move was her head, slowly at first, then, once her eyes met the brown spider sitting on her shoulder, her chin recoiled into her head and she leaped backwards. She flicked the spider to the sidewalk, dancing around on her tippy-toes as if not just one spider was still attached to her, but many. In fact, she combed her entire body, making sure the spider was nowhere on her body.

Drenelle couldn't help but laugh at Latona, her phobia in spiders.

As Latona nearly had a panic attack, Drenelle located the spider.

"What you doing?" Latona yelled out.

"Chill, would you?"

"Chill? Don't tell me to chill! You chill!"

Drenelle ignored Latona, blocked out all of the yelling she was firing away at him, and pulled out a can of Altoids from his coat inner pocket. He emptied out the mints and placed them inside both of Latona's cupped hands.

With hands full of mints, she asked Drenelle, "What in 'da hell you want me to do with this?"

"I dunno," Drenelle said, shrugging off Latona's bickering. "Put 'em in your pocket or something."

While Latona did as Drenelle asked and stuffed as many mints into her pockets as her blue jeans could handle before bursting at the seams, Drenelle reached down and picked up the spider with his bare hand.

"See, Latona," he said. "He's cool—"

"Drenelle! What you doing?"

"It's all good, Latona," Drenelle said as he carefully placed the spider inside the empty Altoids can.

"You've lost your damn mind, that's what it is."

"It's just a spider, Latona."

"Just a spider? That thing almost killed me."

"Nah," he said. "He ain't no killer. He just hanging out. That's all."

"Besides, I thought you hated spiders," Latona said clearly. "In fact, last time I remembered you were terrified of 'em. So what changed, Drenelle?"

Drenelle looked Latona in the eye. She was still terrified, still shaking a little from the minor scare.

"I guess I just look at 'em in a different light," he said to Latona.

"But you used to be—"

"—*Used to be*. But I think when I was little I used to like 'em."

"You liked spiders as a child?"

"Yeah," Drenelle said. "I think so."

"So, what? You regressin' now like my Aunt Miranda?"

Drenelle didn't respond to Latona's assumptions about his mental health.

Instead, he closed the lid and placed the can in his coat pocket.

Latona smirked.

"New pet, huh?"

Drenelle shrugged and stood to his feet.

"Old habits never die, I guess."

"Old habits, as in collectin' little ole spiders?"

"Yeah, so? Gotta problem?"

"To each his own," Latona said under her breath and then nodded toward the intersection ahead of them. "Let's go already," she said, louder.

"A'ight, a'ight," Drenelle said and followed Latona to the intersection.

"So, don't you need to poke holes in that or something? Won't it suffocate?"

"He'll be good for the time being until I can find him a better home."

"*Better* home? You should listen to yourself, Drenelle."

Again, Drenelle didn't respond.

He'd rather listen to Latona.

✂

WHEN Drenelle and Latona made it by foot to one of their favorite spots in Chinatown called The Tea House, Inc., Latona couldn't shut up about how starved she was, but mostly she couldn't keep her mind off waffles with green tea ice cream, which was like a staple dish for anybody who visited the famous tea house.

Drenelle came for the *oolong* tea; however, by the way his interest was more focused on the three young men hanging out a few tables away, it appeared to Latona that Drenelle had another agenda in mind.

Latona took her eyes off the waffles and asked, "What you keep looking at?"

"Nuttin'."

"Drenelle," Latona said, "you hadn't spoken a word since we got here."

"I just like watchin' you eat. That's all."

"From what I can tell," Latona turned her shoulder and glanced at the group of young men at the other end of the tea house, "you ain't just watchin' me."

"Who? Them?"

"Yep."

"I don't know them."

"You act like you do—"

"—But I don't."

"Whatever," Latona said dismissively and noticed Drenelle glancing down at his phone. "Any word from Corey?"

Drenelle puckered his face in disgust from the sound of his name and let out a loud and exaggerated sigh.

"You still talkin' to him, ain't you?"

"Nope," Drenelle said, *popping* his lips from the letter p. "I'm done with that nigga. Corey Grugier. Nigga need to change his name. He ain't even French."

"You still got me, Drenelle," Latona said.

Smiling from ear to ear, both cheeks ballooned outward like a puffer fish from the food still balling in her mouth.

"You will always have me, gurl."

Latona continued to eat the waffles, savoring each bite.

Meanwhile, Drenelle moved his eyes back to the three men huddling over the table, whispering to one another in secret.

One man, who was wearing a raggedy Western tee shirt, broke away from the other two and stood behind a quiet homely woman in line.

Without her knowing, the man extended his arm behind her back, positioned his phone flat, camera-side up underneath her skirt, and took a picture.

The young woman suddenly rotated around and asked what the man was doing.

He shrugged innocently and said, "Nothing. Just drop something."

She wasn't fully aware of what the stranger behind her had just done; however, from the way she retreated back into herself in a restless state of anxiety, it appeared to Drenelle that she knew *exactly* what happened but she was too afraid to say something. Both her legs inched closer together, so close that the heels of her shoes were nearly touching one another. She moved her pocket book in front of her shaky body and folded both her arms tightly across her chest, as if she was wearing her arms, as well as the pocket book, as some sort of protective shield.

The young man didn't bother ordering anything, which was another red flag.

Instead, he walked back to the table he came from, huddled close to his other buddies, and showed them the recent photo he had just taken on his phone.

With a wide grin on his face, the man started texting or writing something on his phone while the other two couldn't keep themselves from laughing.

"You know," Drenelle said to Latona, as he removed his eyes from the three men and sipped from his oolong tea, "it's supposed to be a full moon tonight."

"So, what?" Latona mumbled, chewing her food from one side of her mouth. "You gonna turn into a werewolf?"

"I dunno," Drenelle said. "Maybe."

"So, you have any plans tonight?" Latona asked, as she looked back down at the plate of waffles.

Without Latona looking, Drenelle glanced at the young woman grabbing her tea from the server and taking it to a booth in the very back of the tea house.

"As a matter of fact, I do."

"Oh yeah? Like what?"

Once more, Drenelle moved his eyes toward the young woman.

"Just a few things."

"Like what, *Mister* Mysterious?"

"Mr. Mysterious, huh?"

"No," Latona said suddenly and stopped chewing. "Lame. *Super*-lame."

"Yeah," Drenelle said, deflated. "You're right. Cheesy."

"Cheesy? What you mean cheesy?"

"You know, like corny?"

"Corny?"

"Like, I dunno, like something that's overused."

"What didn't you just say 'overused' then?"

"You know, at times, you can be real finicky."

"Me? Finicky? *Guuurl*, like you one to talk."

"Ain't like being finicky is a negative description of one's character. In fact, I wouldn't even call it a flaw. I wish there was more finicky people out there like you," Latona pointed to herself, "*and me*, too. Like just the other day, my cousin was telling me how finicky I was."

"Gurl, your cousin don't know shit from sand."

"Technically, most sand is shit. Fish shit," Latona said as she wrinkled in her nose. "Saw it on one of them nature channels."

"Is that so?"

"Finicky people pay attention to details," Latona said with a shrug. "Without them details, it's like trying to make a batch of waffles without cracking an egg. Sure, you can use that powder mix shit, but you and I know a waffle ain't a waffle without eggs."

"And that's what I love about you, Latona," said Drenelle, raising his cup of oolong tea in a toast. "You *see* the details even when you can't."

The woman, who was sitting in the back of the tea house, suddenly stood up from her seat. Both of her eyes were red from where she had been rubbing away tears. She glared at the three men from across the tea house, grabbed her belongings, and stormed out without trying to make a scene.

Drenelle turned his narrowing green eyes to the three obnoxious men laughing it up a couple of tables down. He already knew what had to be done to them.

For Drenelle, it was already done.

UNDER the harvest moon twelve-two pulsated like a lazy virescent phantom in the corner of Star's eye.

She moved her eyes from the radiant moon and trained herself to focus on the numbers, four numbers, *not* three.

Twelve *o'* two.

Myko is late, Star thought to herself.

Two minutes late.

To Star, it felt like twice an eternity.

But it wasn't the matter of time that disturbed her the most.

I was going to murder somebody.

A real-life person.

The notion alone of plotting away inside her parked car in a seedy alleyway in one of the seediest, most detestable areas of town and doing exactly what her sagacious father warned her *not* to do caused her jaw to tighten with the tamed rage of a tigress.

Star questioned herself, her motives behind the madness: *Is this what it takes to find happiness?*

In that moment of great uncertainty, all Star could think about was time and where the hell it had gone and how, such a precious commodity, like time, was no longer her ally. Mostly, Star thought about her ole dada, Carlos, as if he was an oblique depiction of time and the callousness of its seemingly harsh nature. Star realized how disappointed her dada would've been to know his daughter, his little "Starlight," had jeopardized her own well being by putting herself in a position of eminent danger, even worse thinking, the very idea of taking another person's life. Carlos Walker was dead, been dead for over three years—or three "long" years to his only daughter, Star. Carlos died unexpectedly after his battle with stage-four lung cancer, which had caught Star, as well as her mother and her family, by complete surprise. Carlos wasn't a smoker. Except for taking a toke when he was at a curious-age, he never smoked a cigarette in his life. He had a distant-distant relative who had died from cancer of the brain. Other than that, he didn't have any family members who died from the big c-word. Star always thought it was either the secondhand smoke that killed him or the pollution in the air. He was always hanging around smokers. *They killed him*, she once thought. They were the ones who murdered my father, *the smokers*, and so, too, did the world around him. Eventually, the thought passed. But it didn't change the way Star felt about them. Carlos had better than good genes. Had the kind of genes that most would kill for. Had a greater grasp on maintaining a healthy diet with a balance of work and exercise. Every morning he jogged four miles around The Harbor. Ate right everyday, hardly indulged. However, he seemed prehistoric by the time Star was in grade school. He had Star when he was an older yet relatively fit man strong enough to give Star a queen-esque piggybank whenever their family visited Fantasy World every summer. Carlos's father, Star's grandfather, was one of the first black cartoonists to have his cartoons published in the daily *Bystander*. Which, having survived the Civil Rights Movement, was a big deal for the Walker family. Carlos Senior was a pillar of the community. Some would say, a man who had rightfully earned the title as "legendary." His son made sure to carry on his father's legacy through his own artwork and creations, as well as a foundation dedicated to his late father. Even though these men were long gone, a piece of their presence was very much alive in Star.

Pulling herself from the thought of her dada, Star glanced at the time on the dashboard and thought that maybe she forgot to change it after the end of daylight savings time. She grabbed the phone from the cup holder and checked the time on her phone.

Same.

Two minutes past midnight.

As Star unlocked her phone, a car pulled up behind Star.

"*Finally*," she said under her breath.

One of the headlights of the car was burned out while the other one, the glaring one, shone through the rear view mirror and forced Star to squint.

Once her eyes adjusted to the bright light, Star could hardly recognize herself in the mirror.

Again, she thought about her dada, his disappointment.

"I can't believe I'm doing this," Star whispered as she shut off the engine.

As she held in a deep breath through her nose, she turned her shoulder to the cat carrier in the backseat.

The glow of its eyes materialized in the darkness inside the carrier.

The sight of the creature alone nearly stole her breath; and for a moment, Star forgot to breathe.

As she leaned in closer to the carrier, it released a low-pitch *growl*.

Startled, Star leaned away and took a moment to gather herself.

She reminded herself to breathe. She breathed. Then reached for her purse in the passenger seat and pulled out a pair of purple gloves. First of all, she slipped the glove over her right hand. By the time Star reached her left hand, she paused and thought it over again. Mainly, Star thought about all of those articles she had spent hours skimming through on the Internet before she arranged this very meeting. Mainly, Star thought about her own health risk.

On second thought, she decided to put on an extra pair of gloves over the pair she was already wearing.

With her hands protected, Star cut the engine of her car.

She was first to step out.

Then, Myko.

Star wasn't sure whether or not that was his real name. She didn't care.

As Myko stood by his car, Star opened the backdoor and carefully pulled out the cat carrier.

Confused, Myko pointed at the carrier.

"Hold up," he said suddenly. "What the hell is this?"

"What you mean?"

"Is that thing alive?"

"Of course, it's alive."

"I thought we agreed that y'all kill it."

"Like hell we are," Star said, disgusted. "That wasn't part of the agreement, Myko."

"Have you ever killed and skinned a dead animal?"

"No."

"It's a pain in the fucking ass."

"Then, deal with it," Star said coldly. "Besides, I thought this kind of stuff was your expertise?"

"It is, but—"

"—*But*," Star said over Myko.

"Whatever," Myko said in deflation. He nodded at Star's hands. "What's up with the gloves?"

"I'm just being precautious," Star replied, making sure to keep the cat carrier away from her body.

"Is it contagious?"

"No," Star said. "Of course not."

"Then, why wear the gloves?"

"I *just* am."

"This thing ain't gonna scratch me, is it?"

"Could," Star said, "if you do some dumb shit like poke at it."

Star handed the cat carrier to Myko.

In return, Myko was hesitant about touching the carrier.

"It's not going to scratch you."

"Well, how you know it ain't gonna bite me?"

Star clenched her teeth and inhaled deeply through her nose.

Deep breaths, she thought.

"Don't mess with it and you'll be fine, all right?"

"You sure?"

"No," Star said bluntly.

Myko finally grabbed the handle on the cat carrier.

During the exchange, the cat carrier shook violently.

Myko suddenly flinched.

Star readjusted her grip over the handle and rolled her eyes at Myko.

"Are you gonna take it or not?" asked Star.

"Yeah," he said sharply, like a boy answering a smothering mother's question.

This time, he grabbed the handle and a sudden odor caused his nose to wrinkle. First, he smelled himself. Then, the cat carrier. His head jolted backward.

In disgust, he said, "This fucking thing's gonna stink up my car."

"Roll down a window or something."

"Where the hell did you get this thing?"

"Does it matter?"

"Forget I asked."

Myko lugged the wobbly carrier to his car. He placed the carrier in the backseat of his car and shut the door behind him.

"How long will it take for her to feel the effects?"

"According to my sources, it should take at least forty-eight hours—"

"—Your sources?" Myko giggled. "What? You like friends with someone who works at the CDC or something?"

Star flexed her jaw, her rage lukewarm but tame.

Myko asked, "How sure are you that this is gonna work?"

"Once it's done, my partner will wire the money into your new banking account," Star said, her tone stern like a businesswoman. "You just make sure you follow all of the details he gave you and everything should run smoothly."

"You don't sound too confident."

"It *will* work. Just do your part. Got it?"

"Yeah," Myko said with a stutter. "Got it."

"Are you sure?"

"Yeah," Myko said, more sharply. "*Got it.*" As Star started to walk back to her car, Myko asked Star from behind, "Tell me. What did this woman do to you to deserve to go out like this?"

Star stopped just before she opened the car door.

"It's only a matter of time before she destroys me. If she was in my position, she'd probably do the same thing." Star shrugged her shoulders. "Of all people, you should know what it's like to lose everything—the ones you love—to wonder whether or not you're going to survive the night, spending your waking hours suffering like a wounded animal desperate to be put out of its misery. I'm trying to salvage whatever life I still have left and the only way I can achieve that, Myko, is with her out of the picture."

"You know there are other ways. Simpler ways—"

"No," she said, unwavering. "I know your other 'simpler' ways and they will draw *way* too much suspicion. This right here. This is the *only* way."

"Whatever," Myko said callously. "Y'all just make sure y'all follow up on your end of the deal."

"You don't have to worry about us."

Star didn't even wait for Myko to reply. She got back into her car.

As Myko drove away, Star hit the ceiling of the car.

"Pop-eye," she murmured.

For good luck.

⸙

STAR spent the early hours of the morning disinfecting the entire backseat of her car. She scrubbed and scrubbed until her fingers blistered. Spent at least an hour on the area where she had set the carrier. Once she was done cleaning the seats as well as the floors, she cleaned them again.

ꙫ

DURING the drive to Chop Soy, Star received a text message from Carmen:

I'm going to be running a little late.

Star patiently waited until she stopped at a red light to shoot Carmen a text back; however, her phone was acting up. For some bizarre reason—Star thought it might've been a service issue maybe or something to do with cell phone towers or even the new upgrade, which apparently included the so-called "bug fix"—she didn't receive a decent signal whenever she left Chinatown and entered Little Tokyo. Star started to lose her patience with her phone as she waited until that little white bar moved across the screen in turtle-pace speed.

By the time the text went through, Star was pulling into the restaurant's parking lot.

No worries. I'm almost here.

Eventually, Carmen received the painfully slow text. Then, texted back:

Okay, Early Bird.

Star didn't want to be rude. She had a diplomatic response for Carmen:

I'll grab a table in the back.

Then, Carmen:

Sounds nice. See you soon.

WHEN Star stepped inside Chop Soy, Fay had already grabbed a table located near the back of the restaurant.

Fay spotted Star at the entrance and waved her over.

Star told the giddy hostess that she was meeting a group of friends.

The hostess grabbed a menu and escorted Star to the table.

"If it isn't Lady Justice standing right before my eyes," Fay said, opening her arms.

Star forced a smile upon her face and hugged Fay.

"Hey, girl," she said, her voice climbing in forced excitement as well. "How are you?"

Surprised by Star's glow, Fay said, "Can't complain." She stepped back, her eyes did an once-over Star's toned body, her getup, her hair, then she redirected the question back at Star. "Look at you. Looking all spiffy. You wear the look of a woman who spent a month in Love Town. So, tell me, who's the lucky winner?"

Star paused, her face somewhat recoiling from the remark.

"Please, Star," Fay begged. "I want details now."

With her chin pressed against her neck, Star said, "I don't know what you're talking about?"

"You know you haven't changed one bit, Star. Still as modest as a mouse."

Star sighed away what she took as a harmless insult.

Fay always carried a pocketful of them, she thought to herself.

"So," Star said, cutting through nervous tension, "you've been here long?"

"Just got here," Fay said. "I figured I'd go ahead, grab us a table before this place gets swamped. I read somewhere that there was some Cosplay thingy at the CP Convention Center this weekend. So, you know it's probably gonna be, as the kids say, 'popping' around here."

"A Cosplay thing, huh?" Star nodded at Fay. "That's right up your alley."

"Not really," Fay said, her brow curling with what Star considered as embarrassment. "Haven't been to one in like years."

Star looked around the restaurant, which was half-full. Strangely, the sight of people being in the vicinity of Star felt comforting. From a legal standpoint, Star looked at them as, more or less, witnesses.

Fay pointed at her seat.

"Take a seat."

Star took a seat as the waitress stopped by the table and poured Star a glass of water and asked Star what she'd like to drink.

"Just water," Star said and pointed at the glass of water.

"Just water? Come on. Really, Star?" Star noticed Fay do that slight move with her brow again. "We haven't seen each other in months. Please, don't make these lunches out as if they're chores, Star."

Fay held up her gin and tonic, tempting Star.

"I would, but I have to go back to work."

"So? One drink ain't gonna kill you, girl."

"Yeah, but it can get me fired."

"You're telling me all your lawyer buddies don't have a cocktail for lunch. Thought it was like a requirement for your profession."

"Fine," Star said annoyingly. "One gin and tonic."

The waitress listened, waited.

Star turned to the waitress, who repeated the order and then walked to the bar area.

"That's more like it."

"So, how've you been?" asked Star.

"Same thing, different—"

"—Different day, right?" Star removed her sport coat and placed it over the chair. "So, any new clients?"

"As a matter of fact, I'm working with a new client right now. A comic book artist."

"Really?"

"Strange fella."

Star's cheeks darkened.

"Strange is good, right?"

"The guy's borderline psychotic. I'm talking grade-a perfectionist, like the *autocrat*-type."

Star laughed at the comment.

"One of them, huh? He sounds committed."

"Anyway, he wants me to do an entire facelift on this new book. Fonts, design, everything."

"What's the name of the comic book?"

"Technically, graphic novel."

"I see."

"So, what's this 'graphic novel' called?"

"*Slow Motion*."

Star paused.

"Interesting."

"I know," Fay said. "I don't care much for the title—"

"—Nah. It's good."

"The story is really incredible, though. It's about a gifted girl who can slow down time. People of power—in particular, *men* of power—want what she has so they try to take it from her."

"Slow down time, huh?" Star thought aloud. "Relatable. I think everybody would love to slow down time, especially living in a time that's moving at a thousand miles per hour, you know, with technology and all."

"I know, right? Anyway," Fay said, "this girl ends up using this gift she has for the greater good."

The waitress arrived with Star's drink.

Star made sure to thank the waitress.

In return, the waitress asked if the two wanted to start off with appetizers, but Star insisted on waiting for the others to show up before placing any other orders except drinks.

Which didn't sit too well for Fay.

She was hungry, already half-buzzed. She ordered yet another gin and tonic to keep her busy. Then raised her partially full glass in a toast.

"Well," Fay said to Star, "to the High. . . " Fay looked around at the empty seats around her, ". . . Five."

"Right," Star said flatly. "More like High Two."

"More like the Trusty Two," Fay said. "First to show and last to leave."

"Salut." Star paused before tapping her glass against Fay's. "And, to *Slow Motion*."

"Cheers."

Star sipped from the gin and tonic.

Then scrolled through the messages on her phone.

"Okay, Ms. Modest," Fay said. "Out with it. I want details. Who is he?"

Star put her phone aside.

"I assure you, Fay, there's no 'he,' only me."

Fay tilted her head to the side and stared at Star, as if she wasn't going to say anything for the remainder of the lunch until Star was completely honest with her.

"Okay, geez. You're worse than my mother. There is one guy."

"Now we're talking." Fay leaned forward, rubbing her palms together. "So, what's this one guy's name?"

Star hesitated.

"John."

"John, okay. And what does John do for a living?"

Star thought of the first word that came to mind.

"Nothing."

"Nothing? He's gotta do something."

Star shook her head.

"Nope," she said, more confidently. "He does nothing. Absolutely nothing."

"Very ambitious, this John guy sounds."

"Well, you asked, Fay. I told."

"So, you mean, he sits around the house all day and does nothing."

"Yep," Star backtracked her immediate answer, "well, he doesn't exactly sit around the house all day. Every now and then, he'll get up off the couch and help me out whenever I'm tied up."

Fay furrowed her brow.

"You talking about what I think you're talking about?"

"What you mean?"

"You know?

"What? You mean sex?"

"Star Walker, you *are* a freak," Fay said as she could hardly contain herself. "I knew it. You have a sex slave and his name is John. You never cease to amaze me, Star."

"Careful now with the slave talk, Fay. You are talking to a woman of color."

"Wow, Typical-Star," Fay replied, the tops of cheeks reddening. "You went straight to the race card."

"Well, you did use the word *slave* in front of a black woman."

"Yeah, all right," Fay said. "We get it. I forgot you were so sensitive about the subject, Star." Fay pointed at herself. "I'm a woman of color." She pointed to a dark skinned woman sitting at the other end of the restaurant. "She's a woman of color. We're all people of color. I'm sure, somewhere in the *distant* past, we all had ancestors who were slaves. I'm pretty sure I had relatives who were slaves, having, like, one percent Egyptian in me. You don't see me getting all offended by the word."

"You're a woman of color? You white?"

"Last time I checked white was a color. I mean, if you wanted to get technical, I'm more of an oatmeal-brown."

"Oatmeal-brown?"

Star tried not to laugh.

"As you know, Star, my dad is white. Mother, Asian. Besides, if you look at it from the bigger picture, we're all slaves. Every single one of us," Fay reached into her pocket and pulled out her phone, "only our master isn't a man. It's a machine."

Star took a sip of her drink, her face expressionless.

"You know, I'm just messing with you, right?"

A laugh broke through Star's stern exterior. Fay started to laugh as well.

"For a second, I thought you turned into a snowflake."

"Snowflake? What?" Star said, "Nuh-uh. Not me. But you, damn, girl, you really get worked up about this race shit." Star took yet another sip of her drink. "But that's what I like about you, Fay," she lied. "You get really funny, like hysterical, when you're mad."

"I'm not mad."

The waitress arrived with Fay's drink.

"I think you need another drink, my sister from another mister." Star waited for the waitress to leave. Then said from the corner of her mouth, "By the way, I have a sex slave named John. Yep. He's my bitch."

"*Freak*," Fay said under her breath.

She removed the lime from the glass, squeezed what little juice it had into the drink, and used the handle-part of a fork to stir the drink.

"Too bad they joined the trend and stopped using straws," Fay said. "It's like they're promoting the erosion of tooth enamel and early gum disease. #Fuckyou. I was going to say something earlier, but the waitress is kind of cute and I didn't want to make her feel uncomfortable."

"It's all to save the planet, you know?"

"From what? Plastic?"

"Centuries from now when highly intelligent aliens take over the planet Earth and obliterate all mankind, forcing our entire race into extinction, they'll comb what's left of the earth for artifacts we left behind—traces of our accomplishments and failures—and the only thing they'll discover is, you guessed it, plastic. That's all we'll ever be known for." Fay's eyes widened. "Hey, Earth. What was it that you really needed from those pesky humans? Earth's response: Plastic."

"Cynical-much."

Fay shrugged.

"So, tell me more about John the Sex Slave. Is he a good kisser?"

"If I had to rate him like a movie on Rotten Tomatoes, I'd probably give him around a seventy-six percent—on the lips, that is. However, whenever he's, you know, kissing other places of my body, I'd give him ninety-eight percent because a hundred percent would raise way, *way* too many eyebrows and make it look like the producers 'paid me off' all for the sake of a good score."

"John sounds 'Certified Fresh.'"

"Oh," Star said, "he's got a Oscar-worthy tongue, baby."

"Does John have a sister?"

"No," Star said. "But he has a brother."

"Not interested."

"Speaking of bitches, you still seeing that one bitch?"

"Which one?"

"You slut." Star said to Fay, "I see you still approach your sex life the same way you vote."

"Which is?"

"Undecided."

"You know I'm not all into labels."

"What's so wrong about a woman being with a man? Being a hetero or lesbo or whatever your sexual preference is, none of those things are really considered a 'label.' It's a part of the human condition."

"Really, Star?" she said bitterly. "Why don't you try walking down Jefferson Street holding another woman's hand and you wait and see how many ugly stares you get—"

"—Did you ever think that they're staring because they're probably checking you out," Star said. "What other reason would they be staring at you?"

"Some of them—*some*—have the balls to actually say whatever it is they're thinking. But, for most of them, I already know what they're thinking."

"So, you can read minds now?"

"Good idea for a new comic book: A girl who can read minds."

Star ignored the idea, ignored the triteness behind it.

"Forget about 'em. That shows a lot about their character and how simpleminded they are."

"Well, it happens way more often than it should."

"People will come around. Eventually. They always do."

"Easy for you to say." Fay shrugged. "Ever since I broke up with Steph, I've been O for six on the other team. I'm not hating on your team at all. But, I swear, some guys act as if they're entitled to be with us, like they shouldn't have to put in any actual work to earn our affection."

"Not all guys are dogs, Fay." Star found herself thinking about the comments that she said earlier. "Well," she corrected, "most of them are. You just haven't found yourself the right one, you know, the overly sensitive type who makes you a better person."

Star was eating her words.

Better person, she thought. *Is that what am I?*

She washed down the thought with another sip of her gin and tonic.

"Well," Fay brought Star back into the conversation, "the last two I've been with have ended up in total disaster. It's like I have a magnet that attracts losers."

"When it comes to choosing a man, you're about as picky as a Forty-Year-Old Virgin."

"Men have enough flaws as it is."

"Women have flaws too, Fay. Sorry, Beyoncé. We ain't 'flawless.'"

"The last guy I was with was named Kelly—and by the way, what kind of a man's name is Kelly? Rhymes with belly, as in bellyache. Which makes perfect sense because every time we made out he gave me heartburn. Not only that, his penis was bent like a question mark and half the time, the guy acted as if he didn't even know how to use the damn thing. It's not rocket science!"

"I once read in *Women's* magazine that a curved shaft heightens the pleasure for a woman during intercourse."

As Fay sipped from her drink, her throat clenched in a burst of a laugh, which caused her drink to spill a little bit over the rim.

She cleared her throat and said to Star, "I would have to go on the record here and respectfully disagree with you, Star. I mean. . . have you like seen one?"

"What you mean? Like for real or on the Internet?"

"No," Fay said. "I mean, like 'seen' one, like close enough you could shake its hand." Fay waved her hand in the air. "Hello, nice to meet you!"

"No," Star said, sipping from her drink. "I can't say that I have, but I once dated a guy who hung thirty degrees to the right. At times, it acted like it had a mind of its own. I wanted to anchor it down like a newly planted tree."

"He could've broken it, you know."

Star shook her head.

"That's like an urban legend," she said. "It's not like it's a bone. It's mostly tissue and veins. And we all know you can't break tissue."

"But you can tear it, can't you?"

"I don't know, can you?"

"I think we'll leave that up for Mandy to decide."

"Yeah," Star murmured. "I'm sure she'd know a thing or two about the male anatomy."

"She's a doctor—"

"—A pediatrician. Much different."

"How so? It's no different than a veterinarian. You got to treat a cat, a dog, a lizard, a snake."

While Star glanced down at her phone, Fay studied Star's change in mannerism soon after the name Mandy was brought up into the conversation. She didn't think much of the change—at least, not yet.

"You know," Fay said, thinking, "another thing about Kelly that I couldn't stand—I mean, it drove me crazy whenever we'd go out in public. The clothes he wore. For fuck's sake, he's a grown ass man dressing like he's an eight year old boy. A fucking manboy is what he is. He's always wearing these superhero T-shirts two sizes too small. It's absurd what some men have turned into."

"Was he in shape?"

"Does it matter?"

Star was leaning toward yes, but she said no.

"He's ripped," Fay said. "You know, typical gym-body. The ego matched the size of his muscles. More than likely, he's probably standing in front of a mirror somewhere staring at himself. I swear, put him in a nice suit and tie and he'd make a good news reporter."

"That type, huh?"

"The *Narcissistic Asshole*," both Star and Fay said together in synchronized harmony.

"Well, to me, sounds like you're not over Kelly. You've mentioned his name two times thus far, once in the present tense. One more time and you're potentially looking at regret. Then, from there, I can't help you. We're talking full-on cyber stalking. Checking his Facebook updates. Monitoring his current status—"

"—You're crazy."

Once more, Star looked down at her phone in a strangely tense silence.

Again, Fay noticed the sudden change in Star, her aura.

She didn't know what to think of the expression—or lack of one.

Star looked up at Fay, saw her eyes shift.

"Look who I bumped into on the way over here," said the voice behind Star's shoulder.

In perfect timing, the next two members of the High Five arrived.

Rhonda and Carmen.

Fay was first to acknowledge Rhonda. Then, Star turned around in her seat and saw Rhonda standing behind her. Carmen wasn't too far behind.

Star stood from her seat and greeted Rhonda with the common, "Hey, how are you?" along with an awkward hug, which came across as a full body heave. Carmen was next to hug Star. Other than a drawn out "Hey, gurl," they didn't say much to one another. Fay remained in her chair and greeted Rhonda with an animated wave.

Rhonda sat down to the right of Star while Carmen sat down right next to Fay and reached over to Fay in a half-hug.

Once they were all settled into their seats, Rhonda had some shocking news for the rest of the gang.

"So, did y'all hear about Mandy?"

At a loss of words, Star tilted her head in utter surprise. She embraced for the worse.

Fay and Carmen shook their heads.

Slack-faced, Star said before Rhonda could follow up, "What happened? Is she okay?"

"Yeah," Rhonda said, laidback. "Of course. She's fine. She had to cancel. She said she had a thing."

Both Fay and Carmen let out a sympathetic *awh* while Star was more interested in why Mandy had canceled.

"A thing?" she said. "What thing?"

"A new patient probably. She didn't exactly say. You know how she's always saving lives."

"Yes," Star hesitated, trying not to draw anymore unwanted suspicion to herself. "Well, that's unfortunate, I guess."

"It's not the High Five without Mandy," Carmen whined.

While Carmen turned to Fay and felt her material and complimented her on her fashion taste, Rhonda leaned closer to Star and asked about her life as a paralegal.

"Busy" was the first word that came to Star's mind.

That, and "demanding."

"Still locking up big, bad wolves."

"That's not exactly my job," Star said. "But I've been preparing myself for The Bar. Hopefully, by the end of next year, I'll be on my way to becoming a lawyer."

"Criminal or civil."

"Criminal."

"A friend of mine's husband has already taken The Bar, like, twice. From what she told me, he basically said it's hard to pass."

"Not if you study, it's not."

Star took a sip of her drink.

"You still teaching at Red Valley?"

"They moved me up from ninth grade to eleventh. If I knew I was going to have to work twice as hard, I would've stayed in ninth grade. Eleventh graders treat reading as if it's a chore. Sometimes, I feel so—I dunno—old around them. The worst is when they call me Ms. Abbott."

"What's wrong with going by a miss?"

"It's makes me feel so old."

"You are old, Rhonda."

Rhonda dropped her jaw and leaned back in repulsion.

"You serious? I'm only a few months older than you."

"I'm not saying I'm not old. I am old—"

"—I ain't old," Fay chimed in.

Star received a text from Carmen:

She's going to kill you.

Rhonda couldn't help but notice Star reading the secret text.

Star subtly put the phone away without drawing more suspicion.

"You know I didn't mean it like *that*, Rhonda," she said, trying to put out the fire, which was slowly building inside Rhonda. "Once you step out into the real world, they, the kids, tend to look at you differently. You're no longer considered cool or whatever word they use these days—"

"—They still use the word *cool*."

"My brother still uses the word *phat* to describe things."

"Fat? You mean like fat-shaming?"

"No," Fay said. "*Phat*. Ph-fat."

"I've never heard of that one."

"You're telling me you've never heard of *phat*—"

"—All I'm saying, Rhonda: You're one of 'them' now. The uncool people. Don't take offense to it. I'm uncool." Star pointed at Fay. "You're uncool. Face it. We're all uncool."

"Hey," Fay interrupted, "I don't care what you say. I'm cool."

A chirp of a laugh slipped from Carmen.

"What?"

Rhonda was still caught up—in fact, obsessed—by what Star referred to her as "them."

"Them?"

"You know," Star shrugged, "an adult."

Holding up her glass, Fay said to Star, "Thanks for stating the obvious, Killa of Cool."

"You know what I mean, Fay."

"In a way, they do make me feel old," Rhonda said carefully. "I used to text all the time in high school. Now, it's like texting is their only form of communication." Rhonda sighed. "God, just listen to me. I *am* starting to sound like my mother."

The comment drew a couple of laughs.

Right on cue, the waitress stopped by the table and asked for orders. Rhonda stuck with water while Carmen spent every bit of five minutes grilling the waitress about Chop Soy's tea by throwing random yet legitimate questions at her in which most waitresses wouldn't know, like where the tea came from or what kind of soil was used in the process. The waitress surprisingly answered each question as if she was throwing them at Carmen in vain for attempting to undermine the integrity of Chop Soy and their dedication to their message of being a green company. Carmen swallowed each answer that came her way. Not once did Fay interject her feelings about Star and herself being the only ones drinking alcohol for lunch. She was too preoccupied by listening to the proficient waitress one-up on Carmen as she dropped some knowledge on the process of making tea. Star finished the rest of her drink and ordered another one without second thought.

Star felt as if she needed the drink, as if it had become a necessity for getting her through the next hour.

Once Carmen was done interrogating the waitress, she made her best attempt to draw more attention to the straying topic in the conversation.

"I know exactly what you mean, Star," Carmen said directly to Star. "Everything changed for me after I had Charlie. I feel like a better person. I no longer feel like I have to prove to anybody that I'm not a responsible person. Trust me. I am perfectly happy with being 'uncool.'"

Rhonda cut in, "I was meaning to ask you, Carmen. How was you momcation?"

"Did I miss something here?" Star asked. "What the hell is a 'momcation?'"

"It's basically where you take a vacation from being a mom. Hence mom-*cation*."

"So, what? You went on vacation by herself?"

"That's the whole point, right? Get away from being a mom for a few days."

"Where'd you go?"

"I went to the Cayman Islands. Did the whole works. The full body treatment. Spa. Facial. Massage. After

134

about a week, I felt like a brand new me. If you ever have a child, I totally recommend taking a momcation. It will *literally* change your life."

"I don't have any plans in spitting out a rug rat anytime soon," Fay said from the corner of her mouth. "So, no, I'm good—and forget about this whole 'on-the-clock' bullshit. A woman can have a child at any age. I mean, nowadays, women are giving birth in their fifties."

"Fifties is like the new thirties."

"You are aware that there are many risk factors, including—"

"—So who watched Charlie?" Star interrupted Rhonda.

"Max," Carmen said, shooting a glance toward Rhonda. "Why?"

"He didn't mind?"

"Max?" Carmen repeated. "Not at all; in fact, he's really good with kids. He and Charlie get along very well. Did you not check out the photos I posted on my Facebook page?"

Star shook her head.

"No."

Carmen then turned to Rhonda, waited.

"I didn't get around to it," Rhonda said. "I've been literally swamped with school."

"You got to see these photos," Carmen said, pulled her phone from her purse, and showed the photos to Rhonda. She made sure to describe each photo, where it was taken, what she was doing at the time. She handed off the phone to Star, who only looked at one photo, which was a photo of Carmen sitting on the beach while she was holding a brightly colored drink shaded with a miniature umbrella in one hand and a black pole of some kind in the other hand. Star couldn't quite tell what it was.

"How'd you take the photo?" she asked.

"I brought my selfie-stick, of course."

Fay said in a lowered tone, "You own a selfie-stick?"

"Yeah," Carmen snapped. "Don't judge."

Fay raised her hands, as if she didn't want to fight.

"Next month, I leave for Haiti."

Carmen asked, "Is Mandy going with you this year?"

"No," she said. "Unfortunately, another 'thing' came up. I know, right?"

"That's Mandy," Carmen said. "Always saving lives."

Always saving lives, Star thought as soon as the words spilled from Carmen's lips.

"This year's going to be extra special because of all the destruction left behind by Claudia. Armey, who's head of Mount Zion, is bringing in tons of worshipers from other churches around the country to lend a hand. I talked to Rachel Merger—"

"—Who's Rachel Merger?"

"She's one of my teacher friends from school. I talked her into coming with me. She's looking forward to it. It's going to be a *huge* event."

The waitress returned to the table with Carmen's green iced tea and asked if they were ready to order.

Two out of the four were still undecided.

The waitress said she'd give them a couple of extra minutes to look over the menu; and then, once more, she left the table.

Over the pause, Star asked, "What about your job?"

"The trip takes place right before Fall Break. So, I'll only miss a couple of days of school. I've already got a sub and everything."

"How about starting off with an appetizer?" Fay suggested while skimming through the menu.

"How about lettuce wraps?" Rhonda suggested. "I haven't tried them yet."

"I'm down," Fay said.

"Fay, you're down for everything."

Fay's brow curled.

"What's that supposed to mean, Carmen?"

"You're like a garbage disposal."

"I am not."

"Are too." Carmen put the menu aside and leaned closer to Fay. "Hey, Fay Baby, I'd kill to have your metabolism. You can eat whatever you want and not worry about gaining weight. Me, on the other hand, I eat a bite of ice cream and I can feel my ass getting fatter."

"I'm sure you dread this time of the year."

"Tell me about it."

"I hate Thanksgiving."

"I actually like Thanksgiving, but not because of the food."

"Then, why do you like Thanksgiving?"

"*Duh*," Fay said. "Family, of course. Except for maybe my birthday or a random pop in, it's like the one time of the year I get to spend more time with them."

Carmen said, "Max and I are thinking about getting away after Thanksgiving. We haven't had any 'alone' time ever since Charlie. We've been currently in a jam with the whole 'babysitter' situation. Like this morning, right, it literally took me forever trying to find a babysitter."

Rhonda asked, "What happened to that new girl, Angela?"

"She quit."

Fay narrowed her eyes in a manner that would suggest deviance.

"Let me guess," she leaned closer to Carmen, "Angela was snooping around your house and she found a little 'something-something' that she wasn't supposed to find. Am I getting warmer?"

Carmen shouldered Fay.

"Cut it out."

"Come on, Carmen San Diego. Am I getting warmer?"

Carmen paused, then smirked.

"Warm," she said.

"Okay," Fay said, sitting more upright. "So, Babysitter Angela found something, something that either made her quit or something that forced her to quit *or*," Fay exclaimed, "you," referencing Carmen, "were looking for some excuse to fire her because you didn't like her *or*, even better, you fired Babysitter Angela based on what she found, *but*, instead of telling us you fired her, you decided to say she quit so you wouldn't draw any suspicion to the matter."

"Too late," Star chirped.

"She found Max's secret stash of pot that he keeps hidden in the flower vase in the foyer."

Carmen rolled her eyes.

"Cold."

"Of course," Fay said, "what kind of teenager looks through, of all places, a vase?"

"One who was desperate to dig up some dirt on you. No pun intended."

"No," Fay said, squinting her eyes. "Angela was a curious girl who spent her weekends babysitting when she should've been spending them with her new stud of a boyfriend who was still trying to get some action but hadn't rallied up enough confidence to make a move. After Charlie was put to bed, she was all by herself. Her new boyfriend was out probably partying with the other football players or even hooking up with a girl who showed him the attention. So, Babysitter Angela turned into what most girls her age turned into: Curious. She went through your jewelry and potential items she could pawn off for that boob job she so desperately wanted for Christmas, but—"

"—Cold," Carmen said. "Ice cold."

"*But* Angela's no thief. So, feeling like the curious one she was, Babysitter Angela decided to go through your more 'personal' items, ones that you keep tucked away in the cozy confines of a drawer."

Carmen smirked.

"Warm."

"Oh," Fay said, "I'm boiling, Ms. San Diego. Babysitter Angela started with Max's stuff. Maybe tried on a couple of his things. Maybe she wanted to know what it felt like to be inside the clothes of a man. No. That's not Angela's style. She's crafty, you see. She's like some young Nancy Drew, only way smarter and more bitchin' and has a keen eye for the perverse nature of the human race—"

"—All right," Carmen blurted out. "She found Craig."

"Craig?"

"That's her big black dildo," Fay said with a grin on her face.

Star said, "You have a big black dildo named Craig?"

"That's not all she found," she confessed. "She found all of Craig's buddies, too. She found the whole gang. Believe it or not, it was my idea. I mentioned it to Max out of the blue. He was into it. The next day, he comes after work with bags full of sex toys, gags, and bondage junk."

"Okay, *Fifty Shades of Grey*."

"And what exactly spawned this salacious idea, Carmen?"

Carmen pointed at Fay.

"What she just said?"

"A movie?"

"The book, actually. You've read it?"

"You think I'm the kind of person who would read that smut?"

Star said, "I'd rather watch a porno."

"I thought it would spice up our marriage."

"Let me guess," Fay said. "He's gotta bent dick?"

"Fay!" Rhonda said, repulsed but not entirely surprised by her candor.

"My husband's penis is just fine, and, for your information, perfectly shaped. But I appreciate your concern."

"Well," Star asked, "did it work?"

"Did what work?"

"These, you know, toys."

"What you think?"

Fay said, "And I thought Star was the freaky one of the group. Man, was I wrong?"

"Fay, really?" Rhonda retorted. "Is that necessary? During this current climate of inequality and toxic masculinity, don't you think comments like those have further divided us women when we—collectively—should be uniting around all females regardless of their sexual preference? The woman's image has already suffered enough damage as it is. One side calls us brave for finally standing up for ourselves once and for all; while, at the same time, we're frowned upon by the other side and treated like a bunch of prudes who've never gotten laid before. Let's not dig the hole any deeper, shall we?"

"Not only is she starting to sound like her mother, but she also sounds like your typical Millennial who practices hypocrisy," Fay said as she reached in her pocket and pulled out an Altoid. "Wanna mint to help you feel better? Or," she said, "how about tissue?"

Carmen leaned closer to Fay and mumbled, "Watch it, Fay."

"Guys," Fay said innocently, "I'm teasing."

"Sure you are."

Star asked Fay, "Aren't you a Millennial, Fay? Oh, that's right. I forgot you weren't into any labels."

"Hardy-har-har."

"I think *Millennials*—our age group—gets a bad rap," Star said to the other three, "like the Hippies or Yuppies or Whoever."

"Don't forget about the ever-so precious Baby boomers," Fay seethed from what sounded like across the room. "They use innocence as an excuse for intolerance. By any means, they certainly don't get a free pass in, as Rhonda said, the current climate. All you have to do is pick up a history book. I mean, just look at all the shit your grandparents went through."

"I don't have to look, Fay," Star said, trying to hold back her anger. "I already know."

"I know you do, but still."

"It's hard to compare the two because it was such a different time back then," Rhonda said to Fay. "It's like trying to compare an athlete from thirty years ago to an athlete in today's world. I hear my students do it all the time, like they lived during that time period when, in fact, they weren't even born. Athletes have gotten stronger. Back then, it was just a game. Now, for some, it's like a way of life. So, you can't say one athlete is better than the other. That conversation is a bust. The only way you can justify your argument is by creating a time machine. Last I checked it hadn't been built yet. But until someone does create a time machine, what's the point arguing about it? The world has changed. If anything, the Baby boomers have showed us, by their mistakes, who we should be and who we shouldn't be. That's a good thing, right?"

"I agree, but what does that makes us?" Star questioned.

Rhonda shrugged.

"Opportunists."

"But don't you agree that, as soon as a generation is defined or pigeonholed into a category, it creates a whole new entity completely separate from reality?"

"Yeah," Rhonda said. "Could. But people see what they want to see. Most people just see things to justify their means, as if they're ignoring what makes us unique and only looking at the certain things that give us, as you said, a bad rap."

"Like we're 'entitled,' they'll say. Or, 'spoiled rotten.'"

"'Indecisive.'"

"'Too distracted.'"

"'Too soft or hypersensitive.'"

"*Easily* offended—"

"—'Crybabies.'"

"By the way, Star, who exactly is 'they?'"

"You know," she said, looking around the table, "The Internet."

Baffled, Rhonda said, "You don't really take the Internet seriously, do you?"

"Don't get me started on The 'Internet People,'" Fay said, chewing on a piece of ice.

"That reminds me," Star cut in, her seriousness gathering everybody's attention. "I have an announcement to make. I was going to tell you guys earlier, but I guess, I was waiting for the right moment."

"You're not pregnant, are you?"

"No, Fay," Star said with annoyance. "I'm not pregnant."

Carmen asked, "Is everything all right, Star?"

"Yeah," Star said, looking down for a moment. "It's fine."

"What is it?"

Star paused.

The other members of High Five leaned forward in anticipation.

"Star, what is it?"

"I'm *finally*. . ."

"Finally?"

"I'm finally quitting Facebook."

Carmen gasped.

"What? Why?"

"You've been saying that for months."

"No," Star said seriously. "I quit Facebook."

"Quit? Like done—"

"—Quit, as in I deleted my account this morning."

Fay raised her glass.

"Congratulations, my friend."

Carmen leaned closer toward Star.

"Why'd you quit Facebook?"

"I dunno." Star corrected herself, "I guess I'm just tired of it trying to control my life." She pointed at Fay. "Like what Fay was telling me earlier, before you guys showed up, about machines taking over."

"Really, Fay," Carmen said to Fay. "You brainwashing Star now?"

"But it's true—"

"—I just don't understand the whole 'wanting to share my entire life with the world' thing anymore," Star said. "It's my life, not theirs. I don't want to be *that* person who gets criticized or ridiculed by some troll for a post I made on the Internet. I'm sick and tired of *all* of it. I'm sick and tired of all the fake news, the one-sided point of view. I'm sick and tired of *all* the anger comments showing up in my news feed, starting fights, provoking me to be someone I'm not—articles about 'people' being upset about 'whatever,' some trivial bullshit when, in reality, only a small group of angry people who have nothing better to do with their lives than to be angry about whatever, make a couple of tweets and all of a sudden, its considered headline 'news.' Comments from people I don't even follow, as if it's Facebook or Twitter's way of trying to make me angry all to benefit their companies' profits. The longer I'm plugged in, the more money they make. The more money they make, the more control they have over me. No way. I'm not going to let these people hijack my brain. Then, you have all these advertisers eavesdropping and tracking your every move. I'm sick and tired."

"Over half the Internet is fucking click bait," Fay said. "Like yesterday, I got some web-cam chick following me on Twitter. I checked out her page and it was clearly a spambot."

"Or some Russian dude posing as a web-cam chick?"

"Or that," Fay said. "Whoever it was, they were trying to entice me to click on a link to a naked pic."

"And did you?"

"Hell no!" Fay paused. "But that's not to say I didn't check out the rest of her Twitter page."

Rhonda said, "I once knew a teacher friend of mine whose phone got hacked. A week later after the hack, she found these bogus accounts on the Internet with her picture in the profile."

"Don't be so negative," Carmen said over Rhonda.

"Like you're one to talk, Carmen," Rhonda said. "The other day, you were talking about changing your name on Facebook."

"That's totally different."

"Change your name?"

"Just my middle name."

"You know, I didn't even realize the initials until this jerk, who's been stalking me, pointed it out. Which I'm kind of glad he did."

"What's your middle name?"

"Úrsula."

"Úrsula, huh?"

"I know what you're going to say, Fay." Carmen shot a glare at Fay. "Don't even go there."

"Carmen Úrsula Navarro Treviani."

Fay repeated the full name to herself.

Then, spoke the letters out loud.

"C, U, N—*Cunt*!"

The others couldn't help but laugh.

"Of *ALL* the men out there, you just so happened to pick the one man with a last name that starts with the letter T."

"Now, I see why you want to change your name."

"Well, drop the middle name."

"Besides, Carmen, most women I know drop their middle name after they get married."

"It's *my* name, not yours."

"Then, don't let some loser on the Internet tell you otherwise."

"No," Carmen said, looking down. "It's probably better that I do. I'm saving myself from future humiliation."

"Lately, it seems like it's getting harder to go on there."

"I don't think so," Carmen said. "I personally don't know what I'd do without the Internet. Where do you think I met Max? All the single women I know don't even go out to bars anymore. They're all on some dating site."

Star said, "You can't buy love or a follower. You have to work for it."

"Star's right," Fay said. "*But* I can't quit Facebook. So, what if it's for like old people. I need it to help promote my business."

"I go back and forth from Instagram to Facebook. But I like Facebook better."

"I still use Facebook," Rhonda said. "I probably use Facebook more than the other social media pages."

"Yeah," Fay said. "You're old, remember?"

"You're hilarious, Fay."

"Why thank you," Fay said politely and then nodded at Star. "I think eventually I'll quit Facebook."

"Eventually is another word for never."

"Facebook has complicated my sex life," Fay said. "For instance, last week I wanted to share a gorgeous photo I took while I was kayaking at Devil's Throat, but I was like, 'Oh, shit!' I totally realized I told a 'certain someone' that I didn't want to go out with her because I was too busy working with a new client."

"Why didn't you just tell this 'certain someone' the truth?"

"You mean you haven't lied to someone because you didn't want to hang out with them at that moment in time."

"Yeah, but why not just tell this person you didn't want to hang out?"

"I just met the chick," Fay said. "That's probably the last thing you want to say to someone you just met. I ended up posting the photo and then deleting the photo like a day later, but it was already too late. It was already 'out' there."

"Did she see the photo?"

"She hasn't returned my texts. So, yeah, more than likely, she did."

"Wasn't Devil's Throat the place where the police found all those bodies?"

"That's right," Carmen followed. "I remember hearing about that in the news last week."

"Technically," Fay said, "they didn't find the bodies until like a month or so ago. So, the lake is perfectly safe. Besides, a couple of dead bodies ain't gonna stop me from kayaking—"

"—Have you seen a dead body before, Fay?"

"I heard it was more than a couple."

The waitress was back at the table, anxiously waiting to take orders.

The morbid conversation came to a sudden halt.

Rhonda took charge and spoke for the rest of the group.

"First, we're going to start off with some appetizers," Rhonda said. "The lettuce wraps—"

"—A cup of miso soup," Carmen ordered.

"And some spring rolls," Fay said abruptly. "Don't forget spring rolls?"

"And the spring rolls," Rhonda said and looked around the table. "Anything else?"

Star shook her head.

"That's just about does it," Rhonda concluded.

With a smile on her face, the waitress jotted down the orders on a notepad in one swift stroke of her pen and once more, glided away.

"Doesn't it freak you out, though?" Carmen asked, watching the waitress as she walked back into the kitchen. "Just the thought of kayaking so close to where something awful happened?"

Resilient, Fay shook her head.

"Not really," she said and tapped her finger against the table. "People die all the time, Carmen; *in fact*, I bet ya someone died right here at this very table while eating their lunch. He—*or she*—was probably enjoying their miso soup when all of a sudden he—*or she*—felt a sudden tightness in his or her chest and then, all of a sudden, he—*or she*—had trouble breathing and then—"

Star laughed off the awkwardness of the joke.

"Really, Fay?" Rhonda said contemptuously. "Enough already."

"I'm just saying 'death' happens all around us," Fay said in defense. "It's the only one thing we *all* have in common. Can't we at least embrace what unites us instead of what divides us?"

"Really, Fay?"

"They should give that maniac the death penalty," Carmen said as she tried to break up the soon-to-be scuffle between Rhonda and Fay.

"You know, I actually heard somewhere that The Snipper wasn't the only one who committed all of those crimes. Instead, he had a crazy cult do all his killings for him. Like that one guy—"

"You mean Charles Manson?"

"Him."

"Yeah," Star said with slight hesitation, "but the people he killed weren't exactly saints either."

With exaggerated disgust, Rhonda said, "You actually agree with what happened to all those poor people?"

"No," Star replied. "Not really. But people should take a hard look at themselves before they start throwing around judgments."

"Typical Star," Rhonda said over Star. "You haven't changed a bit. You're just like you were in high school. Always sticking your neck out for the little man who blames society for all of the world's problems." Rhonda said to the others at the table as if Star was no longer sitting right next to her, "Remember when Star went out with that mumbling little pimple-popper, Justin Blaylock, in order to lift up his self-esteem—"

"—Justin, the Zit Machine? If a zit could talk, it'd sound just like Justin."

"I so did not go out with him," Star said louder. "Even if I did, who cares? It was high school."

"He was a creep."

"He was nice."

"Yeah," Carmen said. "And he had a face that would be perfect for a creepy stalker in a horror movie."

"Star, the psychopath was a 'se-ri-al kill-er' who butchered its victims with a pair of scissors and justified it by claiming these people were awful people—"

"—Bullies."

"Whatever," Rhonda dismissed Fay's side remark and then faced Star. "That still doesn't give a person—"

"—A monster."

"It doesn't give him a right to kill people. How can you defend some 'thing' like that?"

"I'm not defending him."

"More like *It*," Rhonda clarified, her tone more bitter. "Not defending *It*."

"I heard somewhere that he killed his victims with the same scissors he used to make his outfits with. Reminds me of that one dude from *Silence of the Lambs*. Buffalo Bob. What a creepo!"

"Buffalo Bill."

"No," Carmen said. "I'm pretty sure it's Buffalo Bob."

"Carmen," Star said, "that's just a movie, you know?"

"Wasn't it based on a true story?"

"I don't think so."

Star checked her phone, googled the movie, *Silence of the Lambs*, and in the matter of seconds, she had the answer for Carmen.

"Nope," Star said, flaunting her phone in front of Carmen. "Fictional. Based on a book written by Thomas Harris. And by the way, it's Buffalo Bill, not Bob."

Rhonda said over a tense silence, "I think what's so disturbing is that it happened so close to home? I actually contemplated moving to another city—"

"What about your job?"

"There will always be other teaching jobs."

"There are psychopaths in every city," Fay said while making a figurine with her napkin. "Just the other night, somebody got shot not too far away from where I live. Like hell I'm going to move. It's the world we live in. There are clinically insane people out there. Probably some right here in this very restaurant."

"Yeah," Carmen said. "One's talking right now."

"Hilarious."

The other members of High Five laughed, except Rhonda.

"You're serious about moving?"

"Not really," Rhonda said, shrugging. "But I'd be lying if it didn't cross my mind. Mandy told me that she swore she saw St. Croix at the House of Tea a few months back in Chinatown. She mentioned something about a weird-looking guy with bleached blonde hair staring at her from across the restaurant. She said there was something 'off' about him."

"He could've been scouting out his next victim?"

"Who knows?"

Fay asked, "Did you guys hear about how he was captured?"

"All I know is that the cops found like blood or something that matched one of the victims."

"Yeah, but do you know how they found that blood?"

The others didn't respond, which Fay took as a no to her question.

"The aunt borrowed the scissors The Snipper used to kill his victims with and loaned them to *her* sister, The Snipper's other aunt, who was going to make one of those human chain decorations to display at a birthday party for her son, The Snipper's nephew. Somehow, The Snipper's nephew got a hold of the pair of scissors while his mother wasn't looking and while he was running around the house with the scissors, he accidentally tripped and fell onto the scissors; ended up stabbing himself."

Star asked, "You're shitting me?"

"I shit you not, Star," she said bluntly. "Tragically, the kid died. Apparently, there was an investigation into his death, even though his death was later ruled an 'accident.' Cops seized the scissors, 'The Snipper's weapon of choice.' Found a trace of dry blood on the pair of scissors. The investigators matched it with The Snipper's latest victim. The cops put the two pieces together. Arrested Drenelle St. Croix, aka The Snipper."

"Talk about karma."

"When police raided his aunt's house and found all those eyes he kept in jars in his studio, one of the reporters said the eyes were positioned in a way that faced his workspace, as if, in a bizarre way, all these eyes were watching him while he worked. They were like his own trophies or his audience—"

"—Can we talk about something else, please," Rhonda said, extremely irked by Fay's morbid interest. "That's all you ever hear about in the news nowadays. It's like everyday they're reporting something awful that's happened. A stabbing. An active shooter. A protest. A riot. A maniac on the loose. Someone murdering someone because of *this* or *that* or because no reason at all."

"You call it news," Fay said blandly. "I call it entertainment."

Rhonda ignored Fay.

"Like a couple of weeks ago, I heard that somebody somewhere in Chicago, I think, was standing in line, waiting to order food, when out of the blue he pulled out a gun and shot somebody in broad daylight because he didn't—how do I say—he didn't 'agree with' the clothes he was wearing."

"Now that you mentioned it," Fay said, thinking, "I remember hearing about that story. The guy was from West Virginia; in fact, it was odd because there was another similar incident not too far from the shooting. Guy and woman arguing. I remember the woman was from West Virginia too. She was visiting Chicago or something. She went all psycho and killed the guy. Stabbed him to death or something like that. What was even more odd was that the two murder-suspects went out the same exact way. Both ran out in front of a car. *But* that wasn't the strange part. The strange part was they had third-degree burns on random parts of their bodies. Yet, there wasn't any indication that there had been a fire or anything of that nature."

"Talk about strange."

"Very."

"There's one theory circulating that it was some kind of botched government experiment, an outbreak of a 'new' disease."

"Here we go," Carmen said and dismissed Fay by getting lost in her phone.

"Fay," Star said, "don't be *that* girl, dear."

"Don't you guys question these certain types of things?"

"Unexplainable things happen, Fay. When it comes to all these theorists, why is it always the government's wrong-doing?"

Nobody was paying attention to Star.

Everybody was looking directly behind Star.

"Mr. Klopper!"

Star heard an old yet familiar voice behind her.

"If it isn't the *Young Professionals!*"

Surprised by the resonant voice, Star turned her shoulder.

Standing directly behind Star was a hunched over man in his early sixties but looked much older from the frailness of his body, as if he had been through several bouts of major heart surgeries. He was Star's twelfth grade English teacher, Mr. Eugene Klopper. Standing not too far away was Mr. Klopper's wife, Remy.

"The lawyer," he said, touching Star's shoulder.

"Not yet," Star said, forcing a smile. "Still a paralegal."

Mr. Klopper pointed at Rhonda.

"Teacher."

Then, pointed at Fay.

"The artist—"

"—Technically, Graphic Designer."

Then, Carmen.

"The Violinist."

"Ex-violinist," Carmen corrected Mr. Klopper. "Now, full-time mother."

"How many?"

"One, for now at least."

"How old?"

"Just turned three."

"Boy or girl?"

"Boy," Carmen said. "It took me forever trying to find a babysitter to look after him."

"I love 'em when they're that age. Enjoy every second. Before you know it, they'll be all grown up and hating your guts."

"Well, I'm just glad the terrible two's are over. I've heard its all downhill from here—"

"—You mean uphill," Fay interrupted.

"Is that what I said?"

"You said 'downhill.'"

Mr. Klopper said over the two, "Uphill. Downhill. Either way, you'll be just fine." He looked around the table. "So how you doing ladies?" Before the others had a chance to answer, Mr. Klopper threw his finger in the air as if a thought had just come to him. "Wait a second," he blurted out. "I believe we're missing one, aren't we? Where's the doctor?"

A smooth, silky voice crept up behind Mr. Klopper.

"*Standing right behind you,*" the voice said.

Each member of the High Five remained in a state of shock, except for one.

Star.

Who appeared reserved from the sound of the voice.

Mr. Klopper rotated around and said, "Mandy? How are you?"

Mandy hugged Mr. Klopper.

"I'm good," she said. "And you?"

"I can't complain."

"I thought you weren't going to make it?" asked Rhonda.

"Well," Mandy said, "here I am."

"The last time I saw you ladies was a few months back."

"Every four months, we have our quarterly lunch."

Fay said, "It's like 'our thing.'"

"I think that's swell," Mr. Klopper said kindly, "keeping in touch like that. I remember the last time I went to my high school reunion, except for a couple of old buddies, I couldn't recognize a single person there."

Quarterly Lunch, Star thought.

Even the term, quarterly, sounded like it was a word used by an anal-retentive teacher. Star figured it was Rhonda's only way of keeping tabs on each member of the High Five. *But really*, why did she need to *keep tabs on us? What was she really up to?*

Star didn't think too long about Mr. Klopper's presence.

She had another scheme on her mind.

For Star, it was game time.

Mandy sat down in her seat next to Rhonda.

She said hello to the other three. Finally, once she reached Star, she said with a serious expression, "Star."

Then, Star returned, "Mandy."

"Well, I better let you ladies go so you can play catch up," Mr. Klopper said to everybody. Then, he specifically pointed at Carmen. "If you ever need anyone to watch over the little one, ask Rhonda here and she'll give you my number."

"I couldn't—"

"—I don't mind at all; as a matter of fact, I'd be more than happy to babysit. With all this free time now, I'm always looking for something to do."

"I will."

"Till next time, ladies."

"Bye, Mr. Klopper.

"Bye, Eugene.

"Eugene?"

Rhonda shrugged.

"We still keep in contact."

"You still talk to your old English teacher."

"I'm a teacher, duh," Rhonda said to Carmen. "When I was starting out, he was the first person I contacted. Eugene gave me a lot of pointers."

"Who the hell uses the expression 'more than happy?' Nobody's ever more than happy."

"It's just an expression, Fay," Star said.

"Well, it's insane."

"So," Mandy said over a sigh, "who's hungry?"

"Thanks to Fay here," Rhonda teased. "I think I lost my appetite."

"What I do?"

Star said, "It was actually Carmen who brought up The Snipper."

"The Snipper?" Mandy said in a superior manner. "And how exactly did that creature get thrown into the conversation?"

"We were talking about Devil's Throat."

"I see," Mandy said. "Are you still kayaking?"

"Twice a week."

"So, you girls order yet?"

Right on cue, the waitress returned to the table with appetizers.

Lettuce wraps, miso soup, and hot spring rolls with house made duck sauce.

"Here are your appetizers," she said and placed the appetizers on the table.

"I see we have a new one," the waitress said, turning to Mandy. "Shall I give you some time to decide on your order?"

"No," Mandy said, not even looking at the menu. She couldn't help but look at Star in the corner of her eye. "I already know what I want. I'll take the Udon."

The waitress asked, "Your choice of meat?"

"Beef, please."

"I swear you order that same exact dish every time we come here, Mandy?" Fay asked. "Why don't you try something different? You know, experiment. Be a food taster."

Mandy said to Fay, "Whoever said I *wasn't* a food taster? Besides, Fay, I've been waiting all week for Beef Udon."

"And what would you like to drink?"

"Saki," Mandy said to the waitress. "Lots and lots of saki."

The waitress went around the rest of the table and gathered orders.

Fay ordered Vegetable Tempura as well as a California roll; Carmen, Yakitori, which was skewered chicken; Rhonda, Chicken Teriyaki; then, finally, Star, who wasn't at all hungry, soba noodles, which, now that she started to think more about it, was probably a bad choice but she had to order something and soba noodles was the first—*and only*—thing that came to her mind.

Once the orders were placed, the appetizers were passed around the table.

Fay went on an alcohol-induced rant about sushi and how she had been on a sushi-craze for the past month.

Star grabbed a hot vegetable spring roll from the plate and nibbled on it like a bird; and when the lettuce wraps were handed to her, she immediately declined.

Carmen nodded at Mandy.

"Saki, huh? One of those days?"

Mandy sipped from the glass of water.

"It's been a day, all right," she said, unfolding the table napkin and placing it over her lap.

Rhonda asked, "How'd everything go with work?"

Mandy paused.

"I wasn't at work," she said quietly. "The truth is. . . "

Once more, a pause of silence swelled over the conversation. The pause was long enough to draw concern around the table.

Carmen asked, "Is everything all right, Mandy?"

"It's Jack," she said finally. "Jack and I had a fight." Then she said to herself. "It was—how do I say?" She paused. "I'd say *epic* is probably the word I'm looking for. Like one for the record books."

"That bad, huh?"

"Worse."

She hung her head in solemn.

"I've never seen Jack so upset," said Mandy.

Rhonda asked, "What were you two fighting about?"

Mandy faced Rhonda, who was sitting to the left of her.

"He wants to have another child," Mandy said, turning her eyes to Star.

Surprised, Star said to Mandy, "Child?" She quietly cleared her throat. "But I thought you said you wanted another child."

"I did," Mandy said. "I mean I do want a child. Having a child right now is not a good time, though."

"You go, girl," Fay said. "Never ever let a man force a child on you. After all, it's your body. *Not* his."

"But it's not like that, Fay."

"To me, it sounds like he's only thinking of himself."

"Jack's a good man," Mandy said.

Without even knowing, Star's jaw began to tighten with hot anger. It wasn't until she stepped back inside herself that she realized how she might've looked to the others. Nobody was looking, though, except for maybe Mandy, who kept Star in the corner of her eye. Star unclenched her teeth and took another sip of her gin and tonic to help loosen the nerves.

As soon as Star placed the drink on the table, she received a text message on her phone:

She knows.

Carefully, Star removed the phone from the table and held it down in her lap.

She slid open her phone and read the text once more.

The sender was Jack Leland.

"She knows," read the text.

Star took her eyes from the phone below and looked up, specifically toward Mandy's general direction.

Mandy was still talking about Jack. She went from describing him as good to great. All of a sudden, Jack was an extraordinary man who was one of the smartest, most handsome men Mandy had ever had the privilege of knowing.

Star read the text message again.

She knows.

Another text suddenly appeared right below the "she knows" text:

Heads up.

Star quickly responded by sending a text to Jack:

How much does she know?

Then, Jack returned with a reply text:

Everything.

Then, Star:

What do you mean 'everything'?!?

Star pulled her eyes from the phone.
Mandy asked, "Is everything okay, Star?"
"Yeah," Star hesitated. "Why wouldn't it be?"
"You just look like you're not with us?"
"No," Star said. "I am. It's just a new client. He's been giving Frank and I a real headache."
"Frank's probably one of the best lawyers in the city," she said. "I'm sure there's nothing he can't deal with."
"Right."
Star's phone beeped.
Jack texted:

EVERYTHING.

Star texted back.

I'm going to tell her the truth.

As soon as she sent the text, Star's phone suddenly rang.
She answered the phone before it could ring a second time and secured the receiver of the phone against her chest and said, "Excuse me for a second."

"Ms. Worker Bee," Fay said, "always working."

"I got to take this," Star said to the others but was really speaking directly to Mandy.

Star walked outside.

As soon as she was in the clear, she said into the phone, "Are you *trying* to draw more suspicion than there already is, Jack—"

"—Don't use my name."

"How much does she know?"

"Lower your voice, Star."

"She can't hear me," Star said to Jack. "I'm outside."

"So, did she say anything to you?"

"No," Star said, peering back into the restaurant through the window. "But I need to tell her the truth. About us. About everything."

"She already knows, Star—"

"—How?"

"She found an article of clothing you left behind."

"How could you be so careless, Jack?" Star immediately retracted the blame as soon as it reached her lips. "I'm sorry. It's my fault."

"No," Jack said. "Don't do that, Star. If anybody's to be sorry, it's all me."

"Well, there's absolutely no way I can go back in there now."

"You have to, Star," said Jack. "Just act like everything's normal and please, whatever you do, please do not make a scene—"

"I'm not going to make a scene, Jack."

"Just act normal, okay?"

"How can I act normal, knowing that one of my good friends knows that I'm screwing her husband?"

"Listen," Jack said urgently. "I gotta run. I think it's best that we lay low for a while. Just until things calm down a bit."

"Jack, does she know about our plan?"

Jack's phone started to break up.

"Jack?

The other end of the phone went silent.

"Jack, you there?"

Star noticed the call had been dropped.

"Shitty-ass service," she seethed.

Once Star cooled off, she leaned close to the window and checked her face in the reflection and then stepped back inside Flying Lotus.

Mandy was missing from the table.

Star interrupted Rhonda and Carmen, who were gossiping about some recent news report about airlines adding extra leg room inside their airplanes, "Where's Mandy?"

"She had use the restroom, I think."

Star started to walk toward the restroom; however, she stopped after taking three steps, paused, turned around, walked back to the table, and sat back down in her seat.

Fay asked, "Who was on the phone? Boyfriend? Ex-boyfriend? Or, better yet, your sex slave?"

"Fay!" Rhonda called out.

"I'm sorry," Fay corrected. "Boy toy?"

"For your information, it was Frank."

"Sure, it was."

"You know, Fay, I don't think you've had enough to drink."

"Are you being sarcastic? Because, if you are, then you're terrible at it."

"Yes," Star said with frustration. "I was being sarcastic."

Trying to keep the peace, Rhonda asked, "So, what did Frank want?"

"He wanted to talk about a case. Boring legal stuff."

"Doesn't sound boring."

"Trust me," Star said to Rhonda. "It's a snooze fest. Five minutes of Frank talking starts to feel like you just took an Ambien."

Fay asked, "So, what did you two talk about?"

"You know I'm not supposed to talk about that kind of stuff. It's confidential. Plus, I could lose my job."

"Yeah, but I'm sure you talk about cases all the time with your lawyer buddies."

"Enough, Fay, please," Star said seriously.

Silence hovered over the table like a bad stench.

Rhonda tried to break up the sudden awkwardness by asking Fay about her work even though Rhonda didn't have any interest whatsoever in Fay's work—or at least, tried not to show it even though her voice had a particular way of indicating the truth even if her voice wasn't telling the truth. Star was clearly aware of Rhonda's feelings about Fay's profession of choice and how, not too long ago, in fact, the last time she saw Star, she called it in sharp criticism, not a job, but a hobby behind Fay's back. For someone who decorated the walls of her classroom with literary posters, which were designed by graphic designers, like Fay, the jealousy in Rhonda's voice couldn't sound more palpable. Star had a nose for these kinds of things. She'd say she got it from her dada.

FIVE AWKWARD MINUTES LATER

MANDY returned from the restroom in a state of obvious yet seemingly exaggerated disgust.

"We were starting to wonder if you fell in," Fay said to Mandy.

With a sigh shooting from her mouth like a bullet, Mandy sat down in her seat with a heavy thump.

"There was a line," she said. "Can you believe that?"

Star thought it was strange. She didn't see any line when she poked her head toward the restrooms.

"*And*," Mandy emphasized, "some asshole peed all over the seats."

"I hate when they do that," Rhonda said, shaking her head.

"You know," Fay said, "you never saw that before these restaurants started converting their restrooms to gender-neutral restrooms. Honestly, I think men do it deliberately. To rub it in our faces. To show us who's in charge—"

"—I thought you were all for gender-neutral restrooms. So, why the change in heart?"

"No," Fay said. "I am, but still. I think, if you're a man, you should be conscious of the fact that a woman might use the bathroom after you."

"Maybe they're not thinking of that, Fay," Carmen argued. "Maybe some men just pee on the seat. It's like science—"

"—It's like common courtesy."

"Unless you're sitting down to pee—which, I'm pretty sure, most men ain't doing—pee splashes when it hits toilet water. Take Max for instance. Every time he uses the toilet, I have to clean up after him."

"Yeah, Carmen, but he's decent enough to raise the toilet seat before he takes a piss."

"He raises the seat. But, like I said, Fay, the pee still splashes. I once found pee on one of the paintings I have hung up on the wall."

"The man must have one helluva prostate."

The comment drew a couple of laughs around the table.

Star forced a laugh. She couldn't help but draw her attention toward Mandy, who, in return, caught Star in the corner of her eye.

As the tension started to mount, the waitress stepped in between the two and set the tray of steamy food against the edge of the table. The waitress handed out each dish, except for Mandy's Beef Udon. She told her that the Udon was just about ready, and then she went back to the kitchen.

The chatter was tame but steady. The quiet commotion inside Star pulled her away from the topic of discussion, which morphed from gender-neutral restrooms to sexual harassment in the workplace and the stark differences between compliments and flirtation. Star zoned out completely, as if all of the chatter around her had been reduced to nothing more than faint murmurings, like bees buzzing, background noise. She mindlessly made it through a few decent bites of her soba noodles. Occasionally, Mandy would move her eyes toward Star and strangely watch her eat without actually watching her eat.

Before Star could acknowledge Mandy's interest in Star's lack of involvement in the conversation, her Beef Udon finally arrived.

All of a sudden, Star plowed through all of the noise, pushed past the quiet storm inside her, and paid close attention to Mandy as she "dug in."

Mandy removed the sleeve of paper from the pair of chopsticks and rubbed the two chopsticks together as if she was honing a blade with a whetstone.

As Mandy did with Star, Star watched Mandy take her first bite without actually watching her.

Mandy made sure to capture all of the flavors into one single bite, grabbing each ingredient with the grip of the chopsticks. A little bit of the Udon noodle. A little bit of succulent Hida beef. A little bit of the fish cake called Narutomaki, which, to the average guest, looked like a piece of candy with its white star-like shape and a red-pinkish swirl in the center. Then, for garnish, Mitsuba and green onion. She lifted it all to her mouth before it could fall from the tip of the chopsticks and opened wide. Mandy took a bite, chewed twice, savoring each flavor. She closed her eyes, closed off the world. In her closed-off state, Mandy did what only came natural. She reacted with sound, her sound, her own designated noise.

A moan of great pleasure rolled from her tongue and ricocheted off the interior of her closed mouth.

The sound drew eyes toward Mandy.

Star was first to ask, "How is it?"

"*Dee*-licious," Mandy said, holding the food in one side of her mouth.

She swallowed.

Took another bite.

Savored it.

Then, took another.

Savored.

"They make their own dashi broth in house," Mandy said as if she was promoting her dish to her own crowd of curious buyers. "That's what makes the beef so tender."

"What's dashi?"

"It's similar to a vegetable or beef stock."

"What kind of beef is it?"

"I'm not entirely sure," she said. "Maybe prime rib? Whatever it is, it's out of this world."

"Everything they make here is so fresh."

Fay asked Mandy, "Can I have a bite?"

"Only if you give me a taste of your vegetable tempura."

"You got yourself a deal, young lady."

Star said suddenly, "Fay, I don't think you'll like it."

"How you know what I like?"

"But Fay," Star urged Fay, "I've heard the cows they get their meat from are loaded with antibiotics."

"Nice try, Star," Mandy said. "They're grass fed."

"Okay, Fake News."

"You sure?"

"Positive."

Rhonda said, "Not like it's going to kill you, Fay."

Fay forked out a bite of vegetable tempura while Mandy pinched out a bite of Beef Udon with chopsticks. She held her hand underneath the chopsticks, making sure no broth and beef juice spilled onto the white tablecloth. They traded bites.

First, Mandy took a bite of vegetable tempura, savored it, then swallowed it. She nodded her head in agreement.

Next, Fay took a bite of the Beef Udon.

"Wow!" Fay said while chewing. "Delish!"

Mandy turned to Carmen.

"Want a bite?" she asked.

Carmen broke off a piece of chicken, passed it over, and, in return, tasted the Beef Udon. Carmen wasn't exactly a beef-girl. She considered herself a vegetarian, even though, from time to time, she would eat chicken or fish.

"Not bad," Carmen said after she finished swallowing the Beef Udon. "Very hearty. It'd be the perfect dish during the wintertime."

"Oh! I can eat it anytime," said Mandy.

"How about you, Rhonda? Want a taste?"

As Carmen did, Rhonda traded a bite for a bite.

She acted as if she really enjoyed the Beef Udon. She wasn't a good faker.

"It's okay."

"Just okay."

"It's good," Rhonda corrected.

"Star?"

Star immediately held up her hand.

"No thanks," she said.

"But you haven't even tried it before."

"I have," Star said defensively. "I didn't care much for it."

"It's really good, Star," Fay said. "And you know I don't even like beef."

"Come on, Star," Carmen nodded. "Try it."

Then, Rhonda: "You'll like it."

"Okay," Star said.

Mandy broke off a piece of Hida beef, handed the chopsticks over to Rhonda, who, in return, placed the Hida beef on the edge of Star's plate.

Before Star tasted the Hida beef, she looked around the table and it was as if the four members of High Five were encouraging her to take the bite.

She finally did.

Mandy asked, "What you think?"

"It's good," Star said as she carefully chewed the piece of meat. "Better than I thought it'd be."

"Told you," Fay said and went back to her vegetable tempura.

Without the others noticing, Star discreetly spit out the Hida beef into a napkin and waited for the right moment to excuse herself to the restroom.

As soon as Star was away from the others' view, she rushed to the restroom. She didn't have to wait. She went right into the restroom and locked the door behind her. She hurried to the sink where she rinsed out her mouth with water. She even grabbed several squares of toilet paper from a damp roll and used the toilet paper like a toothbrush by scrubbing her teeth, as well as her tongue. Then, she'd rinse her mouth with water. Gargled. Then, she'd grab another couple squares of toilet paper. Scrubbed. Gargled. Then, rinsed. Rinsed and scrubbed. Scrubbed and rinsed.

Lastly, she leaned closely to the mirror and opened her mouth wide, really wide, wide enough to stick her fist into her mouth.

Using the flashlight on her phone for light, Star peered into the depths of her mouth, checking for anything out of the ordinary. Which meant anything "moving." She didn't see anything moving around in there. Everything looked fine.

Once Star felt safe enough to proceed with lunch, she exited the restroom and walked back to the table.

Halfway toward the table, she noticed somebody—one of the staff members, a cook maybe—standing above Mandy. He was dressed in a white chef's attire.

As soon as Star realized who the man was and possibly *why* he was standing there, her heart started to beat faster. Her eyes swelled. Her face went slack. Her chest tightened. Breath swallowed. Her legs heavy. Her walk was unsteady, and she moved toward the table as if she didn't know whether or not to turn the other direction and run for the back exit.

Only a couple of feet away from the table, Star suddenly turned around and started to walk the other way.

Mandy called out from behind, "There she is!"

Star stopped and slowly turned around.

"Where you going, Star?" she said foolishly and waved Star over. "Get over here."

Timidly, Star inched back to the table and sat down in her seat.

She asked, "What's going on?"

"Star, this here is Myko," Mandy said excitedly as she showcased Myko as if he was an exquisite work of art. "I ran into Myko on the way to the restroom."

Star turned to Myko, who acted as if he didn't even know Star.

"Myko and I go *waaay* back," Mandy said as if she had come from an ancient time period where radio was still a custom of quality family entertainment.

"That's right," Myko said and looked down at Mandy. "I hardly even recognized you." Then, turned to Star's direction. "I was complimenting Amanda on how great she looked. Doesn't she look great?"

"Yeah," Star said and forced a smile on her face. "She does."

"Stop, Myko," Mandy said and playfully hit Myko on the arm.

"She's like a ten." Myko corrected himself, "I mean, for real, you were always a ten on my scale. Even back then. But now, you're like a legitimate ten. Like a ten-plus. No joke. It's just too bad you're still married."

Star couldn't quite tell if Myko was being sincere or not.

Or, she wondered, was there *something else* going on.

"Not only is she married, but she's also married to a man who cuts up people for a living," Fay said.

"You're on a roll, Fay," Rhonda said, as if she was talking to a disobedient adolescent. "I mean, really? Why would you even say that? Is that necessary?" Rhonda turned to Myko, who was rather smitten by the complimentary male presence. "Forget all about what you read on the Internet. He's one of the best heart surgeons in town. And he's quite handsome. Dapper, one might say. *And,*" she continued, "not only that, he's an exceptional painter, too; in fact, I bought one of his paintings."

"You make him sound like the complete package."

"Excuse me, Rhonda," Mandy said playfully, "that's my husband you're talking about."

The others laughed, except Star.

"Well," Myko smiled and turned to Star, "he's a lucky man."

"Lipo, a couple of facelifts, and don't mention, a heavy dose of Botox will do that to a woman," Fay said indirectly.

"Lately, I've been thinking about getting the 'Mandy Treatment' myself, but Max says he likes me just the way I am."

"You've met Jack before, haven't you?" Mandy asked Myko.

Once more, Myko turned to Star, then to Mandy, then shook his head.

"No," he said unsurely. "Don't think so."

Nodding in Myko's direction, Star said, "So, where was it you said you two met?"

Mandy looked up at Myko.

"It was right outside that pawn shop, wasn't it?"

"Sigmund's," said Myko. "Yes."

"That's it," Mandy said.

"Believe it or not, Amanda saved my life."

"And you saved mine," Mandy said, glancing up at Myko with tears in her eyes.

"He did?"

"If it wasn't for you, I'd probably be dead."

"You were in a bad state of mind," Mandy said to Myko. Then, turned to the others. "We *both* were in a terrible place, mentally and physically. At the time, I was a resident at Pointe Medical. I was going through a lot of issues, depression, anxiety. I'd lose weight. Then, put on weight."

"You never told us this, Mandy," Carmen cut in.

Then, Rhonda.

Then, surprisingly, Fay.

"I was too embarrassed, I suppose," Mandy said, rounding up sympathy from everyone at the table—except Star. "After awhile, it felt as if my world was starting to cave in all around me. Then, on one rainy night, I came across this young man—"

"—Boy," Myko corrected.

Mandy held Myko's hand.

"He was about to do something terrible," Mandy said. "We talked for what felt like hours. We talked about a lot of things—very *personal* things. Eventually, Myko changed his mind. I brought him back home with me and gave him a place to stay for the night. I helped him get sober. He helped me sort through a lot of my issues. We both helped out each other as if we were going through the same thing, only we weren't. I found Myko here a temporary part time at Pointe Medical to get him back on his feet." Mandy looked up at Myko. "You redefined a sense of meaning as to why I wanted to become a doctor." Then, she turned to the others. "He gave me purpose. I suppose, you can say it was one of those gifts life miraculously hands you every now and then."

Star asked Myko, "So what was this terrible thing you were about to do?"

The others appeared shocked by Star's question as if Star wasn't at all in a position to inquire more detail into Mandy's heart-warming story.

"He was going to rob the owner of the pawn shop," Mandy said bluntly.

"It's true," Myko said. "I was."

"But you didn't?"

"Obviously."

"A week later after I found Myko—or better yet, when Myko found me—I heard about a story in the news: a robbery attempt at that very same pawn shop. A man pulled a gun on the owner. The owner shot the robber. Killed him."

"That's some story," Rhonda said in disbelief. Then, she asked Myko, "Have you ever thought about writing a book about it?"

"Me?" Myko pointed at himself. "No. I'm not the Shakespeare type."

"You can always hire one of those—what you called them?"

"Ghostwriters."

"Them."

Myko waved off Rhonda's offer and turned to the kitchen.

"I think I've found my calling right here," Myko said.

"Well, the food is probably the best I've ever eaten and I'm not just saying that to be nice or anything. If you don't believe me, check my Yelp page."

"We all saw your Yelp page, Carmen. *Everybody* in Newbay has seen your Yelp page."

"What can I say? I'm Yelp-Fabulous."

Fay and Rhonda ignored Carmen and all of her braggadocio and then complimented Myko on the food.

"Thank you," Myko said and turned to Star last. "And how you like the food, Star?" he asked with a ghost of a smirk creeping through the corner of his face. "Is it everything you *expected* it to be?"

The question stabbed at Star, sending thousands of pinpricks throughout her entire body.

All of a sudden, she began to feel lightheaded. Myko's face started to double, then triple; then it was as if she had taken a freeze frame of his ugly face and pinned and mounted it to the forefront of her mind.

To Star, Myko made a face. It might've not been the sportive smirk on his face or the distant twinkle in his eye. Nonetheless, it was a "face." The others couldn't see it nor could they sense it. But Star saw and sensed it clear enough to have its own Instagram page.

The only thought that ran through Star's mind. . .

I have been duped.

Star suddenly stood up from her seat and staggered for a moment. She drew her eyes downward at the bowl of soba noodles. Like Myko's face, the noodles doubled, then tripled, then shifted in and out of focus. For a moment, she actually saw the noodles moving.

As her legs started to buckle, she flung her hand outward and grabbed a hold of the edge of the table as if it was a crutch.

"If you would excuse," Star murmured, her words faint and choppy as if she had recently run a marathon.

While the others remained wordless, Star rushed to the restroom.

She used the closest objects that she could touch for support, the very back of a guest's chair, even another guest's shoulder, then, finally, the wall. She stayed close to the wall, using it whenever she felt as if she was about to fall over like a drunken sorority girl. She hadn't drunk much, only enough to ride a buzz, but she felt as if she was beyond wasted, like college-drunk wasted. She questioned herself, questioned her drunkenness. She tried to tell herself that her current wobbly state was from drinking hard alcohol on an empty stomach. But there was a voice inside her head. *That brain noise.* And it was telling her another story.

Star made it to the restroom without passing out. She reached for the greasy door handle. Her hand slipped from it. She reached once more, strengthened her grip, and tugged on it like a loose tooth.

The door was locked.

She tried once more, this time twisting her wrist.

The door still remained locked.

She resorted to *knocking* on the door but didn't hear a sound behind the door. Then, she balled her hand into a fist and banged hard enough to shake the hinges. On the third pound, Star heard a sound behind the door. A voice.

"Just a second," the soft, drawn-out voice said with a ring of vexation.

Following the voice, she heard the sound of water running and then the grating *schrrpt* noise of paper being torn from the dispenser.

The door opened.

The woman was slow to exit.

Not wasting anytime, Star pushed her way inside, nudging shoulders with the woman.

"Excuse me," the woman barked.

Star slammed the door in the woman's face and darted toward the toilet.

Halfway there, the vomit started to climb up her throat. She caught some of it in her mouth but some of it projected from lips and hit the side of the toilet.

In a second hurl, Star hunched over the toilet and violently pushed as hard as her body would let her. For the next thirty seconds or so, her stomach did push-ups against her chest. Each time, less vomit came out and whatever managed to escape was as acidic as stomach bile. Then came the dry heaving. That lasted for about another thirty seconds or so. Eventually, Star wore herself out and used the toilet seat to push herself upright from her squatted position.

As Star was about to flush the toilet, she noticed a slight movement below her eyes. She peered closer at the murky toilet water and once more, saw something moving under the soba noodles, something red in color and as thin as a wire. Star scrambled through her thoughts and retraced everything she had eaten. She ate a protein bar for breakfast. But *it wouldn't be that*, she thought. *That* would've already been digested. Then, she had a glass of orange juice to wash down the protein bar—maybe it could've been an extra long piece of pulp. *No*, she thought, it, like the protein bar, would've already been digested. Or, *maybe* it could've been the cabbage from the spring roll. With the edge of her knuckles, Star rubbed the backside of her eyelids in clichéd fashion and looked yet again. The soba noodles weren't moving. Only one was, that reddish gray one. Star soon learned it wasn't a soba noodle. It was something else.

More intrigued, Star pulled out a tablet pen from her phone, reached down, and picked up the rare toxioplexus, a worm-like parasitic creature that was better known for its nickname "snake worm," from the clumpy toilet water.

Star held the snake worm up to her face. She realized it looked much different than what she researched on the Internet. For one, the snake worm was much more longer and scalier than she expected. Two, she could actually see that it had a face with two beady black eyes and a mouth filled with jagged, razor sharp teeth as small as the tip of a thread. She suddenly recoiled and flung the dangerous snake worm back into the toilet. She stuck her index finger down her throat and once more, tried to rid whatever thing it was that she ingested. She had hardly anything left in her stomach. She dry-heaved until all that came out was the spit that remoistened her mouth.

What the fuck did you do to me, Myko, *you son of a bitch*?

Crying, she called Jack who answered after the second ring.

The best she could, Star explained to Jack what happened to her; however, he couldn't understand a word Star was saying.

She emphasized *Myko*'s name and how he *tricked* her.

Jack gave Star specific instructions to drive herself to the nearest emergency room ASAP.

Star didn't want to hear anything Jack had to say.

Not anymore.

Her own well being was the very least of her worries.

She was out for blood.

As before, Jack's phone started to break up.

The last words Jack said to Star before the phone went dead were "*Don't do anything stupid.*"

Star flung her phone against the wall, fracturing the touch screen.

Parts of the phone ricocheted against the toilet and slid underneath harder-to-reach areas.

But like her own well being, the phone was the least of her concerns.

She was *out for blood.*

It wasn't until Star felt her skin crawl, specifically a twitch in the corner of her eye, that she realized Jack had every reason to be serious in instructing her to go to the emergency room.

Hoping the quick remedy which she had used ever since she was a girl would save her from all her troubles, she hurried to the sink and splashed her face with cold water. She removed her hands from her face and looked into the mirror. Her left eye twitched similar to a muscle spasm.

Mindful of the creature in the toilet, Star punched the corner of the mirror. A perfectly triangular piece of glass fell into the sink. Star grabbed the piece that closely resembled a knife and held it close.

With her left hand, Star pulled down on her lower eyelid while keeping the shard of glass close to her face.

She didn't see anything at first glance.

Star pulled her eyelid down until it stretched across her upper cheekbone.

Again, she saw something moving below her eyelid.

Not a muscle spasm.

Not an eyelash or grain of dirt or sand that got caught in her eye.

Whatever it was, it was moving.

It was *alive.*

Star wanted it dead.

WHEN Star returned to the table, her face was all cut up and strings of blood were running down the side of her face like ruined mascara. In her right hand, she held onto that shard of glass, which was covered in her own blood. She was shivering too. And struggling to stand upright.

As soon as Star rounded the hallway, she set her blood-stained eyes on High Five, who were all laughing it up and having a "good ole time," an expression Fay picked up from her firecracker of a mother *who* spent her days riding the tequila train to Margaritaville and bathing in the artificial sun three out of the four seasons of the year to match Star's blackness, wearing it like a cool costume opposed to actually living in it, *who* took overly wide turns opposed to cautiously hugging the curb and being mindfully aware of other drivers on the road, *who* spitballed the first glint of a thought that manifested inside her mind which, at times, seemed like the size of the universe. All of it made perfect sense—now that Star thought about it—as to why it was Fay who branded their so-called gang as High Five, not High as in being rec-reational drug users who often got high, but *high*, as in higher than everybody else. Privileged cloud surfers.

Star noticed one person was absent. Myko. A man who was neither high nor low but landing somewhere in a tedi-ous gray area where the crimes being committed were ques-tionable and assured dissension. He was no longer standing next to Mandy. He was off somewhere being gray in the kitchen. Star told herself that she'd deal with that assclown later.

As Star returned to the table, Mandy directed her atten-tion toward Star, who had become the sole oddball of the gang. Neither belonging or accepted. "Just" there. Just was a word she commonly used to describe herself to others who questioned her loyalty to High Five. She was "just" a friend. Or, simply "just" there.

"You don't look so hot," Fay said, noticing Star's fragile state.

Of all the members of High Five, Fay was the only one to notice Star's unusual behavior. Mandy, Carmen, or Rhonda didn't even pay attention or at least act the least concerned for Star's fragile mental state or how she appeared to be bleeding all over the freaking place.

Star ignored Fay and sat back down in her seat while Mandy raised her teacup of warm saki. She insisted the members of High Five raise their own glasses in what appeared to be a toast.

"That includes you, Star," Mandy said, urging Star to raise her glass. "Come on. Raise it up."

Star placed the shard of glass on the table and with her bloody hand, raised the glass of gin and tonic.

"I want to thank all of you for coming here today," Mandy said as she looked at the others seated around her. "All of you are my friends and I am truly grateful to call you friends. Of all of you, there is one who rose to the occasion and became more than a friend. She became my very own special friend. All this time, she was right under my nose. Her name is Star," she said directly to Star. "You showed me the person who I am and who I could be. I want to be that better person. I will be that better person, Star, that better doctor, that better wife, that *better* lover. I'm deeply sorry for my actions, which have resulted in my own husband to find connection with another woman. However, if it weren't for what happened between us, *Star*, I never would've fully understood your devotion to our kinship. Now, I do." She raised her glass higher. "To High Five. Most importantly, to my *new* bestie, Star Walker."

As Mandy sipped from her drink, Star stood up and flung the rest of her gin and tonic in Mandy's face.

"Tell that to Jack, you bitch," Star seethed.

"Star," Carmen blurted out, "what has gotten into you?"

"Shut up, you fake bitch."

"Star?"

"You texted me about how much you hate coming to these 'lunches,' yet here you are," Star said, towering over Carmen. "Why are you really here, Carmen? To play catch up?"

Carmen asked, "What other reason would I be here, Star?"

"You and I hardly even talked to one another in high school," Star said. "So, why, all of a sudden, do you want to rekindle a relationship with me? I tell you. *Because* you're a fucking lonely, pathetic person who hates herself so much that she has to cling to others. *Because* you sit at home all day long, caring for a child whom you regret having. No," Star said, her red eyes widening in madness. "I know what it is! You figured motherhood was going to be a piece of cake. Then, once you became a mother, you found out pretty quickly that it's a lot harder than it looks on TV. I admit. You put on a good show. Always posting photos of that ugly-looking thing you call a child on the Internet, showing him off, trying to impress everybody, trying to prove to them that you're not that same phony-ass bitch you were in high school when, deep down inside, you're still that same fake, PC, wannabe, *phony*-ass bitch always following the crowd and wanting acceptance by rubbing that shit-stain of a child in everybody's face. Did you ever stop and think what your kid's going to think of you when he's older? When he has to explain to all his friends why some kid in his class is ridiculing him in class because of some ridiculous photo his mother posted of him when he was a child without his permission? What the hell do you think it will do to his self-esteem? What's he going to do when he steps out into the real world and realizes that he's not special? Did you ever stop and think for a second of the repercussions for sharing every single *iota* of information that pops into that empty hole of a head of yours? No. You know why. Because you don't give a *shit* about that fucking kid. Fake bitch. That's all you are. That's all you'll ever be. A plastic bitch. I mean, do you have any dignity? Any shame? Do you hold nothing sacred anymore? Or. . . " Star looked over Carmen and sneered at her as if she was way down there, ". . . has *this* what you've reduced yourself to? This insecure, *little* thing who posts pictures of her child all for a *like*? Or, a *follower*? Do everybody a favor?" Star leaned in close to Carmen. "Keep it to *your*-fucking-self."

Everybody in the restaurant turned toward Star's direction. Some watched as if they were witnessing some real-life suspense movie unfolding before their very eyes while some went about their business and ate with modest consumption and then there were some who talked among themselves. Most were silent.

Rhonda suddenly cut through—then bludgeoned—that awkward silence with a "Really, Star? Seniors in high school do it all the time. Don't you remember how we used to post baby pictures of ourselves in the back of the yearbook? I don't remember kids making fun of me."

The word *yearbook*—even the whole idea of the yearbook, Star's high school yearbook, and how it had portrayed Star—sent Star into a red glow of unadulterated rage. A flood of red memories washed over her, gripping her so tight that it stole her breath away, images of Star being the "black girl" who was always seen clinging to not only the white girls but also those "cool white girls" who would, over the boredom of summertime, hold their tanned arms next to Star's arm while sitting on the edges of the country club pool and parade a sense of benign audacity to tell Star, their black friend, that their skin matched Star's color. Snapshots of rushed moments printed in the most popular book in school. Snapshots only showing one side of the story without revealing the other side, the truest side. She was the girl who wore a smile that ran a mile across her face, the girl who, at the last second, hurried into a group shot before the school's designated cameraman, who happened to be some goofy foreign exchange student from Germany named Ryan, blurted out, "Fahrvergnügen." She was the girl who was always seen with part of her cropped out next to the school's most popular crew, her so-called gang, her "besties," the girl who was accepted but never belonged, the girl who was visible but wasn't, the just-girl. Books like *The Great Gatsby, Of Mice and Men, A Tale of Two Cities,* or Star's favorite, *Anthem,* once monuments representing a time lived decades, even centuries ago, the messages rich and vibrant and left to be digested by a young scrupulous mind, nonetheless, stories only to be cast aside and rejected by the generations to come, paled in comparison to the very moment in time that would inevitably present itself at the end of the school year when the yearbooks were handed out.

"Star," Rhonda shouted, sliding from her chair, "how dare you talk to her like that? How *dare* you!"

"Don't get me started on you," Star pointed at Rhonda. Her finger, sharp and deadly like a shard of glass before her, kept Rhonda frozen in her seat. "Mother-fucking-Teresa. During our senior year, you started a little charity to help raise money for families who were left homeless after the Cayenne Wild Fire. Operation *Getup*. You remember?"

Rhonda didn't answer.

Instead, she glared at Star.

"Of course, you remember," Star went on. "Your goal was to clothe all those poor people who lost *everything* in the fire. And what did you do? You took all that money you *stole* from all those gullible people and you kept it all for yourself."

"Star," Rhonda murmured, "Don't you go there. . . "

"Star, you got it all wrong," Mandy interrupted. "Rhonda helped clothe hundreds of people. I was there when she handed out the clothes."

"And where exactly do you think she found those clothes?"

"She bought them with the money she earned."

"She didn't buy shit," Star snapped. "For two weeks straight, she was stealing clothes from the Samaritan's Hand where she volunteered in the afternoons and peddled them as if they were brand new. She even donated her own hand-me-downs. And what exactly did she do with all the money? She used it to buy a new iPhone and told everybody that her father bought it for her because all of her hard work. I was going to expose you, Rhonda, for who you were. A manipulative bitch who thought she was better than everybody else. And now you use your missionary trips as vacations—"

"—That's not true!"

"Don't fuck with me, bitch. I saw your pictures you posted on Facebook last year. You're no different than

Carmen. Like peas in a pod. Fake and phony." Star pointed at Fay and Mandy. "*They* might not be able to see you two for who you are. But I do."

The waitress came by the table and respectfully asked Star to calm down; otherwise, she'd be forced to get the manager.

Star wasn't fazed at all by the waitress.

"Go on," she shouted. "Get him! What's he going to do? Call the cops—"

"—Star," Fay interrupted, "I think you've had too much to drink."

"And you," Star seethed, "you fucking flake. You disappear after our senior year and want nothing to do with me. Now, what? You're back in my life like nothing ever happened?"

"Star," Fay said, "you've known all about my situation, my sister—"

"—Don't you dare use her as an excuse for your lack of loyalty."

"I'm sorry."

"Last but not least," Star turned her red eyes toward Mandy, "the ungrateful bitch who doesn't know what a decent man looks like even if he fell out of the fucking sky and landed directly in her lap. You don't deserve Jack."

"What? And you do?"

"Yes," Star said. "More than you."

"What about you, Star? What the hell makes you so perfect? Why don't you find another man who's not already taken?"

Carmen leaned toward Fay.

"What's going on with her?"

Fay whispered in Carmen's ear, "I think she's having a meltdown."

Star suddenly roared, "I AM NOT HAVING A FUCKING MELTDOWN!"

The manager finally arrived at the table, the waitress not too far behind. Several others employees were poking their head out from the kitchen and elsewhere. Star had herself an audience.

"I'm afraid I'm going to call the police if you don't calm down," the manager said to Star.

"Don't tell me what to do!"

"All right," the manager said, holding up his hands. "I'm going to have to ask you to leave right now."

"You want me to leave?"

"Yes, ma'am," the manager said, his hands shaking.

Everything about him was shaking, even his voice.

"And what are you going to do if I don't?"

"I'm going to call the police," he said.

"You are?"

"Yes."

"So, you call yourself a man? If you want me to leave, then *make* me leave. Don't just stand there like some coward. If *you* want me to leave, *you* make me. Not the police. You!"

The waitress handed the manager the phone.

With a shaky hand, the manager dialed 9-1-1.

Star waved off the manager.

"Forget you," she said. Then, to the High Five, "Forget all of you!"

Then, Star stormed out of Flying Lotus.

Didn't look back.

The High Five was officially dead to Star.

She'd later say that it was better to thrive among living rather than trying to keep up with the dead.

Her dada was a great man.

The best.

🐾

ONCE all the drama was over, Myko exited through the back door of the kitchen carrying the cat carrier with the glaring sign that read "DO NOT TOUCH." He checked both sides of the alleyway and then, once he realized it was all clear, he carefully set the carrier on the ground.

As he reached for the lock of the carrier's door, the beige paw of what looked like a cat reared back with its claws out and scratched Myko on the backside of his hand.

Myko leaped backward, his hand curling into his body.

"Little shit," he whispered as the scratch on his hand started to bleed.

He grabbed a handkerchief from his back pocket and wrapped it around his hand in order to stop the bleeding.

Then, he grabbed a broom, which was perched against the side of the building, and used it as a distraction by banging the handle against the back end of the carrier while he set the would-be cat free.

Once the door was open, Myko took a couple of steps away from the carrier. He held the broom close to his body, ready to strike or defend himself whenever the moment of acting was upon him.

Eventually, *finally*, the scraggly feline emerged from the hazy darkness of the carrier. It was, in fact, a cat—or at least, the remnants of what was left of an orange tabby. Its body was as thin as a skeleton, its rib cage exposed underneath its scaly skin. Yet, the cat moved ever so gracefully, as if it was being controlled by *something* else.

Something more primitive.

The cat moved its red-stained eyes, which were crawling with maggots, up at Myko. A swarm of flies hovered over the cat as if they were acting as some sort of strange force field. Even the repulsive stench emitting from it, caused him to take a couple of extra steps backward. He did so with the utmost caution, hoping not to disturb the grotesque thing.

The cat suddenly snapped its attention toward Myko, ropes of drool swaying from its rabid mouth like dreadlocks.

It opened its gummy mouth and let out a hiss so sharp and stingy it caused his body to cringe and curl inward. His skin swelled with tiny goosebumps. His hair stood up like the quills on a porcupine.

The cat wound up its foot in a slow step toward Myko.

As soon as its paw touched the ground, its ears shot up and turned to the stirring of damp cardboard sloppily stacked directly behind it.

Its ears flickered and acted like antennas.

Myko swore he heard the faint *squeak* of a rodent as well.

He remained in a statue-like pose and listened closely.

Once more, he heard yet another noise, a squeak so high-pitch that it might as well been outside the range of human hearing.

But, strangely, Myko heard it.

The cat suddenly darted toward the direction of the noise and plunged itself into the pile of cardboard.

A struggle ensued underneath the loose cardboard.

This time, the *squeaking* sounds were more evident.

The cat crept out of the cardboard with a dead rat hanging from its mouth like a bloated sausage. The rat's fur was disheveled-looking. It had several bare spots along its body from infection or battle wounds from former scuffles with competitors. Its tail was red and raw and the tip of it had been severed and it was hanging loosely from the end as if it was a tug away from being torn off.

Myko was safe.

But only for the time being.

While the cat began to nibble away at the rat, Myko inched toward the carrier, which wasn't too far away from the cat. Keeping the cat close in his view, he leaned down and saw something strange moving in the corner of his eye.

With his nose covered by the collar of his chef's jacket, Myko peeked inside the carrier, only to find the insides covered with gray worm-like parasites crawling and wiggling around the carrier.

Snake worms. . .

Myko suddenly flinched!

He picked up the carrier, hurled it into the nearest dumpster, and then rushed back inside the restaurant.

Meanwhile, the cat continued to pick apart the rat for it was completely undisturbed by the commotion Myko was making.

Not so much as a distant holler of a man from the street ambience outside the alleyway seized the cat's attention.

It was devoted and unwavering to its basic needs, which were required for the survival of its species.

THE special report aired on the nine o' clock TV spot as what the people in the TV biz called an "interview in silhouette." You've probably seen it before (more than likely on the couch while channel surfing through an abyss of late-night television shows or, every now and then, on shows like *The Predator Catcher* or other crime related shows like the narco, cartel, or mafia-related crime movies or shows where the victims or witnesses—or as gangsters put it politely, "rats"—chose to remain anonymous in order to protect his or her identity), but you didn't know it actually had a name. But it did.

Interview in silhouette.

The interviewee, whose name had not yet been leaked to the press, was disguised in classic silhouette form in order to protect *her* identity. Face blacked out. Skin. The entire body looking like a dark shadow. The only detail that stood out was her long, wavy hair, which appeared blonde, strands of frizzy hair glowing in the faint overhead light like tethered yarns either caused by too much static in the carpet or, in most cases, an old, overused hairbrush; however, the camera lighting made it hard for the average viewer to distinguish. Most of these specific types of interviews didn't require the interviewee to conceal his or her voice by lowering it—or raising it—depending on the producer. In this instance, the interviewee's voice was disguised as deep as Darth Vader.

Noelle Brice, a respected journalist who had been with the network for eleven years, not in silhouette, conducted the interview with the woman whom she simply addressed simply as "you."

The Accuser, "You," plowed through the first scripted answer to the scripted question that she and Noelle had skimmed through prior to the interview.

During the sudden breaks in the interview, she reminded herself that she was human and humans breathed.

After the opening nerves of the interview faded, Noelle skipped the foreplay and dove straight into the juicy stuff, the "why" in why "you" were here. Noelle asked the Accuser how she came to know Miles Straum, the individual who was being accused of rape twenty-two years ago.

"We knew each other from work," the Accuser said, the nouns in her voice thin and shaky. The broad shoulders of her silhouette swelled and rose slightly as she made a noisy inhale through her nose. "At the time," she said, more patiently and thoughtfully, "Miles was an editor at our local newspaper, *The Courier*."

"What was your job at *The Courier*?"

"At the time, I was working part-time in the mailroom. It was slow work, but it helped pay for college."

The Accuser's breathing slowed.

"Where did you attend college?"

More confidently, she answered, "I attended Darmill University where I was studying to become a journalist."

"How old were you at the time when you started work at *The Courier*?"

"I started when I was twenty," she said. "I just turned twenty-one at the time of the office Christmas party?"

"And how old was Miles?"

"He was around thirty-five, I think, possibly a couple of years older—" she corrected, "—Thirty-six. He was thirty-six, now that I think about it. I remember Miles specifically mentioned the number to me because there had recently been a lottery a few weeks prior to the party. He used the number on his ticket."

"So, did you and Miles know each prior to working at *The Courier*?" Noelle paused. "What I mean is 'Were you two on a first name basis with one another?'"

"No," the Accuser hesitated. "Lansdowne was a small town in Oregon. We were about fifty miles outside Eugene. I grew up in the Holly Springs area, which was about three hours away. I had only seen Miles every now and then in town. But, no, I didn't actually know him until I started working at *The Courier*."

"How well did you know him during your time at *The Courier*?"

"Pretty well, I guess," she said, her dark voice sounding deeper. "I mean, we weren't close, but we talked. Mostly small talk, that is. He'd ask me how I was doing. He'd ask about what I was studying to be. School stuff, work. Small talk. He was nice, but. . . "

The Accuser held her head down, her sniffle sounding like a tear of paper.

"Take your time," said Noelle.

"*But* I always felt like he'd go out of his way to talk for 'other' reasons."

"Were you attracted to Miles?"

The Accuser nodded.

"Yes," she said. "I was. He wasn't like most guys I know. He was, I dunno, really sensitive. Miles acted as if he had a good heart, but I knew something was troubling him. Whenever we would talk, he always had this, I dunno, this *look* in his eye, like he wanted to make an advance towards me but didn't want to in the workplace. Despite what happened between us, he was considerate. A part of me knew he wouldn't make any moves, but another part—a more convincing part— knew I was only kidding myself. There was always that 'what if' in the back of my mind. *What if* I looked at him a certain way? *What if* I said something to him that gave him the wrong impression? *What if* I mistakenly gave him a signal that I was interested in furthering what I considered a civil relationship? I hated that feeling, like it was me who was carrying the burden, not him. I just wanted Miles to stop looking at me that way. After awhile, I started to get uncomfortable talking to him."

Noelle asked, "Did you start to feel this way before or after the party?"

"Before," she said. "Then, after the party, it just got worse between us. So much so that I ended up quitting *The Courier*."

"Was Miles aware of how he made you feel?"

"No," she said, backtracking. "I mean, I dunno, really. If Miles did know, he didn't show it."

"Did you ever think about confronting Miles?"

"Yes," the Accuser said. "Many times."

"Why didn't you?"

The Accuser paused for a moment.

"I was scared."

"Scared of Miles or scared of how it would affect the workplace environment?"

"No," she said. "Scared of him, of Miles."

"Why did you go to the party?" asked Noelle.

"I was invited," said the Accuser more aggressively.

"I didn't mean it that way," Noelle corrected. "What I meant was, presuming the way Miles felt about you, did you feel it was necessary to be in the company of Miles, especially at a more relaxed place environment where alcohol was going to be served?"

"Actually, I remember debating on whether or not I was going to attend the party."

"Why?"

"Well, for one, I had class the next day. Two, I wasn't much of a partier. I'd rather stay at home and read a book. I was more of an introvert than an extrovert. And three, I *knew* Miles was going to be there. I *knew* there was going to be alcohol. I knew that, if I didn't go, then he would win.

Why should I let a man prevent me from doing what I want to do? That's no way to live life."

"How did you know Miles was going to be at the party?" asked Noelle.

"I specifically remember preparing myself before the party, spending hours trying to decide what to wear. I didn't want to wear anything that would suggest that I was attending the party for 'other' reasons."

"Such as?"

The Accuser paused.

"I didn't want to come off as a slut," she said bluntly.

Noelle asked, "Did you and Miles talk at the party?"

"Yes," said the Accuser as she took another moment to gather herself. "We did. But only for awhile."

"What did you two talk about?"

"I don't remember exactly. I made sure to avoid him throughout the party."

"Then, what prompted you to talk to him?"

"I bumped into him by accident."

"Did you consume any alcohol at the party?"

"Yes," she said. "I had a couple of drinks, but I *wasn't* inebriated."

"Was Miles drinking?"

"He was," she said. "He was pretty drunk."

"Do you remember anything that you might've said or done that would lead him on?"

"No," she said stuttered. "Of course not."

"To the best of your memory, can you describe the moments leading up to the sexual assault?"

"It happened when I was making my way toward the restrooms," the Accuser described. "He jumped me from behind and carried me to one of the offices. The lights were off. I remember it being dark. But I could see Miles's face in a beam of light. Those dark eyes glistening in the light."

"How sure are you that it was Miles?"

"One hundred percent sure."

"When he grabbed you, did you resist?"

"Honestly, I didn't know what to do," the Accuser said. "He threw me on top of a desk and started to remove my clothes. I just wanted it to end."

Noelle asked, "Did you tell him to stop?"

"Yes," said the Accuser. "Many times."

"And did he?"

"No," she said sharply. "He did not."

"After it was over, did you tell anybody in the office what had just happened to you?"

"No," the Accuser said, tearing up. "I felt paralyzed."

THE night of the interview, Miles dreamt of something moving behind the walls.

A rodent of some kind. Its tiny claws beating against the sides of vent shafts, as well as the backside of walls like a drunken tap dancer.

Miles suddenly bolted upright from his sweaty dream and woke to the sound of *tapping* outside the door.

At first, he thought it might've been the echoes of his dream piercing through his reality.

The tapping continued in intervals of three.

Tap, tap, tap.

Then, a pause.

Then, again, *tap, tap, tap.*

What the hell, Miles said to himself as he rolled out of bed.

Miles checked the door where the tapping was more evident.

With one eye closed, he looked through the peephole and witnessed a young woman standing outside his neighbor's apartment. She was carrying a cup holder with two beverages along the bend of her arm while her other hand, the free one, was tapping on the door with her purple nails. The woman had an orange janitor-sized key chain which looked like a slinky with enough keys to unlock the door of each resident inside The Lofts of Dover loosely worn around her wrist, and that, too, was striking the door.

Miles's neighbor answered the door in an oversized shirt that was barely covering her underwear.

She greeted the woman with a hug and then a peck of a kiss on the lips.

The hardwood floor below Miles suddenly *creaked*!

The woman, neighbor included, turned their attention toward Miles's loft.

Gradually, Miles, feeling the slow burn of their eyes moving through him like a fever, eased away from the peephole.

He waited a few seconds.

When he returned to the peephole, the women were nowhere around.

He heard the *kla-clunk* sound of a door locking.

"Maybe they're European," Miles said exuberantly to himself as if he was his own best audience.

With the warm blood throbbing through his veins, he scuttled into the kitchen and fixed himself a pot of coffee.

Miles couldn't help but direct his attention toward the flat-screen TV hanging from the living room wall.

It was glaring at him.

The blood in his veins turned cold.

Miles told himself that he wouldn't dare turn on the TV. Even if boredom set in throughout the day, which, most likely, it was going to do, he'd remain poised in his protest of no television for at least twenty-four hours—possibly forty-eight, that was how long these things usually blew over.

He walked into the living room, picked up the television remote from the coffee table, and held it in his hand as if it was paraphernalia used for a drug.

"What the hell?" said Miles as he turned on the TV.

The "headline" was on every single channel, every singly network, every single station—even local.

Miles was left stunned by the wall-to-wall coverage. The highlights, clips, as well as sound bites, from last night's "shocking" interview with Miles's Accuser were running on loops while analysts, contributors, and correspondents were strategically yet passionately breaking down each word, each gesture which was used in the interview. On one of the broadcasts, a child psychiatrist was instructing the parents on how their sons should treat and talk to the girls in their classes.

Miles remained glued to the screen, floored by the overwhelming coverage of the story.

Miles's phone rang.

It was *his* parents.

He didn't want to answer, at first. He spoke to them almost everyday. And if he didn't answer, then they might start to worry.

He answered.

It was his mother. She was watching the news, as she ritually did ever morning in her recliner chair with her red and black Minnie Mouse cup of steaming hot coffee in hand. His stepfather was somewhere on the line too, Miles soon realized once he heard Ronnie grousing at the TV set. Surprisingly enough, the story even made it to their "favorite" channel.

"It's not true, Mom," Miles said. "It's all fabricated. Didn't I tell you not to watch that channel? You know how they're well-known for blowing stories out of proportion."

"It's not only *our* channel, Miles," his mother said. "It's everywhere—"

"—Mom, let me talk to Ron."

"You're on speaker."

"Ron," his mother said to Miles's stepfather.

"Yeah," he snapped. "I'm here, Miles."

"It's all bogus, you know that right?"

"It's a smear," Ron said. "That's what it is. A goddamn witch hunt!"

"Ron," his mother called out, "your blood pressure—"

"—All right, all right," he groaned.

Miles could hear his stepfather's coughs becoming less and less blusterous as he stormed out of the room where the two habitually watched daytime television.

"Do you know the woman?" his mother asked, her voice softer.

"No," Miles said. "I've never met her before."

"Why would she disguise her face? It doesn't make any sense, Miles. Even if it did happen, why wouldn't she go to the police after it happened?"

"Mom," Miles yelled out, "it did not happen! Okay?"

Miles still heard the muffled echo of his voice on speakerphone. He removed the phone from his face and gritted his teeth.

"Didn't I raise you right, Miles?"

"I'm not having this discussion right now, Mom. Listen," he said, "I got a lot of things to do today." Which was a lie. "I'll talk to you guys later." Which was yet another life. "*And* don't watch that nonsense. It's not healthy."

Miles hung up the phone before his mother could say goodbye.

He received yet another phone call.

It was a longtime friend, an old female colleague of his at *The Courier*.

Miles was too ashamed to answer. He sent the call to voicemail. Following the call, he received more texts from other colleagues. He received a text from an old buddy named Gus whom he frequently went out with for beers on slow news days. Miles read through the texts.

One caught his eye:

> How does it feel to go from Mr. GQ to the most
> hated man in the world?

Miles decided to text back.

> Not funny, Gus.

Gus texted back:

> Don't sweat it, brohem. Everything will work
> out. It always does.

Miles texted:

I don't know, Gus. You know how the story
goes. My life is ruined now.

Then, Gus:

Think of it as a blip, brohem.

Miles:

I don't know what I'm going to do around here.
I haven't 'not' worked a day in my life.

Gus:

Think of it as 'me time.' Run some errands.
Hitting the gym always works for me. Think of
it as an indefinite vacation.

Miles:

I don't think it'd be wise to leave home right
now.

Gus:

Hang in there, Miles. It'll be all over soon.

Then, finally, Miles:

Will do.

For the remainder of the day, Miles piddled around his
loft: he cleaned; he did laundry; even washed his bed sheets;
he dusted, he scrubbed the bathroom; the shower; he emptied his entire refrigerator; threw out whatever was expired
or rotten, like week-old Thai food, spotted vegetables, some
covered in balls of green and blue fuzz, slick deli meat,
sweaty leftover casserole inside containers of Tupperware.
Miles even cleaned out the trays inside his refrigerator
doors.

After the cleaning spree, he tidied up and rearranged the furniture in different positions, which made the loft looked almost new.

By the time he was finished with everything, it was already dinnertime and he was starved. Miles ordered takeout from The Flying Lotus, which was located only a few blocks away from Miles in Little Tokyo. While he waited on the food, he picked out a book from his impressive library of books. He decided to go with one of the longest ones in his collection: *The Fifth* written by Ellis Kross. It was a monster of a read, nearly a thousand-pager. The story was about a young man in pursuit of the American Dream. In a way, he could relate to the story. He wanted to push the reset button and start over and rediscover the American Dream—the real one, that is.

He only read through a few chapters until he was disrupted by a shrill voice shouting outside his window.

He couldn't quite tell what the person was shouting but one word was clear to him.

The word, *rapist*.

Miles placed the book aside and inched toward the window, only to witness a woman in a brown hoody standing on the street below. Her dark eyes were wide and mad and she was homely-looking with matted greasy hair hanging down her chest like a raggedy mop. She was looking up toward the direction of Miles's loft and shouting out the word, *rapist*, over and over.

As soon as he got a better look at the woman below, Miles suddenly ducked back inside the dim light of his loft.

The woman kept screaming.

"Show you face, you rapist!" she cried out, gathering attention on the streets. She pointed up at Miles's loft and said to a passerby, "A rapist lives in this building! And his name is Miles Straum!"

Miles heard a sudden *clanking* sound coming from the coffee table!

Startled, he snapped toward the noise.

The phone was on vibrate within a silent mode; however, he must've perched it against a metal ashtray whenever he was rearranging the furniture.

Miles picked up the phone and as he had been doing throughout the day, sent the call to voicemail. He inched back toward the window and peeked outside.

Strangely enough, the woman was no longer standing on the sidewalk. However, he could still hear her voice in the distance.

THAT night, Miles found himself rehashing the same dream from last night.

A remake.

In this new, updated version, he dreamt of a rat infiltrating his loft.

The rat managed to burrow a hole into the space on the wall between an abstract painting which he called *The Squares* and Amish-handbuilt bench that he bought a local thrift shop. The rat fell onto the edge of the rustic bench, then fell onto the ground like a beanbag. The rat rolled to its feet and scurried around his loft, going through Miles's things, like his food, the fruit inside the weaved basket on the kitchen countertop or his tennis shoes resting near the front door.

Then, finally, the rat paid Miles a visit.

Its body was revealed in the amber-colored floodlight, which cast a machete-like beam of light along the base of Miles's queen-sized bed.

The rat was obsessed, scabrous, disease-infested.

Miles woke, sat upright against the leathered headrest, and stared at the rat in his bed.

The two made eye contact.

Across the room, Miles heard that same *tapping* sound, only louder.

Tiny claws beating against drywall.

The sound doubled, tripled. Soon, it was in the hundreds and thousands.

An entire clusterfuck of beating claws.

Soon, the wall started to tremble.

The floor shook.

Miles woke shaking from a dream within a dream. He was covered in a coat of sweat. His breath labored. He reached over and hit the snooze button on top of the alarm clock, which lit up the time. It was a quarter after two o' clock.

Disturbed by the sight of the time, Miles let out a sigh and rolled out of bed. He switched on a lamp and lifted up the comforter on his bed. He checked underneath his bed sheets but didn't see any signs of rats or spiders or whatever the hell he dreamt. He wobbled to the window and looked outside at the street below. He heard the sound of giggling coming from the sidewalk. He pinpointed the sound to a suspicious couple drunkenly sashaying hand-in-hand along the sidewalk.

A man and woman, Miles noticed. Nightowls.

The well-dressed man occasionally pulled the woman close and kissed her.

Miles carefully watched the two. They stumbled to a luxury car parked along the curb. The man opened the passenger door for the woman, who, from Miles's point of view, appeared more intoxicated than the man.

Once the two were inside, they made out yet again.

A couple of minutes later, the headlights switched and the car drove away.

"Lucky bastard," Miles mumbled.

As Miles was about to return to sleep, he heard a strange noise coming from the hallway outside. First, he checked the peephole and peered out into the darkness of the hall-way. In his mind, he wielded the neighbor's door to open and reveal the source of the sound. He stared, eyes burning and unblinking.

The door cracked open halfway!

Miles witnessed a small creature in the corner of his eye. He looked down at the floor and saw what looked like a rat slipping into the dark loft. He had to inform the neighbor of the soon-to-be nuisance and possibly catch the rat before it scurried away. Or, was that really the reason why Miles decided to check on his neighbor? Was something else going on? Something darker?

Quietly, Miles exited his apartment and walked across the hallway toward his neighbor's loft. He knocked on the opened door, which, in return, opened several inches farther.

Miles was unsure whether or not the neighbor had let the rat inside.

Or, he thought, was it another rat that managed to open the door?

If they could open doors, what else could they open?

Or worse, *what else could they do?*

Miles called out to his neighbor.

He didn't know her name.

"Ma'am," he said even though she didn't look like a ma'am. Miles stuck his head into her loft. "Excuse me," he said. "It's your neighbor, Miles," he remembered the story on TV, the accusation, his once respected name among the media world reduced to mud. He corrected, "Devon Miles."

Miles didn't hear anything in return.

He fully opened his neighbor's door, but it appeared as if nobody was home.

"Ma'am," he said as he cautiously took a step inside the dark loft.

He stepped into the kitchen, which, similar to his own, was located at the front of the loft.

Except for the stairs leading into a sunken living room— Miles soon realized as he stumbled forward—the layout was the same. He grabbed a hold of the wall, preventing him from crashing into an invisible glass table.

He heard another noise, this time coming from the bedroom. He approached the bedroom. He could see two moonlit figures on the bed. One of them was lying on the bed while the other one was position at the base of the bed.

One of them sounded as if she was moaning.

Miles knew what he was doing was wrong. Him being here was not only an invasion of privacy, but also, in most cases, a crime. He mentally told himself to turn around, go back home, use your shirt to close the door behind you, and go to sleep. They'll never know you were here. He started to think about why exactly he would use his shirt to close the door. Of course, because of the fingerprints he had left behind. Miles started to think more about the things he might've touched inside the loft. He remembered touching the wall. But, of course, it'd be nearly impossible to wipe the fingerprints from the wall, especially in the dark.

Miles eyes adjusted to the darkness of the room.

The two dark figures were women, one of them being his neighbor whom he only knew as "ma'am." She appeared as if she was the one lying on her back. As for the other one, she appeared much shorter, almost stubby. He wasn't quite sure if it was the same woman delivering coffee and a kiss for her head was deep between his neighbor's legs and she appeared to be going down on her.

The strange woman raised her head from his neighbor's legs.

Miles first acknowledged that, unless she was wearing a mask, she wasn't human. Its head was covered in scraggly brownish fur. Its eyes were glossy, beady, and black, and when the soft moonlight hit them they gleamed like white marbles. Its nose was long, like a snout with pointy whiskers protruding outward from its face. Its ears were pointed too, bare and veiny. It was that moment when the creature opened its mouth that Miles knew exactly what it was.

Miles's eyes bolted open.

Hit by the light of a red dawn, he gasped for air.

Once he gathered himself, he checked the time on the alarm clock.

6:49 AM.

The dream—or better yet—nightmare was still fresh. The images were vivid and easily accessible.

The teeth.

Those two front woodchip-like teeth chomping up and down, up and down as if it was inaudibly talking to Miles.

Miles shook away the images from his head and went about his daily morning rituals.

First, he checked his phone.

He had fifty-seven text messages and twelve missed calls.

All Miles could think about were those two front teeth.

And coffee.

Plenty of it.

☙

AFTER the accusation, the second day started out the same as the first, with yet another shocking headline.

Apparently, last night more women came forward on late night TV. Three, to be exact. One, a middle-aged woman named Natalie Eisner, was the guest on the late night news program, *Caught in the Midol*, with the notorious whistle-blower, James Midol. On Midol's show, the new accuser, Ms. Eisner, claimed that Miles sexual assaulted her six years ago. She even brought a picture of the two standing together with Miles's arm wrapped around her waist as they posed for the camera. Miles had absolutely no idea when or where the photo was taken. She claimed it was taken at a sports bar called Trendy's, but Miles had never been to any place of the name. She claimed that it was later in the night when Miles lured her to his apartment where he "at-tacked" her.

On the TV, news anchors were talking about the high-lights from last night's broadcast. Later in the live broad-cast, they were going to have all three of Miles's accusers join the show to shed more light on Miles's past criminal acts.

From inappropriately touching or forcing himself on other women, to sexual harassment among coworkers, to exposing himself, to sexual assault, all of these new accusa-tions made their rounds across airwaves, bouncing from one network to another. It was an all-out smear campaign to defame Miles Straum, a chivalrous man who, overnight, went from one of the most respected, qualified investigative journalists in the business to America's number one sleaze-bag.

Two days ago, women would gladly bare Miles's offspring.

After the new accusations, women hated Miles.

In fact, some women would gladly watch Miles burn to a crisp over a flaming stake as he screamed out in bloody horror.

Of course, Miles knew these claims or accusations were exactly what his lawyer had described: false allegations, with an emphasis on *false*.

Miles's lawyer, Samuel—"Sam," he called him—wanted to meet up and discuss *all* of the litigations and whatnot. Somebody was going to fork out money to repay Miles for all of the damage that had been done to his good name and it certainly wasn't going to be coming out of the accusers' pockets.

Those who knew Miles well thought it was all a conspiracy, a political stunt; and "fixers" with deep pockets were behind it all. Possibly someone in charge of a competing network, a man in a high castle, a Wizard of Oz, someone powerful who was paying these women—actors—to make allegations against Miles. Women Miles had never even met before, let alone seen in real-life.

An hour into the news, flipping from one channel to another, Miles was done with the TV and all of the garbage spewing from the screen. He switched off the trash TV and in a sudden burst of outrage, slammed the remote to bits against the floor. He turned "off" his phone. He was tempted to break that too, but he took a moment to think about the consequences of not having a phone. Which, as of now, wasn't all that bad. But he was so tired of watching it glow and pulsating in the corner of his eye, as if it was screaming at him in a strange way and reminding him of how much of a loser he was to find himself in such an awkward position. He didn't want to hear or talk or explain anymore about himself or whatever illegal act he most certainly did "not" commit.

Miles didn't bother with the coffee. He needed some fresh air.

Then coffee.

With a black White Sox hat worn low and tight over his scalp, Miles grabbed his textbook-sized book, *The Fifth*, and exited his loft.

Miles stepped into the elevator and as the doors were about to close, a woman yelled out, "Hold that door, please!"

His initial reaction, especially with everything going on, was to flinch, protect himself, then run.

Once he realized she meant no harm, he pressed the button on the side panel but the doors still closed.

At the last second, he threw out his arm between the crack of the doors.

The elevator doors hit his arm, causing the doors to slide back open.

In front of the elevator stood his neighbor.

Miles made brief eye contact with her as she warily stepped inside the elevator.

All Miles could think about was the news and he hoped she wasn't the type to get involved in it. Even if she did watch the news, he prayed that she wasn't the type who was brainwashed by it. For Miles, she didn't look like either type.

A tense silence filled the elevator as soon as the doors closed.

Two levels down, Miles turned to the attractive woman and said, "I'm Miles. I think you're my neighbor."

"Apartment 815?"

"Yes," Miles said, a smile curling over the side of his face. "That's right. I live directly across from you."

Miles reached out his hand.

"Nice to meet you. . . "

"Leelu," she said skittishly as she held her fingers outward and barely shook Miles's hand.

She already knew, he thought.

It was her tone, the slight tremor in her voice.

Either she was socially awkward around new people or she saw my face plastered all over the TV.

Her hand shot back into her body.

Miles saw her take an extra step away from him, her body leaning up against the very corner of the elevator.

"Did you just move in?" asked Miles.

"Two weeks ago," she said shortly.

The woman, Leelu, could hardly make eye contact with Miles. She kept her attention mostly at the doors before her. She pulled out her phone and started to scroll through it, as if it was her way of ending the soon-to-be conversation.

Miles faced forward, his eyes moved down toward Leelu's phone below and he noticed that she had the numbers 9-1-1 dialed and her finger was hovering over the green call button.

All of a sudden, Miles was overcome by a heat flash. He faced turned warm, his palms started to sweat, then armpits. He found himself shrinking.

The elevator arrived at the first floor.

Leelu jetted out the doors as soon as they opened.

"Have a nice day," Miles said, his voice cracking.

The woman returned her head held down with a strained smile on her face.

Miles remained in the elevator in a state of shock. He tried to wrap his mind around the fact that this woman, Leelu, by her actions, was absolutely terrified of him.

Then, again, maybe she wasn't comfortable around strangers.

Miles wanted to believe it was true, that she was only shy, for he, too, was no stranger to the shyness, which consumed most of his adolescent years. When he was a little boy, he had his own internal battles. Eventually, after college, he slew that dragon which was anxiety.

But he could feel it rising again.

From that dark cave, its orange eyes narrowing.

<hr />

INSTEAD of driving, Miles decided to walk to a café, The Cup, which was located a couple of blocks from his loft.

About halfway toward the café, Miles saw a woman giving him an icy glare as she stepped into her car parked along the side of the curb. Doubts crept back in. He couldn't help but think of the young woman in the elevator. The look she gave him. The sound of her voice. The fear in her. He tried to put himself in her shoes and wonder as to why an individual would feel such a way in front of someone whom he or she hadn't met before. He thought more directly; maybe she had a *bad* experience with a man who treated her poorly. Maybe she felt threatened or intimidated by men. Or, maybe she was not attracted to men in general. A lot of maybes ran through Miles's head and not a single one of them had any concrete resolution. He tried his best to ignore what happened in the elevator, even though it was at the forefront of his mind.

For the rest of the walk, Miles kept his head down. He passed a rowdy group of teenagers, all male, catcalling at young woman who was dressed in a provocative dress. The young woman turned to the kids and gave them a look of disgust. Miles approached the kids, asked them if that was necessary. They recognized his face from the Internet.

"Like you one to talk, you hypocrite." The kid pulled out his smartphone and blew up Miles's face on his touch screen. "Lookie here, Miles Straum." The kid read a couple of comments on his phone. "Guess what? You're trending and not like the good kind of trending."

"Yeah," another kid said. "Like the dead-kind of trending."

"That's Miles Straum," the other one said. "You're dead, didn't you know?"

"R.I.P.

"Yeah," another chimed in. "Rot In Peace."

"Shouldn't you be in school, getting an education?"

"Well, shouldn't you be like in jail or something?"

Miles shrugged off the group of teenagers and grabbed a newspaper from the dispenser in front of the café. He made the second page. He threw the newspaper in the trash and entered the café.

As Miles waited in line, he could feel wandering eyes pounding down him. He directed his scattered attention to a middle-aged woman with a stony face sitting with another stony-faced woman at a table not too far away. One of the two women pointed at Miles. The other one turned her shoulder and glanced at Miles. They started talking while, at the same time, shooting glares at Miles. He tried to ignore them.

He'd direct his attention elsewhere and find another woman, younger, staring at him.

As Miles turned away, she started texted on her phone, laughing while doing so.

Miles thought one woman took a photo of him from across the dining area.

Miles closed his eyes for a moment.

The chatter around the café increased.

He eavesdropped on several conversations. He heard his name thrown in the mix. *Miles*. Then, *the guy*—no—the *slime on TV*. Then, he heard the word *trash* a few times.

Then, the word *next*.

"Sir?" the young barista said.

Miles looked around the café.

Again, the barista said more clearly, "Next."

A woman standing behind Miles tapped him on the shoulder.

Miles flinched and rotated around.

"Are you going to order or not?" asked the woman.

"Yeah," he said and stepped forward.

The barista wasn't pleased to see Miles.

When she asked for his order, she did so in a manner that suggested that either she didn't want to be here at this miserable job, or she didn't want to serve a customer, like Miles, who treated women as if they were pieces of meat. Miles leaned toward the latter because, just a couple of customers ago, she was laughing and smiling and she told one of the customers to enjoy the rest of her day.

"One tall medium roast," Miles said, struggling to look the barista in the eye.

"Anything else?"

"No, thanks. That's it."

Miles pulled out his wallet, then his debit card.

Before he was about to pay for the coffee, he noticed the price of the coffee was much higher than the last time he was here; in fact, it was three dollars more than what he paid a week ago. He checked the menu above and noticed the price was different, cheaper, three dollars cheaper.

He moved his eyes toward the barista, kept them there on her. Another wave of heat came over his body.

She narrowed her eyes and pointed at the touch screen.

"Slide your card," the barista demanded.

Miles hesitated for a moment, looked at the differentiation of prices on both the menu, as well as the card swiper below, then looked at the barista standing in front of him.

"Slide your card, Sir," she said once more, this time in a hostile tone.

Miles swiped his card.

"Name on the coffee?"

"*Straum*," Miles said confidently as he stared at the barista, "Miles Straum."

As Miles waited in the far corner of the café for his coffee, he saw his face on the TV above the lounge area. Several customers were gathered around on what looked like an inviting sofa and shaking their heads with distaste as they watched the news. The sudden distraction gave the barista enough time to hawk a loogie into Miles's coffee while Miles wasn't paying attention.

The barista called out Miles's name.

She handed him the coffee.

Surprisingly, his name was spelled correctly. Next to his name was a doodle of a smiley face.

"You have a wonderful day, Miles Straum," the barista said with exaggerated glee.

"You too," Miles said modestly.

Miles walked over to the self-serving station adjacent the cash register. He opened the lid of the coffee, first inspecting it for any spit and then smelling it. It seemed fine. He poured cream and sugar into the coffee.

As Miles turned around, a woman suddenly came charging at him with a cup in her hand. She flung hot coffee toward Miles's face and shrieked, "Burn in hell you fucking pig!"

Miles ducked his head.

Hot coffee hit the side of his face, but most of it landed on the self-serving station behind him.

The woman turned to the barista and asked for the manager, "How can you serve this pervert? This man is a rapist!"

Her husband was trying to calm her down.

With the side of his face burning, Miles placed his coffee aside and delicately touched the side of his face.

A young man stepped in and grabbed a handful of napkins and started patting coffee from Miles's shirt.

"Thanks," Miles said to the young man.

Miles grabbed his coffee and hurried to the exit door while customers glared at him and called him all kinds of names behind his back, like "creep," "misogynist," "pig," "bully," "scum-of-the-earth," and even worse, "monster."

Of all the names—or words—*monster* was the one that stayed with Miles the most. Throughout his brief existence, he had been called many names before, but not that one in particular.

As soon as Miles stepped out of the café, the customers cheered in jubilation.

Miles couldn't help but think about the one word and the meaning behind it. Even his once thick skin started to feel strangely thin and brittle.

THE sickness crept in during the latter part of the afternoon when the softening glow of twilight approached and didn't make its presence known until around ten o'clock that night while Miles was plowing through *The Fifth*. His body was hot, feverish. His throat incredibly sore and scratchy; and every time he swallowed, his throat stung. His nose as runny as a dripping faucet. The tip of it red and raw from constantly rubbing it with a tissue. His glands were also swollen and throbbing, a telltale sign he was coming down with something nasty. To make matters even worse, he had a blister on the side of his face the size of his palm. He read somewhere that popping a blister made it harder to heal and would possibly lead to scarring. He left it alone for the time being and figured he'd sleep on the right side of his body, which was opposite of the normal position he slept. The idea of sleep, lying in the confines of his own bed, in that keyed up darkness, closing his eyes, trying to go to sleep, and eventually, dreaming: these were like milestones to Miles. Unwanted choirs. He knew sleep was going to be a challenge and his only temporary remedy was over-the-counter medication until he could schedule a doctor's appointment the next morning. Miles was the holistic-type who preferred to catch a cold before it turned into a flu or pneumonia or let a virus runs its course by treating it with a proper diet, which included leafy greens and fruits, hot soups or broths, hot teas with ginger, lemon, and honey, and loading up on an alphabet of vitamins, particularly vitamin C and D, which were known to ward off ailments and boost an immune system, rather than run straight to the doctor for a quick fix. He went through a phase in college where he experimented with drugs; however, they never wrecked his life or caused any irreparable damage like some he knew. Back then, whenever he got sick or came down with a mild fever, he'd take a pill without thinking twice.

After Miles brushed his teeth and gargled his mouth with warm saltwater, he opened the medicine cabinet and debated whether or not to take anything to aide his face, as well as help him sleep. He came across a bottle of NyQuil, unopened, waiting there like a life raft. For the first time in many years, Miles grabbed the bottle without hesitation and chugged it. He turned off every light in his loft and slept hard in blackness. He slumbered in a deep, dreamless state.

A sudden *BANG* at the door!

Miles jolted upward from his deep, recuperative sleep.

Once more, the door violently rattled from the *bang, bang, bang!*

Miles ripped the covers from his sweaty body as if he was unwrapping a gift and catapulted himself from the bed. The blast of coldness punched his hot body.

He picked up a cardigan close by, threw it on, and stomped toward the closet where he stabbed his feet into a pair of slippers.

Then he stomped toward the front door. He checked the peephole first. Nobody was there.

With a balled-up fist, Miles swung open the door. He looked to his right but didn't see anybody in the hallway. Then looked to his left. Miles saw a shapeless man dressed in black rounding the end of the hallway. Miles chased after him.

The chase continued on the stairs. Miles arched his body over the railing and spotted the dark figure fleeing down a flight of stairs two levels below him. Miles pushed past any reason and pursued. He heard a door swing open then close as he made it to the seventh floor. He wasn't sure if it was the fourth floor or the fifth. He was still riding that bluish-green wave of NyQuil, neither drowsy nor alert but gripped by what felt like a mild hangover.

Panting with exhaustion, he made it to the fifth level.

He walked down a dark hallway that was blocked off. A cardboard sign that read WET PAINT was attached to a piece of caution tape, which had been stretched from one side of the wall to the other. The sign was moving, as if it had recently been disturbed. Miles hunched his body underneath the strip of caution tape and found the man in black anxiously waiting in front of the elevator in the next hallway.

Miles got a better look at him. He was dressed in all black, hoody, jeans, and boots. A walking cliché. The agent provocateur turned to Miles. His face went slack. He was a white young male, he concluded. And scared.

Scared white.

"Hey," Miles called out to him.

The man—or boy, Miles didn't know how old he was—took off in the other direction. He went through a door, possibly one leading to the other staircase.

Miles paused and thought for a second.

He knew exactly where the stairs ended.

It led to only one exit.

With a new plan in mind, the elevator let out a *ding* and the doors opened.

Miles took the elevator to the first floor.

Instead of exiting through the main lobby, he exited through the back exit.

He waited in shadows behind the building until the exit door swung open. He jumped the person from behind, pushed him to the ground, and kneeled over him.

"What the hell do you want from me?" asked Miles, as he grabbed the young man by the collar of his hoody.

"Get the fuck off me!"

Miles picked up the difference in the voice.

It was shriller.

The hoody suddenly flipped backward as Miles shook the young man.

He soon realized it wasn't a man.

It was a woman. Her hair was pulled back in a ponytail. Her cloudy cheeks were trembling with either rage or fear, Miles couldn't quite tell. Her eyes, however, were piercing. He didn't know the woman, hadn't seen her face before, but he knew the look in her eyes. The hatred.

Miles's grip loosened from the collar.

"Why are you doing this to me?" asked Miles. "Huh?"

"You belong in prison!"

"Prison? For what? You're the one who came at me!"

"You're a rapist!"

"What?" Miles backed off. "You're serious? You actually believe that shit you hear about in the news? It's all bogus. Smoke and mirrors."

"Rapist!" she screamed. "RAPIST!"

Eventually, after the sixth shriek of the word *rapist*, she paused to catch her breath.

"You don't even know me, lady—"

"—I know enough."

The woman stood to her feet and thumbed the drop of blood on the corner of her lip.

"Now, I'm gonna sue your ass," she said.

"Listen," Miles said, acknowledging the minor injury. "I didn't know."

"What? That I was a woman?"

The woman puffed out her chest.

"You're gonna pay for what you did," she seethed.

Miles held out his hands and took a step back.

"Whatever," Miles said, making his way to the exit. "Just leave me the fuck alone or else, next time, I will call the cops."

"Go ahead," she said over Miles. "Call them. It still won't stop us."

"Us? Who the fuck is us?"

"The world, Miles," the woman said as Miles opened the door. "Didn't you hear? Your life is finished!"

Miles went back to his loft.

When he finally made it back, the door was wide open. The lights were off inside. He cautiously stepped inside, grabbed a fire extinguisher from the wall, and held it close like a weapon. He flipped on every light switch to every room in the loft. Lastly, he flipped on the lamp in the living room. Hanging from the ceiling fan was a noose.

And it had Miles's name written all over it.

MILES remained awake for the rest of the night and well into the early morning.

As soon as the doctor's office opened, Miles called to make an appointment. The doctor had an opening at ten-thirty. Miles made the appointment and tried to go back to bed. He managed to doze off for about an hour or so until he heard a commotion on the street outside.

"What the hell is it now?" Miles asked himself as he rolled out of bed.

He staggered to the window and looked outside, only to find an angry mob of people protesting outside his apartment building. Protesters were holding up professionally made black and white signs with words like *rapist* and *criminal* and phrases like *"lock him up."* Others signs were much more garish, showy and glittery, with the lettering hand-written with Sharpies. Some of the signs were politically based or inspired. Signs with the theme of blame or shame: blaming the current administration for the erosion of our society, blaming the government for the moral decay or lack of civility, but most importantly, signs meant to "shame" not only Miles, but also his fellow sex, as if Miles himself was no longer an individual responsible for his own actions but the sole ambassador of all men.

Most of the crowd consisted of women and extremists who attended the protest for other more sinister reasons. Women were crying and screaming at Miles. To Miles, the scene was surreal to say the least. Miles didn't know whether or not he was still dreaming. He didn't know what was happening, really.

All he knew was that he was here, in the present.

He looked down at his shaky hands and lifted them up to his face. He started to touch his face, feeling each corner and groove.

He was here.

He couldn't say the same about the people below.

Was she right about what she said last night?

The world being after me?

Surely, he thought, the world hadn't become so shallow to rush to judgment.

Who was manipulating these people?

Was there some hidden force, a grand power dwelling underneath the shadows, pulling the strings behind the whole charade?

Was it technology?

Miles looked down at his phone on the nightstand.

Then, he turned to the TV.

Was it people like me? Am I to blame for all of this?

After all, Miles thought to himself as he stared at the people below, *I started all of this.*

An overwhelming sense of glum settled over his body like a thorny coat.

I had to finish it.

The thought alone that he himself was responsible for all of the madness on the streets caused a sharp, thorny pain to knot in his gut.

He rushed to the bathroom and stared at himself in the mirror.

He looked like shit, worst than shit. He looked like the kind of shit that drew flies. The left side of his face was infected. He was wearing dark baggage underneath his eyes, which had made him look twice his normal age.

Miles knew his health was more important.

In time, he knew, the truth would come out—*it will*.

For the first time in a long time, Miles prayed the truth would come out much sooner than later.

WHILE keeping a low profile, Miles avoided the mob by exiting through the parking deck.

As soon as he pulled out of the parking lot, they were waiting for him. Miles shielded his face with his jacket. Somehow, they knew it was him. If they knew exactly where he lived, then, surely, they knew exactly what make and model of car he drove.

He crept through the crowd, projectiles as well as hands hitting and slapping at the sides of his car.

A woman tossed her coffee cup at the windshield.

Creamy-brown coffee spilled over the windshield, forcing him to hit the wipers.

One woman jumped out in front of the hood of the car, flopped like a professional soccer player to the ground, and started wailing and rolling on the ground as if she was badly hurt.

A man tended to her for a moment. Then he came charging at the car. He elbowed the side of the driver's side window, shattering part of it but not entirely breaking it.

Miles feared for his safety.

He gunned the car into traffic, knocking over a couple of protesters onto the street.

He thought for certain he injured one of them, but he kept driving.

MILES'S condition worsened by the time he pulled into the doctor's office. He met with the nurse first, told her all about his symptoms, the sore throat, the sneezing, the runny nose, the fever, and the most obvious, the burn on his face. Miles was afraid and jumpy at times, knowing, in the back of his mind, she might scold him for what he was accused of doing to a woman. She was professional, though. The issue was never brought up. She treated Miles as if she was unaware of what he was going through. The attention was centered on his well-being, not accusations, false or not.

The nurse left the room.

His doctor, Doctor Delhi, entered soon afterwards.

He went over the chart.

Miles informed the doctor about his symptoms.

The doctor didn't hesitate. He prescribed him medication to help reduce the symptoms. He also prescribed Miles with a strong cream to apply twice a day to his face. Then, lastly, he referred Miles to see another doctor.

Confused, Miles looked over the name on the piece of paper.

"A shrink?"

"Trust me," he said, his hand on Miles's shoulder. "It'll help, Miles. Maybe she'll be able to prescribe medication to help with the anxiety."

"Anxiety?"

"I know what you're going through Miles."

"You do?"

"Everybody does," he said. "It's all over TV. Have you ever tried disguising yourself when you're in public?"

"I shouldn't have to disguise myself," Miles said. "I'm an innocent man."

"What I meant to say is disguise yourself for the time being, you know, until everything cools down. By next week, everybody will forget what happened."

Miles hung his head.

"You know they left a noose inside my loft."

The doctor folded his arms across his chest and shook his head in disgust.

"Did you call the police?"

"No."

"How these individuals break into your home?"

"I must've left the door unlocked," Miles said, unsure. "I don't know."

The doctor leaned in close to Miles and placed his hand over his shoulder.

"You need to take care yourself," he said with concern. "Don't let this get to you." The doctor paused. "My mother, who was a doctor herself, a highly intelligent woman who had an extraordinary gift to identify problems, always told me to 'consider the source.' As a child, I never understood what she meant by those words until later on in high school. 'Consider the source,' she'd always say. Till this day, those words have guided me, not only in life, but also in my practice."

"Right," Miles said emotionlessly.

The good doctor pulled out a notepad from his breast pocket and wrote Miles another prescription.

"I'm going to prescribed you with something that will help you sleep. Make sure you take only *one* pill a night," the doctor emphasized. "It's potent stuff, but it works."

"Thanks, Doctor."

Miles stood from the table and shook the doctor's hand.

"Hang in there, Miles," the doctor said and showed Miles the door.

AFTER Miles left the doctor's office, he killed time by driving around the city for a while until his prescription was ready to be picked up. He wondered about the pharmacist, if it was a woman, and if so, would she slip in a different medication, possibly something that would make his condition even worse. Or, worse, something that would kill him.

He started to think about these things, even during trivial times of the day, such as running common errands like picking up medication from a pharmacy. The pharmacist turned out to be a man. Which was a relief to Miles. However, he realized all of that worrying he was doing in the car was all for nothing. And, if he went about his days like this, the constant worrying, then he was going to give himself a stomach ulcer. Or, even worse, Miles was headed straight to Looney Town.

As Miles stepped out of the Med-Mart, he suddenly gagged from the smell of smoke in the air. He covered his nose and mouth with the loose collar of his tee shirt and spotted the smokestack-like column of black smoke spewing into the air. He traced the smoke to his car engulfed in flames. Some people in the parking lot were fleeing from the fire while others were gathering around the fire like a tribe. One face in particular caught Miles's eye. A shaky pale face of a young woman. She crept from the growing crowd, her red eyes moving around the chaotic scene in what Miles recognized as paranoia. She turned her body toward the front entrance of Med-Mart and for a brief moment, locked eyes with Miles. Underneath the stiff collar of her leather jacket, she had a foreign tattoo running up the side of her neck like a serpent. Miles couldn't help but stare at it, that tattoo.

Furious, the strange woman clenched her teeth, the sides of her jaw like tiny bulges.

A man behind her hollered out something like *call the police* to a friend.

The woman flinched from the man's voice. She back-pedaled from the crowd and speed-walked to a noisy Honda hatchback across the parking lot and peeled away, her car leaving behind a trail of smoke.

The tattoo, Miles said to himself. *That* tattoo.

He replayed the images in his head. Found himself diagnosing the image.

Durga.

The name came to him out of the blue.

The tattoo was of a fierce woman—a goddess—a multiple arm-formed goddess from the Hindu scripture. In one of her many arms, she was holding a sword in her hand and slaying an evil demon while riding on top a tiger.

The more he thought about that one name in particular, the name *Durga* with an emphasis on the *Durrr*, the more Miles thought about her, the bearer of the tattoo, the bartender from V Lounge, most commonly known as V to weekend warriors who drank there every festive weekend.

What was her name?

BY the time the firefighters arrived at the scene, the car was all charred and burnt and nothing much remain of it but a blackened shell with a dark melted interior.

The woman's name suddenly came to Miles when he was speaking to the police officer on the scene.

The cop mentioned the word *after* and then *exited*

(*After* you *exited* from Med-Mart. . .)

Strangely enough, those two words were the magic keys to unlock the memory gates.

"*Alexis*!" Miles blurted out as he stood next to the police officer on the sidewalk next to Med-Mart. "Her name is Alexis!"

Strange how the mind works like that, Miles thought, certain words bringing forth trapped memories that remained tiny and unlit, waiting to be wiggled loose into the blazing light of consciousness.

"Girlfriend?" said the police officer.

"No."

"*Ex*-girlfriend?"

An emphasis of the *ex*.

Miles hesitated.

"No."

"She's a bartender at V."

"V?"

"The V Lounge."

"I see," the officer said as he wrote it down on a piece of paper attached to a clipboard.

Miles pulled out his phone and looked this Alexis up on Facebook. He had no luck. He went on V's Facebook page and saw her face in one of the photo albums. He scrolled through the timeline and clicked on the face, which sent him to her profile page. There, he found her full name.

"Alexis Welding," Miles told the officer.

Miles showed the officer a picture of Alexis on his phone.

The officer wrote down the first name.

Then hesitated before writing down the last.

"Welding?"

Miles spelled it out for the officer.

The officer jotted down the last name.

Miles searched through the contacts in his phone.

He completely forgot that he still had her number in his phone.

"So, how do you know this woman, Alexis Welding?" asked the officer.

"We've met before," Miles answered. "She used to serve me drinks at the V Lounge. Plus, we have mutual friends."

"Do you have any kind of relationship with Ms. Welding?"

"We have no relationship, at least not like that."

"But you two do *know* each other?"

"Yes," Miles said. "I guess you can say that."

Miles directed his attention toward the police officer writing. The officer appeared bored with Miles, as if he was going through the motions.

"You're going to catch her, right?" asked Miles.

"One of the detectives will be contacting Ms. Welding," the officer said.

"She's going to say that she didn't do it," Miles said with frustration. "If you don't believe me, then take a look at the footage from the surveillance cameras."

Miles pointed at the camera mounted on the corner of the Med-Mart building.

"Don't tell me how to do my job," the officer said seriously.

Miles backed off.

"I'm just saying."

The officer continued to write.

MILES ending up taking a UBER back home.

He told the UBER driver to drop him off a block away from his building.

Just to be safe.

If the mob was still there, then he had no protection.

Miles knew he had to be smart about how he'd sneak into his building. The thought alone of "sneaking" in somewhere was ridiculous. Miles felt as if he was sixteen years old again, sneaking into his bedroom window in the middle of night while desperately trying not to wake the sleeping giants.

Miles heard a commotion coming from the street ahead. The closer he came to the commotion, the clearer the words became. He heard screaming, the chants. They were *still* there, still raging. Miles made it to an intersection, poked his head around a corner, and saw the mob outside the front of his building.

Like before, he decided to enter via the back of the building; however, when he arrived in the back alleyway, he saw a crowd gathering around the door. Miles was no *Spiderman*, even though the thought of scaling the building like the web-slinger came to him. *Imagine the possibilities!* But that was all fictional, a world Miles wished was real. Another idea came to Miles, two ideas actually, and both of them he learned from his rogue days in high school.

Bomb threat was clearly off the table.

Bomb threats were taken too seriously, especially given the circumstances of the situation.

However, the other one could work.

He called one of his neighbors, Martiez, his workout partner and the occasion wingman on Saturday nights. Fortunately, Martiez worked from home. He happened to be in the building when he called. Miles asked him for a favor.

A "huge" favor.

THE building cleared from the fire alarm.

As the residents exited the building, Miles shouldered his way past the crowd and entered the building undetected.

Miles hid inside the last stall of a bathroom while the firefighters were called to the building. One of the clunk-sounding firefighters entered the bathroom but was called upon by one of his colleagues to exit the building once they realized it was the false alarm.

MILES spent the rest of the day hunkered in his loft. He blasted heavy metal jams through his headphones to drown out the mob outside but could only listen to the music for an hour or two before his ears grew sore. Toward late afternoon, that time in the day when the news was preparing for five o' clock, various news vans showed up at the scene. Right on cue. Cameramen, as well as reporters, some of whom Miles personally knew, were among the mob.

When night *finally* arrived, Miles was tapped out yet still jacked up from the chaos outside. It felt as if he was on a combination of both uppers and downers, as if he just got done slamming five shots of fireball. His body wanted to pass-out, but his mind wouldn't shut off; and at times, he felt as if it was the other way around, like he had a switch inside him and some bratty little shithead kept flipping it on and off, on and off, on and off, singing the words *nana nana boo boo, stick your head in dodo.*

Out of mere curiosity, Miles decided to turn on his phone. His voicemail was overflowing with messages. Same went with text messages. He had hundreds of emails in his inbox. One of the messages stood out the most. It was a voicemail from Noelle, a colleague from the network. She sounded worried about Miles and she wanted to meet up and talk about what was going on—what they were going to do.

Miles hesitated to call her back.

As before, he didn't.

He turned off his phone and took a pill to help him sleep.

THE rats were back.

Hundreds and thousands of them chewing and clawing through the walls and moving like a brown tidal wave through his loft.

Driven by an innate hunger of human flesh, the rats climbed onto his bed.

Miles was stuck inside a dream. He woke but was still asleep. He curled his chin into his neck and peered down his body, only to find a pack of rats crawling up the base of the bed, arching their heads upward as they sniffed Miles's scent, craving his pungent aroma. It was as if they could smell the terror emitting from the pores of his skin, like that mustardy-colored gas in the movies. They crawled up his feet, legs, waist, and settled onto his chest.

With his eyes swelled open, Miles tried to move, tried to wake from the horrible nightmare, but he was completely paralyzed. He was struggling to catch his breath. The weight of the rats made each breath more taxing than the one before.

The rats were smothering Miles.

As the dream started to spin out of control, Miles suddenly woke up from his deep sleep, brushing away the rats from his body. There were no rats, Miles soon realized as he caught his breath and flipped on the lamp.

It was a dream, Miles told himself.

A nightmare.

"It's not real, Miles," he said audibly to himself.

It's not real.

He rolled out of bed and dragged himself to the bathroom. He flipped on the light. In the corner of his eye, he saw something unusual, something darker. He turned to the mirror. Except for his hair, his entire face, as well as his body was as dark as a silhouette. His skin a deep black. He reached up with his black hand and touched his black face. He couldn't feel his hand. He continued to reach farther into the blackness. His hand kept moving farther into his head, going deeper and deeper as if he was reaching into his mind and that, too, was pitch-black. . .

Once more, he suddenly woke up from the dream!

As before, he dragged himself to the bathroom.

As before, he checked his face in the mirror, his eyes, his nose. He reminded himself it was only a dream. He sipped water from the faucet.

With distant images of the strange dream still battering around his mind, he walked to the spot where the rats had emerged from the wall. He turned on a light and noticed a quarter-size piece of drywall on the floor. He picked up the drywall chip and matched it to a bare spot above the electrical outlet.

It's not real, he told himself.

Or was it?

THE next morning, Miles heard a bunch of people talking on the street. The mob had settled down; however, they were still there, loitering around as if Miles's loft and the street that surrounded it had all become an amusement park and they were waiting for the rides to open. Some protesters were gearing themselves up with signs while others were fueling themselves up with coffee.

Miles decided to take up his doctor's advice about wearing a disguise.

He did have a disguise.

A good one.

Miles pulled himself from the window and splashed his face with cold water from the bathroom faucet, which helped relieve the soreness in his face.

Outside, the crowd was starting to get stirred up by a megaphone.

Once more, he checked on the crowd outside.

A handful of protesters, ones that Miles never saw the day before, were fired up and shouting out the word of the week, *rapist*, as if it was a new trend that had graduated into the Hall of Names, which would be used like slander against future political opponents. He thought they looked like out-of-towners. People who had nothing better to do than try to ruin an innocent man's reputation. Miles couldn't understand how these people receive a great deal of satisfaction in bringing added stress to a man's already stressful life. But *maybe that was the whole point*, Miles thought. *To break me down. To drive me out of town.*

As Miles stared at the faces below, he felt nothing but a raw resentment for them and their ability to be easily persuaded.

Miles stormed back into his bedroom and pulled out a shoebox from the top shelf of the closet. He set the box on the floor and removed the lid. Inside was a long blonde wig, as well as various cosmetics, gold tubes of lipstick, a silver stick of mascara, a clamshell-shaped container of powder, a small mirror. He grabbed the wig from the box and held it up before him.

At that moment, Miles knew exactly what had to be done.

Miles was no longer known as Miles Straum when he stepped out of his loft. He was a handsome young blonde named Scarlet, as in the color red. The name, Scarlet, had come to him from the sight of the tall teepee shaped scarlet runner in the botanical garden inside the courtyard of his building. Miles couldn't help but notice the capital A shape of the plant. Plus, Miles liked the name, Scarlet. It was elegant and rolled off the tongue like a wave.

The first person to acknowledge Scarlet was his neighbor, Leelu.

Or, he thought, was it Leila?

She held the door open for the woman in the red dress as she stepped outside. The neighbor stopped in her tracks and gave Scarlet what she thought was a rather flirtatious look.

Miles thought, *Was she checking me out?*

Scarlet pushed the thought aside and thanked her neighbor for being polite.

"You new here?" asked the neighbor.

Scarlet paused and cleared her throat.

"I guess you can say that," Scarlet said, smirking.

She turned and walked away as if she was playing hard to catch. Making just the right impression that would stay with Leelu for the rest of the day. Scarlet had no intentions at all about pursuing any kind of relationship with his neighbor. He liked playing The Game, one where he was the only one who came out on top.

Scarlet pushed her through the small crowd, then walked around a larger one. Nobody looked at Scarlet twice, except for a couple of built fellas who were talking amongst themselves. Scarlet ignored them—or at least tried to. She still received looks, but this time it was mostly coming from men.

They don't know, he thought. *If I've gotten this far, then why not go a little further.*

What the heck?

So Scarlet did. She walked to Miles's once favorite go-to spot for caffeine, the same café where he had hot coffee thrown in his face and heckled out by loyal patrons. She stepped inside the cafe. Surprisingly, Scarlet received similar attention as Miles did the last time he was here. She received glares from men, same from women; however, a couple of women, like Miles's neighbor, appeared as if they were checking out Scarlet.

Not to draw any suspicion, Scarlet ordered the opposite of what Miles would normally order. At first, he thought about tea and how good a cup of hot lemon ginger or chamomile tea would be; however, he was feeling adventurous. He had never tried one of those fancy-schmancy caramel drinks with whipped cream on top and a swirly straw before. Frankly, Miles was too embarrassed to order one in public. What better opportunity to try something different?

The same barista as before greeted Scarlet with a much better jovial attitude, which Scarlet first interpreted as phoniness.

Scarlet waited for the barista to unravel and reveal through her actions, even her words, that she was completely aware of Scarlet's game.

Scarlet vigilantly watched the barista and waited for a sign, the slight lowering of a lip, a dark spot in her eye, a drop in tone, a clearing of her throat, a twitch or sudden fidgetiness of her body, any movement or gesture that indicated that the barista was not only playing the game, but was also battling for the sole rights of dominance.

The barista remained poised and friendly, didn't miss a beat when Scarlet ordered a Caramel Frappucchino.

She smiled at Scarlet. She stayed with character, an extremely cordial barista who had a heart the size of the world, who bent over backwards to make Scarlet's visit the most comforting experience.

The two even started talking about the weather and other things, like the different types of new autumn flavors, which had been recently added to their limited fall collection. The barista talked about what a nice day it was going to be, but strangely enough, she was glad to be right here at the café, working her tail off on a cheap salary shy of minimum wage, and concocting hot as well as cold beverages for thirsty patrons.

Scarlet pushed aside Miles's tongue-in-cheek pessimism.

For the first time all week, Miles felt optimistic about the future. Except for all the preparation involved in the whole transformation process, including all the extra garments worn to make himself plumper in areas that were flat or shaving areas of the body, which weren't meant to be shaved, or the waxing and all the burn and hot pain that followed afterwards or applying more lotions and creams to his skin, or the plucking of rogue or unpleasant hairs or the constant changing of his voice, which, Miles knew, over time and repetition, he'd be able to master, or being able to have an open mind when it came to picking out colors, figure out which ones worked well together, and then dabble in various shades that he normally wouldn't wear or, lastly, possessing a steady hand while applying a new face, he sort of liked being this "new" person.

Despite all of the effort and dedication, Miles didn't understand what the fuss was about.

Besides the looks or maybe a few pounding stares he received every now and then, Miles thought, it wasn't all that bad.

Once Scarlet's Frappucchino was ready for pick up, Scarlet, like the neighbor before, thanked the barista for her politeness.

As Scarlet was about to walk away, the barista asked Scarlet if she liked to run.

Scarlet's face went long.

"Run?"

"Yeah," the barista corrected. "You know, like jogging."

"Oh," Scarlet said and giggled. "Sure. I like to jog."

"This weekend, a few of my girlfriends are getting together for a benefit. If you don't have any plans, feel free to join us. The name's Lou, by the way."

Lou, huh?

Scarlet thought over the invitation.

"That sounds nice. I'll have to check my schedule."

The barista wrote down her phone number on a blank receipt and handed it to Scarlet.

"Give me a call or text me if you're going to come." Lou grinned. "I'll text you the location."

Scarlet looked over the number, smiled back.

"I will," she said. "Thanks."

Scarlet left the cafe and enjoyed her Frappucchino on the patio outside.

She couldn't help but think of how nice the day was going to be.

AFTER Scarlet left the café, she looked up the nearest car rentals in the area. She found one a few miles away; however, it was beyond walking distance. She decided to grab an UBER.

While she waiting, she spotted a curious man waiting behind a Prius as if he was using it to conceal himself. Scarlet remembered seeing him at the café; now that *she* thought more about it, she remembered his scrunched-up face, his gray eyes wrapped in bitter wrinkles.

She checked her phone.

The UBER driver was seven minutes away.

Seven *long* minutes.

Either the guy knew Miles was pretending to be a woman named Scarlet or the guy had other sinister intentions and was most definitely eyeing Scarlet.

A minute in, Starlet decided to cancel the UBER and lose the guy on foot. She walked down the sidewalk bustling with pedestrians. During her hasty walk, she turned her shoulder. As expected, the guy was following her.

But not just following, stalking.

Scarlet sped up, didn't run; but she sped up her walk into a power walk.

As she rounded a street corner or jaywalked past an intersection, she looked over her shoulder; and the same guy, with his eyes sharp and shriveled, continued to stalk her.

Scarlet was only a block away from her building. She decided to remove the red stilettos from her feet and take off down an alleyway. She stepped on a jagged rock on the concrete; but as with her preparations into making her coming out party official, she pushed through the pain.

Once Scarlet reached the end of the alley, which intersected with yet another alley, she stood on her toes and stretched out her body until she was as thin as a teenager and hid within the frame of doorway alongside the side of the building. She heard footsteps coming closer, then silence, then the footsteps began to travel in the opposite direction. Then, after a couple of minutes, the footsteps faded into street ambience. Scarlet poked her head from the doorway and checked her surroundings. The guy was gone. Scarlet told herself to breathe.

She breathed.

For a moment, the sun came out and sword-like rays pierced the alley below.

Relieved, Scarlet put her stilettos back on and began to walk back toward her building where she'd grab another UBER to the car rental place.

As she exited the alleyway, the same guy from before leaped out behind her, startling her.

The guy paced around Scarlet, eyeing her body from legs-up.

"Hey there, good-looking."

"Please," she said. "I don't want any trouble."

"Too late. Trouble's already found you, sweetie," the guy said with a smirk stretched across his mean face.

Miles was unsure whether or not the guy was making an attempt at foreplay, as if referring to himself as "trouble," as if all women liked men who were nothing but trouble. She expected to hear a pick-up line about his middle name being "maker."

The guy stepped closer to Scarlet and blocked her path.

Scarlet realized the situation was more serious than she originally thought.

"What's a good-looking woman like yourself roaming back alleyways?"

Scarlet took a brief moment to observe her surroundings, her exits, as well as her weapons.

"I'm just taking a shortcut home."

"And where is home?"

"It's none of your business." Scarlet made an attempt to pass the guy. "Now if you don't mind—"

The guy slid to the right and once more, blocked Scarlet's path.

"I said ' I don't want any trouble.'"

"Nothing's wrong with *Trouble*," he said. "Why does *Trouble* get such a bad rap? Maybe you should try getting yourself into trouble. You don't know what you're missing out—"

"—Please," Scarlet said, backing away. "I have cash."

"Cash?" The guy paused for a moment from the word *cash* as if it was holy word, his God. The guy clenched his teeth, shook his head as if he was shaking away thoughts, and said with wide, lustful eyes, "I ain't here for cash, sweetie."

"Please, I'll pay you whatever you want. Just leave me alone—"

"—Leave you alone?" The guy laughed. "You know you want it, baby. It's written all over you, your face, your body, the way you walk. Relax. Don't be so uptight. Think of me as. . . " the guy paused once more, ". . . as one of the good guys."

"Get the fuck away from me—"

"—Easy, sweetie. What's your name?"

"I mean it," Scarlet said, her hands balled into fists. "Back off."

"How rude of me," the guy said, carefully taking a step toward Scarlet, who, in return, took another step back. "I should've introduced myself earlier. Name's Boe, but you can call me *The Chiropractor*. I'm here to straighten you out."

"Please. . ."

Scarlet made an attempt to run around the guy—The Chiropractor.

He snatched her by the arm. Scarlet tried to yank her arm away, but the guy resisted and threw her to the ground.

As the guy crept forward, a bulge formed in his pants. To Scarlet, he showed no sign of backing off; in fact, he started to remove the belt from his pants.

"Wait!" Scarlet screeched.

"Nobody can hear you scream out here, sweetie," the guy said, his bloodshot eyes widening with madness. "I've had my eye on you for awhile. You're mine."

The guy stepped on Scarlet's ankle.

Scarlet hollered out in agony.

Then he proceeded to lift her dress. He fondled her soft breast, which was made out of balls of toilet paper that had been stuffed and compacted inside the D cup of a bra.

Scarlet suddenly removed the blonde wig from her head.

"Wait a second!" Miles shouted out. "Look! I'm a dude!"

The guy—or soon-to-be rapist—backed off in mild disgust.

"Shut the front door," he said, chuckling.

The guy caught his laugh, his face washed over with seriousness.

Witnessing the fury grow inside the guy's eyes, Miles held his hand outward, signaling for the guy to stop.

"I'm a dude, man!"

"Now, you're going to get it. . ."

The guy clearly didn't watch any TV or keep up with current affairs, Miles thought.

He lurched forward, grabbed Miles by the wrist, and pulled him closer to his body. His eyes swelled and darkened. He started to whale on Miles's face with his fist. He got in at least three to four good licks before a nearby pedestrian, who was walking on the sidewalk not too far away, rushed into the alley and stepped in and broke up the fight. The guy—The Chiropractor—took off down the alleyway while the pedestrian tended to Miles.

"You okay?" asked the good Samaritan.

Miles looked down and found a leather wallet on the ground.

As the Samaritan helped Miles to his feet, Miles secretly grabbed the wallet and slipped it inside the fold of his purse without drawing any suspicion.

"Yeah," Miles said, holding the side of his jaw. "I'm straight."

The Samaritan picked up Miles ruined wig from a murky puddle of water and handed it to Miles. The wig was stringy and soaked with brownish water.

The two shared eye contact.

The Samaritan acted as if he didn't care if Miles was dressed up as a woman.

"To each his own," said the Samaritan.

"It's not what it looks like," Miles said depressingly. "My life has become a living hell. I can't go out in public anymore without being recognized."

"What? You famous or something?"

"Or something," Miles said and started to walk from the alleyway. "Anyway, thanks for jumping in."

"No problem," the Samaritan said with a strange look on his face. "We got to look after each other, right?"

Miles looked the guy directly in the eyes and for a split second, he witnessed a crease in the corner of his right eye, a crow's foot, followed by a phantom of a smile creeping somewhere underneath the right side of his face. He realized that the guy knew exactly who Miles was, the unlucky sap on TV whose face had become the greatest meme used for puns and sharp jabs; and yet, the guy wasn't being so forthright with Miles and it was as if he knew something about Miles that Miles didn't know—or least expect.

After a thorough study of the guy's vague facial expression, Miles didn't respond to the guy's comment.

He already said what he needed to say and then he was on his way.

MILES arrived at his building.

The mob had doubled since the last time he saw it.

One protestor in the middle of the crowd had even blown up Miles's head on a massive cardboard sign and placed it over a piñata. Other protestors were taking turns at beating the piñata with baseball bats, broom handles, and belt buckles.

Miles held up the wig, which looked like roadkill. Then examined the dress, which was partly torn and covered in black scuffmarks and street grime.

Curious, Miles pulled out The Chiropractor's wallet. The man in the driver's license picture wasn't the same man who attacked him in the alleyway. He took a second look at the picture, thinking maybe that the guy had lost a whole bunch of weight or changed his hair color, even eye color. Miles concluded that the man in the picture was *not* the man who attacked him.

Not only was the man a criminal—*a rapist!* Miles thought—but he was also a common thief.

A pick-pocketer?

Miles looked over his phone.

He knew there was only one person whom he could trust.

He had to call her.

Had to.

NOELLE agreed to meet Miles outside an old laundromat in West District.

Noelle arrived shortly after Miles contacted her, reached over the center console of her car, and pushed open the passenger door.

"Get in," she said to Miles, "hurry up."

Miles skittishly checked his surroundings before getting inside the car.

"Miles?"

Miles stepped inside.

"Just wanted to check to see if you were being followed."

"That bad, huh?"

Miles closed the door.

Noelle sped away.

"Look at me, Noelle!" Miles cried out. "Look what I've been reduced to!"

Noelle reached over Miles's seat and grabbed the gym bag in the back seat.

"Here," she said as she tossed the gym bag in Mile's lap, "brought you some clothes to wear."

Miles's zipped open the gym bag and pulled out a tacky yellowish Hawaiian shirt, which looked two sizes too big for Miles, along with a pair of blue jeans, as well as green Chuck Taylors, a brown bomber jacket, and a red baseball cap with the capital A in bold, yellow Princetown lettering.

"I already standout enough," Miles said, annoyed. "Are you trying to get me killed?"

"It's all I could find," Noelle said.

"What the hell is this? A Halloween costume?"

"They once belonged to my brother. Are you going to wear them or not?"

Miles placed the gym bag on the floor mat beneath him.

"Whatever," he said. "So where we going?"

"I was thinking about we drive to up to Oak Hill," Noelle said. "Lay low for the rest of the afternoon."

"Sounds good," Miles said and sat back in his seat and tried to make himself comfortable. "Anywhere away from here."

"So," Noelle said over the silence, "you want to tell me what happened?"

MILES and Noelle grabbed a bite to eat in a rural area outside the city.

"I still don't get it," Noelle said as she sat on the hood of her car, which was parked in the back of a Burger Hut parking lot. "This guy—"

"—The Chiropractor," Miles interrupted.

Noelle sighed and glared at Miles.

"Sorry," Miles said.

"If this guy—The Chiropractor—if he was following you after you left The Cup, then he must've been following you before you arrived at The Cup. What if he was one of the protestors on the street?"

"No," Miles said. "You're not listening. Like I said, Noelle, he acted like he didn't know me."

"Well, you were dressed like a woman, Miles."

"Don't recite facts back to me, Noelle," Miles said tensely. "I'm saying *this guy* didn't know me after the wig came off. I want you to look him up."

Noelle sipped from her iced tea as she looked over the stranger's wallet.

"I don't know, Miles," she said, skeptical. "Don't you have more important issues to worry about?"

"The man tried to rape me, Noelle! What if he is a real-life rapist? What if I'm not the only one? What if he's a serial rapist, Noelle? A man like that cannot be out there roaming the streets! People like that need to be locked up! If we can catch this guy—expose him for *what* he is—then maybe it'll change the way people look at me. Maybe this is our opportunity to change the narrative. People like redemption stories. They eat them up like candy. This can be my only chance to salvage whatever's left of my God-given name. Who knows, Noelle? The people might even forgive me for what I did—"

"—But you didn't do anything to her, Miles! For crying out loud, the woman doesn't even exist! Remember? Don't you start cracking on me now, Miles."

"I'm not going to crack."

"Listen, I'm just as much a part of this mess as you are."

"I wish there was something I could do."

"Just leave it be, Miles."

"He has to pay for what he did, Noelle! He must!"

"Then, tell me, Miles, what exactly are you going to do about it? You talking about street justice?"

"Street justice is better than no justice."

"Seriously?"

"If I go to the police," he said, thinking, "I look like a rat. If I don't take care of it myself, I look like a coward."

"Don't say that—

"—*And* if I do take action and somebody gets hurts, I'm more than likely facing a lawsuit. Even worse, thrown in jail. I'm stuck. Unless. . . "

"Unless *what*?"

Miles faced Noelle, his eyes sharpened.

"We catch him in the act," Miles said. "Deal with him ourselves. If he's the real deal, then he'll strike again. He will!"

Noelle paused, rolled her eyes, and placed her drink aside.

"Miles, the network, they want you gone," she said finally. "These new accusations that keep coming forward have put them in an extremely difficult position."

"But we knew this was going to happen, Noelle. It always does, right?"

"Pressure is mounting," she said as she ignored Miles's cynicism. "They've already assembled a team of lawyers. They're expecting you to retaliate, but you and I both know eventually, with all the legal fees, they're going to bleed you dry. You don't have the money to battle them, Miles."

"You act like they're preparing for war."

"Well, they are, Miles," Noelle said. "Their reputation is on the line."

"Their reputation?" Miles couldn't believe what he was hearing. He stepped closer to Noelle and yelled in her face. "What about mine?"

Noelle remained calm, poised.

"They're not going to let you bring them down. They're going to make a decision soon. *And* it doesn't look good."

"So, what happened to the idea that this whole thing was going to blow over once these new accusations came forward? The absurdity of the other accusations alone would be enough to plant skepticism inside the minds of our viewers. Besides, it's not like you don't have to report it. You still have The Snipper's disciples out there, still carrying out his work. Why not just stick with that story."

"That story's played out. People are getting sick and tired of anything related to The Snipper. They want scandal, not murder."

Miles couldn't believe he thought it, but he did—

What if they could get both?

"We didn't think it'd get this out-of-hand, Miles. Times are changing. People want blood, Miles. *They*, they want your blood."

"Well, they can't fucking have it!"

"Face it, Miles," Noelle said soberly as she walked up to Miles. "You underestimated them. You gave them exactly want they wanted. What'd you think was going to happen? You come out scot-free?"

"So, you're saying I'm going to be out of a job?"

Noelle hung her head.

"Yeah," she said quietly. "It looks that way."

"And you? Are you still going to keep your job?"

"Miles, this was *all* you, the whole idea," Noelle said defensively as the anger rose in her voice. "Not me. I just went along with it. I mean look at what this story has done, all of the money it has brought in. The ratings are at an all-time high. They're through the roof! All the other networks are trying to keep up with coverage, but they don't even come nearly as close to what we did. We have the upper hand—"

"—You mean, *you* have the upper hand. My life is hell, Noelle. Ruined!" he screamed out. "I'm not even on trial for God's sake and they're condemning me as if I'm a fucking criminal!"

Noelle seethed, "You want to talk about hell, Miles, huh? A slow day in the news. That's hell." Her face slackened. She shrugged. "Your words, *not* mine."

"Everything's changed—"

"—Nothing has changed."

Miles couldn't believe what he was hearing. He threw out his hands.

"For all I know, they promoted you!"

Noelle paused once more.

"They did, didn't they? I can't believe these sons of bitches!"

"But Miles, I was going to ask you before I said yes to it but you didn't pick up your goddamn phone!"

"So, that's it," Miles said, frantically pacing around the car. "So, you're siding with the network? What in the hell makes you any different? What you did? You're just as guilty as I am—"

"—That's not the way the network sees it."

"Then," he hesitated, "what about our friendship, huh? Does that mean anything to you? No," Miles said before Noelle could answer, "of course not. What am I thinking? All you care about is money. You cherish nothing of great value! You hold nothing sacred anymore, other than the dollar! It has become your god, your only means of getting up in the morning. I thought you were better than this, Noelle. You disgust me!"

"Hey," Noelle said, offended, "I'm not the one playing dress-up."

"Years from now, when you look back on your life, you're going to remember what you did to me, to us, and how it destroyed what goodness you once had, and you're going to have nothing but regret, Noelle. Regret!"

"Maybe," Noelle said thoughtfully. "But now, *I'm* looking forward."

Miles shook his head in utter disgust.

"What happened to you?" Miles asked Noelle.

In return, Noelle said, "I grew up, Miles. What happened to you?"

Miles threw up his hands.

"I'm done," he said and walked away.

"Miles!" Noelle called out. "Where are you going?"

"Far away from you," he said to himself.

Noelle slid from the car and looked down at the wallet in her hand. She kept the driver's license and tossed the wallet in a trashcan.

THAT night, Miles ended up staying in a shabby hotel just off the main highway. Miles knew that there was no reason to go back home. He was soon going to be out of a job. He didn't have any friends. Except his mother and Ron, he had no other family. He had no place to live. He was stuck. The only thing Miles could think about was the redemption story, *his* story, finding a way to redeem himself from the bogus story that he had manufactured.

At the crack of dawn, Miles received a call from Noelle. Miles was too disgusted to pick up the phone. He listened to the message on his voicemail. In the message, Noelle stated that she decided to research the name on the driver's license. Turns out there actually was a man who was a chiropractor, Timothy Hume, and the name on the driver's license, Abraham Fisher, was a patient of his. Mr. Fisher accidentally left his wallet in Dr. Hume's office yesterday afternoon after receiving spinal treatment and Dr. Hume, The Chiropractor, told Mr. Fisher that he'd return the wallet to him as soon as possible; however, he didn't get around to it. Noelle went on to say The Chiropractor's office was

located a few blocks from the spot where Miles was assaulted.

Thanks to Noelle, Miles had everything he needed to
catch The Chiropractor. He had a name, an address, and
most importantly, a new reason for living.

WITH new information on his attacker, Miles took an
UBER back into city. First, he stopped by a car rental to
rent a car because he knew that he couldn't stake out The
Chiropractor in an UBER. For one, with the unpredictable
nature of a stakeout, it could end up costing a fortune, especially at night, when rates were higher. And two, we all
knew it was a solo job—a two-man job, if you got a partner
dirty enough to share the company and possible blame. Either way, the job was perilous and required the most hated
investigative journalist in America to work in a place where
he worked best.

In the shadows.

Everything was all taken care of until Miles paid for the
rental. First, the associate swiped Miles CREDIT card and
received an "error" message. The associate, like the barista,
recognized Miles from TV. Initially, he thought she was
just screwing with him, her own subtle way of sticking it to
him, hitting him exactly where it hurt: the wallet. She
tried once more by inserting card chip-side into the machine.

Again, the card wasn't working.

Miles handed the associate yet another card, the trusty
gold one.

Like the one before, it didn't work.

It wasn't maxed out, Miles thought. He habitually
checked his bank account everyday, checked his balance,
checked for any suspicious activity.

Miles second thought, *How could this be?*

Miles stepped outside the rental shop and called a number on the back of the card. He had charges on his card
that he wasn't even aware of. Small charges not drawing

any suspicion. Surprisingly, Miles hadn't been keeping up with his account for the past couple of days—considering his unusual predicament. Somehow, an unscrupulous individual had gotten hold of his social security number, as well as his personal information, like phone number and address. He had heard horror stories from other people. He once worked on a story about identity theft and the constant danger that lurks among us. Not once did he ever think he'd find himself in the same position as those poor people he interviewed.

Like them, he was a victim.

MILES had no other way to get around it. He needed a vehicle. So, he decided to steal one. He searched a parking lot not too far away from the rental place. Most of the cars were push-star—Miles cursed new technology.

With all hope lost, he checked one last car, a silver Frontier truck that used a key ignition. He remembered all those movies he watched when he was younger. He thought "hot-wiring" a car—or truck—was something that only happened in the movies, like an action hero using a gun to shoot a tank of gasoline and causing the tank to explode for added special effects or whatever ridiculous tropes Hollywood used to keep their audiences in their seats.

"What do you know?" Miles said as the truck started.

It works.

As far as his attire, Miles wasn't too concerned about disguising himself.

After all, he looked like a tourist.

He camped outside The Chiropractor's office and waited for his last patient to leave the building. Sure enough, it was him, his attacker.

Timothy Hume.

"The Chiropractor."

Miles waited for The Chiropractor to get inside his shoddy Civic before staring up his car. He tailed The Chiropractor to a rundown town home on the outskirts of the city or what most called the "bad part of town."

He waited.

A couple of hours passed before The Chiropractor stepped back outside. He drove off. Miles tailed him, this time making sure to keep his distance. The Chiropractor drove to the nicer side of town. Miles lost him at a stoplight but ended up catching up with him at another. The Chiropractor arrived at his destination, a family-owned Italian restaurant called Luigi's. There, he met up with an attractive woman outside.

"Ole Timmy got himself a date, huh?" Miles said, as he camped outside the restaurant.

She was his next victim, he soon realized.

Tonight was going to be the night, Miles thought. *He tried with Scarlet but failed. The man's a bad wolf, and tonight, he's hungry.*

TWO and a half hours later, the two finally emerged from Luigi's.

The woman appeared tipsy, Miles witnessed, as The Chiropractor walked her to her car, which was parked around the corner in an unlit area. Miles knew these conditions couldn't be any worse: the woman was intoxicated and she was parked in an area which was dark and without any streetlights.

Miles drove closer to the two for a better view. He parked behind a bus stop. They were both laughing and talking and they appeared to be enjoying each other's company, which, to Miles, was good for the woman—great, actually; she seemed happy, okay with her date—but, as Miles thought more about himself, his dire situation, a feeling of melancholy came over him. He didn't want anything terrible to happen to the innocent woman, but in a dark way, he did.

As the woman arrived at the driver's side of her car, The Chiropractor leaned in for a kiss. He wanted more, though,

Miles inspected closer, as she grabbed his hand from grabbing her breast. She pushed away his hand, but he was grabby.

Miles leaned forward.

"Here we go," he said, almost excited.

Suddenly, she pushed him and backed away.

The Chiropractor charged at her.

She quickly reached into her purse for a can of mace and managed to spray him in one eye; however, he struck her in the face.

Dazed, the woman tried to get inside her car.

The Chiropractor snatched the keys from the woman's hand and flung them across the street.

The two struggled.

The Chiropractor was half-blind but he was clearly overpowering the woman.

As he pulled her by the hair and yanked her head in directions it shouldn't be moving, she screeched out, "Help!"

The Chiropractor slammed her head against the side of the car.

She was dazed, but she was fighter.

As The Chiropractor was about to strike her once more, she found an opening and scratched him in the face and then kneed him directly in the groin.

Miles found himself rooting for the woman, but, at the same time, not.

The Chiropractor grabbed his crotch and lurched forward in pain.

This brief pause had given the woman enough time to run away.

Here was the mistake, though.

Instead of running back to Luigi's, a well-lit establishment filled with people, the woman ran into a sketchy, unlit alleyway. Miles didn't understand the intent behind the woman's thinking. Maybe she thought she'd lose him in the alleyway. Maybe she wasn't thinking at all.

Once The Chiropractor recovered, he chased after the woman.

Miles thought about the story.

His story.

Redemption.

If America had given the Jam a second-chance, why couldn't they give me a second-chance?

And if there was one thing Americans loved, it was a real-life hero, like a cop or a firefighter.

Who doesn't like a hero, a savior, a guardian angel?

Each second Miles spent thinking about whether or not he wanted to save the woman reduced her odds at surviving. He got out of the vehicle and chased after The Chiropractor. He heard a muffled scream coming from the end of the alleyway. Cast in a distant floodlight were two silhouettes, the larger one, which Miles suspected was The Chiropractor, straddled on top of the motionless woman who was lying flat on the ground.

Miles yelled out, "Leave her alone!"

The Chiropractor turned to Miles, his devilish eyes glowing in the dark.

As Miles approached, The Chiropractor took off running in the other direction.

Miles rushed over to the woman who was bleeding badly from the face. Her left eye was swollen shut, nose bent to the side, broken. Several teeth were missing from her mouth and Miles didn't know whether she was choking on her blood or her own teeth. He felt as if it'd be a criminal act to examine her body. But he did, briefly. Her blouse was torn open, one leg bent in a ninety-degree angle. Her pants and undergarment had been pulled down to one of her ankles. He saw blots of blood around her inner thighs. He quickly looked away and did all he could do in her final moments.

"Hang in there," Miles told the woman. He reassured her that everything was going to be okay, but he knew it wasn't. It would never be "okay" for her. Even a word like *okay* would soon carry so little merit in the days to come. Eventually, "okay" would turn into something else entirely, a sacred word, one of great reverence. A word in which she'd desperately strive to touch, even finger. *Just okay.* Even if she managed to survive her injuries, which, Miles knew by listening to her breathing was very slim, the internal damage of what was done to her would remain inside her like a new organ, fatty like a liver and spotted-black and shriveled like a smoker's lung, nonetheless, a thing, vital like an organ but unable to be repaired or even removed. Miles knew that she would carry this unwanted thing, this burden, inside her to her grave.

He cried for her, but only for a moment.

Miles held onto her hand and told her how sorry he was for not warning her. He was sorry for what happened to her. Miles was especially sorry for not doing more to make sure people like Timothy Hume never walked the streets again.

The woman's breath grew more swallow and thinner.

Her face stilled, her eyes froze on Miles's.

Miles checked her pulse and found none.

Once sympathetic, now vengeful, Miles pulled out his phone.

The story, he realized.

My story.

There was still a chance to save my name.

He didn't want to do it, but he had no other choice. He needed proof.

After Miles took a photo of the dead woman, he found a purse lying a couple of feet away. He reached into the purse and pulled out a driver's license.

Her name was Rachael Merger.

While Miles was reading her license, one piece of information caught his eye. She was an organ donor.

MILES didn't sleep.

He waited until the light of dawn pushed away the shadows of buildings and drove to The Chiropractor's office where he camped out inside his musty truck. He made a phone call to Noelle, told her about last night and how he had proof that Timothy Hume was a rapist. He opened his photo gallery and pulled up the photo of one dead Rachael Merger.

What?

The photo was gone, vanished—or deleted?

Miles swiped through his most recent photos.

The only one Miles could find from last night was a photo of a dead rat in an alleyway. The rat was lying in a puddle. The floodlight cast a light on the rat, as well as Miles's dark reflection in the puddle.

"I must've deleted it or. . . " Miles said to Noelle.

The idea hit him and nearly left him breathless.

Credit card, he thought.

"I was hacked," he said. "Someone must've stolen the photo from my phone. What if they use it against me?"

"*They?*" Noelle said, her voice drawn out. "Miles, who is they?"

"The Network," he said.

Noelle asked, "Where are you?"

"I'm parked outside Hume's office."

"What are you planning on doing to him, Miles?"

"I'm doing what needs to be done, Noelle—"

"—Miles," Noelle said patiently. "If what you're saying is true, then this is a police matter. You need to contact the authorities right now."

"The police aren't going to do a goddamn thing—"

"—Miles, whatever you're thinking about doing, don't do it."

Miles witnessed The Chiropractor pull into the parking lot next to the office.

"I got to go—"

"—Miles, think it over!"

"I've thought enough," he said vaguely.

Noelle said slower, "Miles, *don't do it.*"

"It's the story, Noelle," Miles said. "It's all that matters."

Miles hung up on Noelle.

Miles waited for The Chiropractor to exit his car, then made his move.

As The Chiropractor was walking to his office, Miles jumped him from behind. He threw him to the ground.

"I know what you did, you piece of shit," Miles said as he started kicking The Chiropractor in the ribs.

The Chiropractor shielded himself by covering his head and curling his body into a fetal position. Miles focused on the ribs, bones that break easily. He broke at least two or three of them. He didn't care. He kept kicking and kicking.

Each time he kicked The Chiropractor in the ribs, the more powerful he felt.

He wasn't going to stop until The Chiropractor was dead.

A couple of pedestrians on the street rushed in behind Miles and tried to pull him off The Chiropractor. Miles pushed them away and continued his assault on The Chiropractor. More people rushed in, but this time they didn't come to The Chiropractor's aide. Instead, they whipped out their phones from their pockets or handbags like weapons and started filming the assault on camera.

Before Miles knew it, he had a whole audience gathered around him filming him as if he was a celebrity.

A woman suddenly shouldered her way through the massive horde surrounding Miles and threw her body in front of him.

"Stop it!" she cried out, as she attempted to push Miles from The Chiropractor.

Through his red haze, Miles glanced at the woman's familiar face.

He couldn't help but look again.

Closer.

She was holding a brown bag lunch in her hair. An apple had fallen from a damp hole in the bottom of the bag and rolled down the sidewalk.

"You?" said Miles.

"Get the hell off him!"

Miles was left in a trance.

The woman's screams, the same ones he heard last night in the alley, snapped him from his trance.

Once more, he studied the woman's face. She was wearing the face of a dead woman.

Rachael's face.

"You're dead," Miles said with confusion.

"What?" The woman furrowed her brow. She placed the brown bag on the ground and waved at several pedestrians who were filming Miles. "Please," she cried, "somebody help my husband—"

"—Your husband?" said Miles.

She tended to The Chiropractor, shielding her body in front of his.

Once she realized the severity of his injuries, she pointed her finger at Miles.

"Get him away from me!" she screamed, her eyes filled with rage.

Miles took a step away.

Another pedestrian called out from the back of the crowd, "That's the pervert all over the news!"

"Miles Straum!"

"Rapist!"

"Pig!"

"Monster!"

Miles rotated around and found himself moving in circles around the crowd. All he could see were the beady black eyes of camera lens aimed directly at him, each one of the pedestrians' faces hidden by the backside of their smartphones. He soon realized he was in the center of the mob. . .

One man stepped forward with his hands curled into fists.

"Miles!" a familiar, more comforting voice shouted out from a distance.

Out of breath, Noelle emerged from the mob. She rushed over to Miles. She first saw The Chiropractor bleeding against the side of the building as he grabbed his abdomen in great agony.

"Miles," she said, "what the hell did you do?"

"You know this man?" one guy yelled out.

Soon, Noelle found herself in the center of the mob, more eyes beating down on her.

Another yelled out: "That's the reporter on TV! She friends with him!"

"Wait!" Noelle said and grabbed Miles by the arm. "He's sick, you see. He needs help—"

"—He needs to pay for what he did."

"This man," Miles said and pointed at The Chiropractor, "he's the rapist. Not me!"

The guy continued to approach the two in a threatening manner.

Others followed suit.

All of a sudden, both Miles and Noelle found themselves surrounded.

Miles leaned in close to Noelle and whispered in her ear, "When I say so, we make a run for it."

"We're outnumbered, Miles."

Miles looked for an opening. He saw one to the right of him. A thin twenty-something woman with a crew cut slouched over with her slick smartphone held directly in front of her face. Miles noticed the satchel she was wearing over her shoulders. From the way it sagged well over her back like a bulky sack of potatoes, it appeared as if the young woman had her entire bedroom stuffed into that satchel. The second observation was the Vans she was wearing. The soles were flat and worn down. One shoe had a penny-size hole near the toe and part of her pink sock was exposed. Which meant she probably didn't get good traction. And not only that, the ground was still slick from last night's rain showers.

When she took her eyes off the smartphone and glanced up for a moment, he witnessed her eyes—or what little eyes she had. Her eyes were beady and black, startling.

She's one of them, Miles thought.

"Just follow my lead," Miles said to Noelle.

"Miles. . . "

"Just follow my lead on the count of three," he said over Noelle.

Miles grabbed Noelle's hand, held it tight.

"Don't you dare do anything stupid—"

"—They're going to tear us a part, Noelle."

"But Miles. . . "

"One," he said.

"Miles!"

"Two," he said over Noelle.

In return, Noelle tightened her grip around Mile's hand. "Three. . . "

Miles lowered his shoulder and charged at the young woman inching closer to him. She didn't even know what hit her. She fell on her back, which gave him an opening.

Both Miles and Noelle ran through the opening in the mob.

Hands suddenly reached out to them, grabbing them, pulling at them, smacking them like tree branches. Miles and Noelle lowered their bodies and treated it as if they were both plowing through dense shrubbery.

Once they were free, they scurried into an alleyway.

The mob ran after them.

Miles and Noelle managed to lose the mob once they crossed a street that was congested with traffic and cut through an abandoned building in Green Heights.

Noelle lagged behind. She was telling Miles to stop.

"I need. . . to catch. . . my breath," she barely said at one point.

She hunched forward and placed her hands along her knees.

"It's imperative that we keep moving, Noelle," Miles urged. "We're not safe in the city."

Noelle placed her right hand over her chest as if she was trying to calm down her beating heart and embraced slow, deep breaths.

"Where'r you parked?" asked Miles.

Noelle closed her eyes for a moment and then cleared her throat.

"Are you okay?"

"Just give me a minute," she said shortly.

While Noelle was recovering, Miles checked out the internal structure of the building. The entire building had been gutted—looked like an old factory, Miles thought. The walls were stripped bare and holey from unfinished work, paint chipped, peeling, and exposing layers of mold. Support beams were badly rusted. Even the floors had been chewed up and picked apart and covered in a wicked combination of dirt, dust, and debris.

Miles tried his best to keep his mind occupied by closely expecting the integrity of the building; however, the cold fear of imminent danger was lurking like a dark shadow in his thoughts. He heard a sudden *clank* of a metallic object being kicked around at the other side of the building.

"You hear that?" asked Miles.

Noelle finally stood upright.

"Hear what?"

"That noise," Miles said and pointed past a set of stairs spiraling up towards what looked like a raised office on the second floor. "Over there," he said softer.

"What's the plan, Miles?" asked Noelle.

Miles was too concerned with the noise and the thing that was making it.

"Miles?"

"Right," he said and snapped from his trance. "Plan. We need wheels."

"I'm parked next to Hume's office," Noelle said. "If you can somehow make some kind of distraction to draw them away, then it may buy me enough time to make it to my car."

"Sure," Miles said, trembling. "I can do that—"

"—Miles," Noelle said, as she grabbed Miles by the shoulders, "we're going to be okay. Think of it this way. By next week, they'll forget all about us."

Miles nodded.

"Okay," he said. "Let's go."

As the two made their way to the exit, the atmosphere inside the building became much darker. Miles thought it was nothing, clouds blotting out the sun.

What Miles failed to realize was that the mob had found them and they were surrounding the entire building. Their numbers had grown substantially, ten times the size back at Hume's office. Hundreds of bodies slowly came forth, each one standing in front of the cracked, murky industrial-sized windows. Their shadowy hands pressed against the glass, faces too, as they peered through the windows.

Miles and Noelle cautiously stepped outside and as they started to walk from the industrial park, two massive hordes of bodies came rushing in from both sides, flanking them. Miles rotated around and tried to make it back into the building, but one horde blocked his path.

Miles pointed forward and yelled out to Noelle, "Run!"

They didn't make it far. Like on the street, they were quickly surrounded.

The horde grabbed Noelle first. Reaching for Miles, she cried out and desperately tried to free herself from their grips. But there were too many hands and they were all grabbing at her, smothering her. When they grabbed Miles, Miles found a way to slip from their grips. He slid from his bomber jacket like a melted candy bar from a wrapper. He crawled under several pairs of legs, as if he was tunneling through holes of flesh. He managed to get ahead of the mob. He ran. He didn't look back as Noelle screamed out in horror behind him. He was tempted to fight off the mob and rescue Noelle. But like she said earlier, they were out-numbered. Clearly. If he *did* go back for Noelle, he'd be dead as well. But, with him having legs to run, Miles had a fighting chance at survival. And if someone was going to make it out alive, it'd be Miles. He thought about all these awful things while running, the odds, his chances being greater than hers. He needed to tell his story and he damn well couldn't do that if he was rat food. The chase pursued into the same alleyway that he and Noelle first entered. He found a manhole in another alley that led to a dead end. Miles had no other choice. He lifted up the manhole and slipped inside right before the mob could spot him.

As the mob entered the alley, Miles carefully closed the manhole behind him. A circular halo of flickering sunlight cast over his right eye as he watched the sea of flesh moving above him, swaying back and forth, all zombie-like. Miles could hear them through the cracks of the manhole, mur-muring among cliques within cliques, lifelessly wandering around like the undead with the craving of human brains, their slick and sophisticated smartphones attached to their hands as if they were ready to film Miles's end game, snap it, tag it, post it, claim it.

After of couple of tense minutes of waiting, the mob eventually moved on.

Miles knew that he, too, had to move as well.

He climbed down the ladder, which lead to the sewers. He followed the narrow passageway, holding his nose from the pungent smell emitting from a stream of shit and piss below. He spent at least an hour trapped in the maze of the sewer system. Each manhole he tried, he heard the mob close by. He kept trying, going from one manhole cover to another. Eventually, he gave up and rested on a piece of cardboard next to the ladder below a sewer grate where a perfectly shape beam of sunlight shone through the opening, making the light interestingly divine.

In his deep trance, he heard what sounded like a footstep. He peeked around the corner and witnessed the stark shadow of a long-limbed man moving gracefully along the round wall. He peered closer, traced the shadow which belonged to a man who was waving him closer. He didn't look like a threat, not like one of them from above. The Phone People. His face was soft and gray; his eyes hidden inside the dark sockets of his skull and glimmering in an overhead beam of sunlight. His posture appeared weak, frail like an elderly man.

"Come closer," the stranger said, his voice thin and raspy.

Despite the imminent danger lurking above him, Miles decided to creep over to the stranger. He was standing in the shadows of a small room, which looked as if it was once a utility room; however, to the stranger, it was home. He had thick sheets of cardboard stacked like a mattress in the corner. Two dead rats were lying next to a hot plate. A rectangular grate along a rather quiet sidewalk on the outskirts of the city was what appeared to be the stranger's only source of light. Miles glanced up at the grate; and occasionally, some pedestrian, clueless of the strange man lurking below, would pass on by.

In the corner of Miles's eye, he was attracted to yet another light, a soft flickering one beating like a pulse. He turned to his right and saw a glowing yellowish light around the corner. He stepped forward, arched his head outward and witnessed a pyramid-shaped shrine of old candles, hundreds of candles; the hot wax that slowly dripped from each one had molded with the other candles resting below, making all the candles appear as if they were one unified candle. In the very center of the wax mound perched what looked like the skull of an animal.

Miles took yet another step closer.

The skull was one of a cat; and its remaining bones were spread out on top of a weathered, slightly skewed table with one uneven leg, which was being propped up by a brick. At the base of the shrine was a Persian rug.

Miles's attention was redirected by a throaty—almost guttural—sound coming from the other side of the room.

The stranger, who was tucked away in the cozy shadows of the room, pointed at a raggedy brown coat draped over a wired rack next to Miles.

"Put it on," the stranger insisted.

Hesitant, Miles put on the smelly coat.

"For disguise," he hissed, his letter s's sounding as if his tongue was as long and split as a snake.

Miles got a closer look at the stranger. He was much younger than he originally thought. Maybe a few years older than Miles himself. But the stranger carried himself as if he was much older, ancient almost, like a rare species undiscovered by man. He was wrapped in rags. His face was skeletal. Miles could see a gray outline of his skeletal structure in the hazy light.

Then, Miles said to the stranger, "Do you know who I am?"

"Ah," the strange man said with fascination, "We know you. My friends here tell me all about you, Miless Ssstraum."

Miles could even smell his breath from where he stood. It was twice as pungent as sewage, deathly. His gums were swollen, and he was clinging onto two or three teeth, which protruded from his gums like fungi.

"Your friends?"

The stranger pointed at the dead rats on the ground.

"Rats?"

"Don't underestimate the rats," the stranger said. "They are the eyes and ears of the city. The unspoken ones. The watchers. 'The silent majority,' if you will. They've been telling me all sorts of things about you. They say you're the chosen one."

Miles soon realized he found himself in even worse danger than the ones that lurked above him. He was in the mouth of the Crazy den. And Crazy had its eyes honed in on him. Miles pointed the other way.

"I'd better get going," he said as he backed away. "Thanks for the coat."

As Miles turned around, the stranger called out from behind, "You can't run away from who you are, Miles Ssstraum."

Miles paused for a moment, turned around, and witnessed the stranger taking a step closer into the light.

The stranger moved robotically.

"How—how do you know my name?"

He opened up the damp rags in which clothed his gaunt body, releasing hundreds of rats from within. Miles flinched and started to back away as rats climbed and crawled over the stranger's body as if they were a part of his body.

The stranger reached into his body, pulled out a rat, and held it in his cupped hands. Miles couldn't help but notice the scaly skin on the stranger's discolored arm and how parts of it appeared infected from where skin had been gnawed away either by the stranger himself or the very rats in which surrounded him.

The stranger petted the top of its head with his bony soot-covered hand.

"We know *everything*," he said, his gray eyes wide and menacing. "They tell me a new king must be crowned."

Shocked, Miles pointed at the rats.

"*They* talk to you?"

"Everything talks, Miles," he said. "The living *and* the dead. All you have to do is listen carefully."

"How did you get here?"

"Like you, I was chosen but," the stranger looked down at his skinny body, "I am not worthy to hold the crown. You see I have what doctors call a bug." Miles couldn't help but look closer at the man's face. He swore he saw his skin move, as if he had a worm or something trapped underneath his skin. "My friends here, they don't get along with Harry."

The stranger's head slowly curled backward, his gums peeled back, revealing not only another set of teeth, but also many sets of teeth, jagged and sawtoothed, like a shark. The stranger suddenly chomped off the rat's head. He chewed, then swallowed it, then tossed the rat's corpse to the ground where the other rats began to pick at it.

"Excuse me," the stranger said with embarrassment as he held his hand over his mouth. "I swear, it had a mind of its own."

"What the hell was that?" asked Miles as he stood defensively.

"Harry."

"Harry?"

"He's my bug."

"Is this a nightmare?"

"Nightmares only exist in the mind, Miles."

"Who the hell are you?"

"I'm Myko," he said. "Or, at least that's what they used to call me."

"What do they call you?"

"They call me all kinds of names. Terrible names." The stranger, this Myko fellow, looked up at the grate above. "I used to have a life up there. Among the humans. A boy with his head in the clouds. Times were innocent back then. Yet, we were blind to the blood on our hands. I used to *be* one of them," the stranger watched a pedestrian stomp by overhead, "optimistic yet unaware of what waits below. If I knew what I know now back then, I don't know what would become of me. Once, you see, I thought the humans were important to the survival of our planet. Then, I peeled back its face and saw its true color." Harry suddenly bared its sharp teeth, briefly showing its hideous face to Miles. The stranger paused and held his head downward, calming Harry as it sensed the blood pumping in Miles's veins. "I often wonder if it was always like, from the beginning. The greed. The consummation. The innate hunger for flesh. Look at us now." The rats crawled all over the stranger's shoulders, even face. He faced Miles, his eyes glimmering. "Look at what we've become. But you, Miles, you are very, *very* special." The stranger stepped closer, the pack of rats following his every step. "We are at the brink of a *New Age* of Transformation. . . Lead us, Miles! Leads us into the new world!"

Miles backpedaled.

"Like hell I am," he said, repulsed. "You're crazy."

"We're all crazy down here, Miles," the stranger said, grinning.

Miles suddenly ran back the way he came from as the stranger hollered out from behind, "There's nowhere to run, Miles! They'll find you! They'll find you the same way they found me!" He ran as fast as his aching legs would take him. "They're like that, you see!" the stranger yelled, his voice trailing off into an echo along the dark tunnels. *"They're smart! They're smarter than you think! In time, you will see, Miles! You will lead them to the New Age! You will! And they will all bow down to you! You'll see, Miles! You'll see. . ."*

RAINWATER dribbled down the slick ladder leading up to the manhole.

Cautiously, Miles slid open the slippery manhole cover.

Exhausted and dehydrated, Miles emerged from the opening.

Dark clouds parted and for a moment, the sun, like before, crept through and a ray of sunlight hit Miles in the face. He was back in the alleyway, same one as before. The mob was nowhere around, which was a good sign. The ground was soaked from a recent rain shower and somewhere high above, a rainbow was cutting through the gray sky. Miles didn't know how long he had been down in the sewers. Hours? Maybe even an entire day? Two days? Three?

The sight of the sun, as brief as it was, comforted him.

As Miles closed the manhole cover, he looked up and saw what looked like an arm hanging from a nearby dumpster. He was overcome by instant dread. He decided to inspect the dumpster. He pushed away the trash bags and other debris. Once he cleared away the trash, he found Noelle's naked body lying among the garbage. She had bruises all over her face, as well as body. Strings of blood caked onto her mouth and nose. He knew Noelle was dead and that she had been dead for a while now, but he checked her pulse anyway.

"Noelle," Miles said and gave her shake on the shoulder. "Wake up. Please, Noelle. Wake up. . . "

Miles fell down to his knees and started crying. He wept like a baby. Miles couldn't even remember the last time he cried. Despite the little tears he shed for Rachael, in a way, it felt good to cry, to let it all out this time, to release an entire week—or month, whatever—of misery into a liquid form of emotion. He wanted to bottle his tears and save them as a reminder of how precious life was. He had no bottle, though. Except for the smelly scraps of clothes he was wearing, he had absolutely nothing. All Miles had left was his shadow and even it seemed crooked.

As the tears turned warm with anger, Miles frantically searched the dumpster for a weapon, anything sharp to run across his throat or wrist, the ultimate delete button. He wanted to delete himself from this very existence but he couldn't even find a sharp piece of glass to cut himself. He fell to the ground, pressed the side of his face against the wet grit, and closed his eyes. He heard something approaching, something big. . .

When he opened his eyes, he witnessed hundreds and thousands of rats flooding the entire alleyway. The rats surfaced from the openings of the streets, sewer drains and manholes, and moved like a sweeping brown wave from the streets, the sidewalks, and stormed directly toward Miles.

In a matter of seconds, the rats completely engulfed his body. Miles wasn't scared, though. Not the least. He embraced them, the rats, as if they were family.

As the rats swarmed all around Miles and helped lift him from his diminished state, a crown made up of old trash, such as soda can sheets and shavings, scraps of compacted newspaper, pieces of cardboard, and discarded electronics, like torn headphone wires and broken interfaces, was brought forth over the brown wave of rats. The rats passed the crown forward as if they were running an assembly line.

As if they were conducting a sacred ceremony, the rats droned the words over and over in harmony: *He who wears the Crown shall rule the Town.*

Two rats carried the wobbly crown on their backs while another one grabbed it by its sharp teeth and together, they placed the crown on top of Mile's head.

The brown wave chanting: *He who wears the Crown shall rule the Town.*

Next to be passed forward was a small cylinder-shaped object.

Miles couldn't make out the object from the end of the alleyway; however, he was incredibly intrigued. He intensely watched the rats, one-by-one, pass the object toward Miles. The object crowd-surfed along the backs of the rats and when it finally reached Miles, it took at least five or six rats to carry it to Miles. Miles knew exactly what the object was as soon as it reached his feet and he found himself smirking by the sight of it. He was starting to see everything take shape as if he had an inkling of a bigger, much broader picture.

He who wears the Crown *shall rule* the Town, Miles thought to himself.

The rats placed the microphone in Miles's hand and they spoke to him.

And Miles listened.

Indeed, he listened to them.

One rat came forward. The other rats made a hole for it. They circled around this one particular rat that was standing in the space between Miles's legs.

"Miles Straum, you are now crowned 'The *Royal* King of Trash,'" it said, its tiny voice high-pitched like a Chipmunk.

Together, the rats chimed, "All hail the king!"

Next to be brought forth through the river of rats was a camera.

Miles had no cameraman.

No problem.

Fortunately for Miles, the rats knew how to operate a camera.

"It's time for you get back to work, Miles," one of the rats said to Miles.

Miles stared at the microphone lying in the palm of his hand and all of a sudden, a wicked smile stretched across his weary, dirty face.

The rats started to pile onto one another, forming a human-size mound. The camera sat on top of the rat mound like a hat.

Miles stood to his feet and cleared his throat. He adjusted the crown with one hand while keeping the microphone gripped in his other. He primped his hair underneath the crown, pushing loose, sticky hair behind his ears.

After he adjusted himself one last time, he nodded his head, motioning to the rats that their king was ready to speak.

The cool red light turned on below the camera.

His listeners around the world were watching.

And waiting.